Once Upon Now

Once Upon Now

Modern Tales with a Fantastical Twist

Danielle Banas, Mikaela Bender, J. M. Butler,
Debra Goelz, Shannon Klare, R. S. Kovach,
Ali Novak, Tammy Oja, Christine Owen,
and Jesse Sprague

G

GALLERY BOOKS

New York　London　Toronto　Sydney　New Delhi

G

Gallery Books
An Imprint of Simon & Schuster, Inc.
1230 Avenue of the Americas
New York, NY 10020

First Gallery Books trade paperback edition October 2016

GALLERY BOOKS and colophon are registered trademarks of Simon & Schuster, Inc.

For information about special discounts for bulk purchases, please contact Simon & Schuster Special Sales at 1-866-506-1949 or business@simonandschuster.com.

The Simon & Schuster Speakers Bureau can bring authors to your live event. For more information or to book an event, contact the Simon & Schuster Speakers Bureau at 1-866-248-3049 or visit our website at www.simonspeakers.com.

Interior design by Davina Mock-Maniscalco

Manufactured in the United States of America

10 9 8 7 6 5 4 3 2 1

Library of Congress Cataloging-in-Publication Data is available.

ISBN 978-1-5011-5526-0
ISBN 978-1-5011-5595-6 (ebook)

Contents

Why Yes, Bluebeard, I'd Love To

j. m. butler

"ARE YOU READING that book *again*?" Anna nudged Emeline with her snow-pink slipper.

"Apparently." Emeline glanced up from *The Inimitable Jeeves* to see Anna, her amazingly wealthy and generally bored friend, standing over her. Such intrusions happened regularly. Lying on the floor in the back of the seating area with one's legs against the wall often resulted in interruptions, but it relieved the tension in Emeline's back and left her feeling marvelously refreshed.

"There are thousands of other books published every day. Why not read some of those?" Anna gave Emeline her patented "there's something about you that needs improving" look, complete with crossed arms and half-shaded eyes.

"I do. But sometimes it's nice to return to the familiar."

1

Emeline rolled up and made her way to the muffin display case. Anna was always finding things to improve about people.

Silas, the Chipped Mug's owner, stood behind the counter. He was exceptionally young to own and run his own coffee shop, particularly one with such impeccable design. On the outside, it looked like a typical cafe, with brick walls and a forest-green awning. On the inside, it was as if it had been plucked from the *Arabian Nights*, with thick carpets woven in intricate designs, ornate wallpaper in burgundies, golds, and ceruleans, and even a few nonworking hookahs and incense bowls.

Oddly, the cuisine bore little resemblance to the decor.

It was also strange that there were so few regular customers. In addition to being quite handsome, with loose, dark curls and twinkling brown eyes, Silas baked the best muffins in all of Walter County. The thick blue apron and the white collared shirt with sleeves folded at the elbows were not enough to hide the fact that he was exceptionally well muscled. Maybe that came from lifting all that flour and sugar.

He set aside the mug he had been polishing and leaned forward. "A good morning to you, ladies," he said with a bright smile. "How can I make your morning better?"

Emeline rewarded him with a matching smile. "Good morning, Silas. Well, I'd love a strawberry-banana shortcake muffin and a cup of green tea."

"Ugh. The same thing?" Anna groaned. "Why don't we go to the Spotted Tiger and try something exciting and new."

"Eh." Silas frowned slightly. "I've got everything the Spotted Tiger's got and more."

"Don't worry, Silas. I'm in love with your strawberry-banana shortcake muffins." Emeline kissed her fingers.

"That's promising," Silas said.

"Emeline, this is sad," Anna said. "I could predict you like a bad nineties rom-com."

"I'll wait for Ryan Reynolds to sweep me off my feet, then."

"Wrong decade, love," Silas said.

"Oh. Then who am I waiting for?" Emeline asked.

"If it must be someone other than me, then Tom Hanks, perhaps?" Silas half lifted his shoulders. "Richard Gere. Maybe Timothy Dalton."

"Oooh, I'd wait for him. He played James Bond too. I could have romance *and* adventure." Emeline picked up a small stir straw.

"You could," Silas agreed.

"Silas!" Anna smacked her hand against the faux marble counter. "You're not helping."

"I may be of better service if you order something." Silas winked at her.

That wink was enough to soften even Anna. "Oh . . . surprise me." Anna turned back to Emeline. "Sometimes you must throw your arms open and take in the universe. Seriously, Emeline, can you imagine how incredible your life would be if you said yes to everything?"

"Oh yes. Everything. I've heard of that. It includes things like jumping off cliffs and not thinking for yourself." Emeline handed Silas a ten-dollar bill and motioned for him to keep the change. "Saying no isn't a bad thing."

"Come on. You know people don't ask other people to jump off cliffs."

"You know, even if there was a one-in-seventy-billion chance that that would happen, it would happen to me."

"Why haven't you entered the lottery, then?"

"Because it would be bad news for the universe if I was this incredible *and* rich."

Anna rolled her eyes. She accepted the orange frappé with green froth Silas offered her. "How about a wager?"

"Hmmm, you're in a betting mood today, are you?" Emeline took a bite of her muffin. The flavors exploded in her mouth, warm and buttery, tart and sweet. "Whoever came up with the idea of combining strawberries and bananas in shortcake was a genius."

"Thank you." Silas bowed his head. "I'm glad you approve."

"If you go twenty-four hours and say yes to everything that comes your way, then I'll donate twenty thousand dollars to your charity, Helping Paws."

Emeline's mouth fell open. "What?"

"Ah, now I've got your attention." Anna sipped the strange frappé and managed an artful smile. Smacking her lips, she gave a contented sigh. "That tastes like new experiences."

"Twenty thousand dollars?"

"Well, to your charity. I think it might be illegal for me to pay you directly. Look." Anna pulled up an app on her phone. "See? I've transferred the twenty thousand into an account right here. If you fail, then it's going to go to . . . what's a charity or organization you hate . . . Oh! The Ku Klux Klan! Wait . . ." She frowned. "If you fail, I'd rather not ruin my own reputation. Umm . . . what if I transfer it to a kill shelter?"

"Anna, you wouldn't." Emeline gave her a stern look. "You're right . . . how about Rich and Proper, a charity that teaches rich people to appreciate their wealth and the finer things in life?"

"Any chance I could benefit from that charity?" Silas asked.

"Looks like you have to be worth at least five million to even get in. Twenty-five thousand is the lowest donation amount. All right. No problem. Twenty-five thousand it is." Anna tapped her screen a few times. "Voilà."

"You're just that determined to get me to hug the universe."

"Yes!" Anna clapped her hands together.

Emeline stared at her for a moment. Anna was odd, eccentric, and prone to being overcritical, but she didn't lie. More importantly, Helping Paws could really use the money. "You're serious about this."

"Absolutely. You make it through, and I'll see to it that the *Morning Gale Post* features your charity and all your wonderful work as well as the twenty-five thousand dollars. Plus this will be great publicity for you. I hope you do meet someone charming today. Wouldn't that be the most awesome how-we-met story?"

"Are you doing all this because you want to set me up with someone?" Emeline demanded, her eyes narrowing.

"Again?" Silas shook his head.

"You'll see." Anna laughed and folded her hands. "Emeline, would you like to try a pumpkin kiwi chia kale shake with soy milk?"

Emeline rolled her eyes. "You're not starting me off easy, are you?"

"Hey, we could go down to Thai Smile and try spiced tarantulas or live octopus." Anna tapped her fingers to her cheek and smiled.

Emeline grimaced. "You're going to make me earn this, aren't you?"

"Pumpkin kiwi chia kale shake with soy milk?" Anna's smile broadened.

"Where are we even going to get that concoction?" Emeline asked.

"Right here." Silas raised his hand.

"All right, fine." Emeline glanced at Anna sidelong. "Anna, would you like to pay?"

"I'd love to." Anna removed her billfold again. "See, that wasn't so hard."

Silas passed her a thick green-brown smoothie with black speckles. He grinned, his mischievous brown-black eyes twinkling. "Enjoy."

"You're too kind." Emeline took a sip. The thick, chalky mixture struggled up the straw and filled her mouth with a strong bitter-and-oversweet-tart combination. The pumpkin and the kiwi dueled for dominance while the kale punched its way down the back of her throat. A few other flavors she couldn't even identify made her eyes water. "Oh, good night!" She grimaced. "That's a special kind of vile."

"I'm so proud of you!" Anna hugged her. "This is going to be fantastic. And I promise you, you're going to meet someone really splendid today."

Emeline wiped her mouth. "I knew it!"

"I promise he's stunning. An absolute one-of-a-kind. Now . . ." Anna gave her a mischievous smile and wrinkled her nose. "Would you like to go for a walk down by the old Victorian bridge on the edge of Grete's Woods? I'll tell him to meet you there?"

"Fine."

"Okay, good. I'll see you soon!" Anna hurried away, the silver bells on the door jangling loudly as she left.

"You know, your problem isn't that you lack adventure or spirit or the ability to try new things," Silas said. "It's that you don't always see the opportunities in front of you."

"Yeah, I suppose so." Emeline snapped a picture of the smoothie.

So much happened in life, it was hard to know exactly what one missed.

"You don't have to do this whole say 'yes' to everything to have an adventure, you know. You could just say 'yes' to other things."

"True, but where else am I going to get an easy twenty-five thousand dollars? There are hungry puppies and kitties to think of." Emeline took another picture, dropping the smoothie into the trash. "Did you intentionally make that disgusting?"

"It needed no help from me." Silas grinned. He cleared his throat. "Would you . . ." He paused, his cheeks reddening as if he was rethinking something. "Would you like to hire me to cater your birthday party this summer?"

Emeline arched an eyebrow. "Et tu, Silas?"

"Hey, business has been slow." Silas smiled crookedly. His

gaze softened. "Besides, I'll take any excuse to see you." He shook his head and coughed. "Of course, if it turns out this fellow's the one for you, I'll cater your wedding. Or if it goes badly, I'll cater your funeral. I mean . . . um . . . not that I want you to get hurt. That didn't come out right." He laughed nervously. "Don't you hate it when bad things happen to good jokes?"

Emeline chuckled. "Don't worry, Silas. I know what you meant. You're a good friend." She didn't actually know what he meant or why he was so flustered, but she didn't want him to feel uncomfortable.

⊱✦⊰

EMELINE SAUNTERED OUT of the coffee shop and took the long path toward Grete's Woods. It was a nice morning for a walk, the air warm for late April. Only a few billowing clouds marred the clear blue sky, and dozens of larks and sparrows heralded her with song. A panhandler on the corner of Cinder and Prince asked for a handout, so she gave him her last ten dollars, and a little girl in a red-and-white-checked dress asked her to play a round of hopscotch.

By the time Emeline hit the edge of the city, the wind had picked up, bringing with it a faint chill. Thankfully, she had dressed for walking. Her periwinkle cardigan warded off the coolness, and her jeans were fitted enough to be stylish without chafing. Lady's slippers and buttercups blossomed in the ravines along the roadside and among the scattered trees; her favorites were the dark patches of trillium and mayapples.

Plucking one, Emeline hummed to herself. Had there ever been a better day for a walk? The only downside was that her cell reception worsened the deeper she got among the trees. It was nearly an hour later when she received a text from Anna. The message had a photo, and she clicked accept to download. But the connection was so weak, it listed the estimated time for completion to be almost three hours.

"Would you like a new phone, Emeline?" she muttered. "Why yes, yes, I would."

"You are Emeline?" a strange voice asked.

Emeline looked up. "I am."

She was still a half mile from the old Victorian bridge in Grete's Woods where she was to meet her date, but an unusual man strode out of the woods anyway. He was quite striking in appearance, wearing a double-breasted charcoal suit. His eyes were light gray, and his features, from what she could see, were quite handsome. Most striking of all was the massive blue beard covering all of his lower face. And not just any blue. No. A blue as deep and as lush as if someone had melted sapphires to color it.

"Hello," the man said. His voice was deep and throaty, almost musical in its richness. He removed his charcoal fedora, revealing even more cobalt hair. He bowed. "It's a beautiful day, is it not?"

"Definitely." Why would Anna bother with sending a picture? All she had to say was he had blue hair.

"May I ask you a question?" the man asked.

Emeline nodded. "Hmmm, yes."

"Will you marry me, Emeline?"

"Pardon?" Emeline's eyes widened.

"Would you marry me, Emeline?" the man asked again.

This stranger had the slightest hint of an accent that shaded his vowels and drew out his *r*'s.

Emeline folded her arms and smiled slowly. "Well . . . Anna certainly isn't playing fair, now is she?"

"Pardon?" The man frowned slightly. He straightened.

"You're Anna's friend, right? The one I'm supposed to meet?" Emeline asked.

He nodded. "Yes, Anna! Dear, sweet Anna. Of course I am." The man smiled, the skin around his eyes crinkling. "Forgive my boldness. It's just that you are stunning. I cannot resist you. Please marry me, Emeline."

What a joke this was. Did Anna really think she would be that easy to throw off the scent? Well, she would show Anna. Emeline's smile broadened. "Why yes, I'd love to."

The man's eyes brightened. "Excellent! Come with me, beautiful one. We shall be married at once."

Emeline laughed. "Well, of course we will! Why wouldn't we be? Now, what's your name, sweetheart?"

"Bluebeard."

"Wow. Bluebeard. Really. That's . . . that's imaginative. I would never have guessed that. Is that your first or last name?"

"Yes!" Bluebeard placed the fedora back on his head. He held out his arm. "Shall we?"

"Oh yes, let's." Emeline looped her arm through his. He smelled like cologne with a faint touch of mildew. "That beard is absolutely brilliant. What brand do you use for your dye? Can I touch it?"

"Certainly."

She dug her fingers into his beard and shook it hard. "Oh, now, that is gorgeous! You must give me your secret."

Bluebeard nodded as if uncertain what to say. Then he pulled her hands down. "It is genetics, I suppose."

"So your beard is naturally this color. Will our children have blue beards, then?"

"Perhaps."

"Even the little girls?"

Bluebeard's mouth worked for a moment, but then he smiled. "That is not how it works, my dear."

"Oh, but it is. There's nothing wrong with being a bearded woman. I knew one. Although my favorite thing about her was how poised and calm she was. I'm sure it took a lot of practice. And—"

"Let us visit our new home. Shall we?" Bluebeard gestured toward the wooded path that turned off from the main road. The conifers, maples, oaks, and elms obscured most of it from sight. Already the new leaves were thick enough to mask the forest in all shades of green.

"Lead on, you blue-bearded devil, you." Emeline removed her phone, snapped a selfie next to him, and then thrust it back into her pocket. "I can't wait to see the magnificent palace that awaits me."

"It's more of a château."

"Well, if a château is the best you've got, so be it. I suppose I can make do."

"You are quite a fine lady indeed."

"You have no idea how fine I am."

Bluebeard opened his mouth to speak and then paused.

Emeline patted his arm. They walked on for a while longer. Bluebeard had little to say, much to Emeline's surprise. And they did not follow the path to the Victorian bridge. Not that that bothered Emeline. She had seen the bridge many times. But after another hour of walking up and down hills straight into the forest, she began to grow weary. Her slim flats were practical enough for short walks, but not for this.

"How much farther?" she asked.

"You are getting tired?" Bluebeard stopped. "Would you like me to carry you?"

Hmmm, that was even more out of her comfort zone. Emeline hesitated. "You're sure you won't drop me?"

Not that it mattered. She *had* to say yes.

"You are but a feather in the palm of my hand. I swear it."

"All right," Emeline said, a little more hesitantly.

Bluebeard lifted her up. He was obviously a good sport. Emeline wondered how much Anna had paid him. His strong arms encompassed her and held her to his barrel-like chest.

She laughed nervously. "We should enter the North American Wife-Carrying Championship. I bet we'd be a cinch to win. Then I'd be worth my weight in gold. Or beer. I can't remember which it is."

"You're already worth your weight in gold to me."

"Oh, go on." Emeline feigned coyness. "Well, you certainly are silver tongued."

"I am quite gifted of tongue."

"Aha. Yes." Emeline patted his shoulder. This was awkward. Bluebeard carried her at least a mile farther. The fallen leaves rustled beneath his feet, some damp and some crisp, making a constant *shooshoosh* sound. It was nearly noon before the path brought them to the front of a large château. It had once had pale-blue paint and black-and-white trim, but now all had faded. The southern portion of the roof was buckled, and nodules of mold grew in clusters around the indentations. Most of the roof had shifted somewhat to the east. A large tower curled up from that east side, the stone fastened tightly together and covered with a thin layer of dull green moss, and the chimney cut through the center. A smaller westward tower jutted out, but it only went up partway. All in all, the château was a slanting mishmash of angles.

"Oh . . . how charming," Emeline said. "Why didn't Anna recommend this place for the Halloween bash?"

Bluebeard chuckled. "Oh, I do not celebrate Halloween."

"I think you should know I don't have any money, and any money that I might come into wouldn't even be enough to fix that roof," Emeline said. Something felt off. But was there something seriously wrong, or was it just her?

Of course, her phone still wasn't working. A glance at the screen revealed the signal was even worse. The message from Anna was 64 percent downloaded. Why wasn't there a read-only option? Stupid phone.

"What difference does that make, my love?" Bluebeard flung open the door and then bowed. "I do not desire you for your money. I desire you for you."

"Well, me is pretty fantastic, thank you very much. You're getting a real bargain."

"Indeed I am." Bluebeard smiled through his beard. His teeth were quite white beneath all that blue. "You have made me a very happy man, Emeline."

"I do aim to please." As Emeline started to turn, he caught her hands in his.

"You please me already."

"My, what strong hands you have." Emeline laughed nervously. She'd noticed it before when he was holding her, but now as she studied his hands, she saw they were massive and had long, thin scars.

"The better to hold you with."

"Hmmm . . . and what a quick wit you have." Emeline smiled.

"My tongue and my wit are both equally sharp."

Emeline laughed again, a little uneasily. "Back to that tongue. Let's wait until after the honeymoon starts, eh, big man?" She was going to get Anna for this.

"Very well. I must go make preparations for our wedding." Bluebeard removed a large metal circlet from his pocket. How that fit in there Emeline had no idea. He took her hand and turned its palm upward. "What is mine is yours. Go wherever you like." He draped a circlet of keys over her palm. With a stern look, he added, "Except the West Wing. Do not enter the West Wing under any circumstances. Do you understand?"

Emeline gripped the keys. "I do."

"It's *important*, my love."

She nodded her head wryly. "I'm sure you'll have to kill me if I sneak a peek."

"I'm glad you understand."

"Oh, I do."

"Then I will see you soon." With that, Bluebeard adjusted his suit, bowed again, and turned on his heel.

"All righty, then." Emeline waited until the great oak door slammed shut and then lifted the circlet of keys. "Well, well, Emeline, would you like to see what's in the West Wing? Why yes. Yes, I would."

Emeline swung the keys around her wrist and started up the sagging grand staircase.

IT WAS QUITE AN EXAGGERATION to refer to this as the West Wing. Even with her limited knowledge of architecture, Emeline doubted that a single half tower on the west side of the house could truly count as a "wing." Then again, they were all playing a game. It was best to stay in the spirit of the adventure.

Emeline continued to twirl the keys as she went up the stairs. The aged steps creaked, each one groaning and squeaking with a slightly different voice. A few even shuddered after she moved off them.

If she had been more of an artist or a romantic, this house might have left her with a more positive impression. It was obviously quite old. The stair railing had intricate designs carved into it, and the faded blue-green wallpaper boasted what was likely an impressive damask pattern. The carpeting—if this wasn't mold beneath her feet—could have been any color. Even white. It was so badly discolored. The scent of rot grew stronger with each step, and a faint *drip-drip* somewhere indicated water leakage.

"I don't suppose you winterized your pipes, did you?" Emeline said aloud.

The landing before the West Wing creaked and groaned as she stepped onto it. Ragged fibers suggested there had once been some sort of rug. The rank scent was even worse here, but it had an almost fruity undertone. The staircase curved upward and continued on to the next floor, but this was the only stop-off point on the west side.

"West Wing," Emeline muttered. "More like West Room."

She fished out one of the keys and inserted it into the rusted lock. The key stuck as she twisted.

"Lucky me, I've got more keys." Emeline removed it and attempted another with a triple-crossed heart in the handle. It didn't go in at all. The third, a tarnished silver key with a skull, also failed to go in. The iron key had too much rust and residue to be used, and the fifth, with its six spikes protruding in all directions, was clearly not right. She whistled a little tune as she continued searching.

A black striped lizard stuck its head out of a nearby hole in the wall, his slick tongue flicking in and out. "Come to hear my song, did you?" Emeline grinned.

The lizard darted back into its hole. Apparently he wasn't such a music fan.

At last, her palms a little sore from the twisting and covered in rust dust, she found the right key. A thick black one with two teeth on the end that was far heavier than it looked. It settled in, and when she gave it a firm twist, the tumblers fell into place, and the door jolted open half an inch.

"Perfect." Emeline slid the ring of keys over her wrist and

pressed her hands to the door. Its wood was black and soft, and it opened with the deepest, heaviest creak Emeline had ever heard. A horrible scent rushed out as if eager to escape.

"Oh, Morpheus, what is that?" Emeline fanned her face and peered inside. Her stomach lurched, and it was all she could do to keep from vomiting right there.

For not celebrating Halloween, Bluebeard had the most elaborate and realistic death chamber Emeline had ever seen. It was almost as good as the Horribly Haunted House in Baltimore, which had reputedly used actual corpses in its macabre tableaux. Blackened blood streaked the walls, mingling with green and black mold. Small congealing pools of blood dripped and drained across the floor, settling into the dips and crevices. Fifteen high-backed wooden chairs lined the water-damaged walls. In all but two of the chairs sat headless women clad in velvet or silk gowns, their heads sitting beside them on small octagonal tables nearby. Their hands were all folded before them as if in contemplation, and on each of their left ring fingers was a lovely sapphire ring. The gowns and bodies were in various stages of decomposition. A couple were little more than skeletons. Some were far . . . meatier.

The woman beside the two empty chairs was recent enough that despite the stench and swelling, Emeline could see that she had hazel eyes and had likely been a dancer.

"Okay . . ." Emeline kept her hand on the door. "Either this is in terribly bad taste, or . . ."

The other side of that statement was quite unappealing.

Anna wasn't above ghoulish—or expensive—pranks, but this was extreme even for her. Besides, how could anyone have set this up? True, it hadn't taken much persuasion to convince Emeline to agree to the bet, so arguably Anna and this Bluebeard could have set up the entire prank long ago.

"Wonderful." Emeline removed her phone and recorded a panoramic view. Her stomach twisted. "You know, Anna," she said, "if you invested this sort of time and money into the shelter, we wouldn't have budget problems."

She finished the picture and paused. The phone and the keys fell from her hand.

A rat was nibbling on the foot of one corpse. Its nose twitched as it kept its shining eyes fastened on her.

Bile rose in the back of Emeline's throat. "I don't suppose you'd eat a rubber or latex corpse, would you?"

The rat cocked its head. Then it returned to nibbling.

Obviously not animatronic. This was not a prank.

Scooping up her phone and the keys, Emeline hurried out, telling herself she had to remain calm. The door locked behind her. "Keep calm, yeah," she muttered, jamming the phone and keys into her cardigan pocket. "Calmly get out of this place!"

She raced down the staircase, desperate to escape before Bluebeard returned. If it turned out that this was a joke, she'd get even with Anna in the most epic way possible. In fact, if she survived, she might do that anyway. As she struck the bottom landing, the front door squeaked open.

Bluebeard stepped inside. "My darling!" He spread his arms wide. A large bag hung from his left hand.

Emeline stopped short. "Sweetheart," she said with far less enthusiasm.

Bluebeard offered her the bag. "A little something for my beautiful bride."

"Oh, you shouldn't have." Emeline accepted it, avoiding the temptation to run. Perhaps another alternative would present itself. Forcing a smile, she peered inside. "Oh! A dress . . . and a ring." Inside the brown paper bag were an elegant blue velvet gown and an all-too-familiar sapphire ring. "However did you guess my size?"

"I have my ways." Bluebeard smiled, his white teeth shining beneath his beard. "And now that I have given you something, do you have something for me?"

"Hmmm . . ." Emeline raised an eyebrow. "I'm afraid I'll need some time to—"

"The keys, dearest love," Bluebeard said. "I meant the keys."

Emeline moved her hand back when she realized that both her phone and the keys were covered in sticky bits of blood and mold. She clapped her hand over her pocket. "Oh, that's not much of a gift, you ridiculous man. Ahh!" She forced a laugh and pecked him on the cheek. "You give me this gorgeous dress and a lovely ring, and you think all I'm going to do is give you some rusty old keys? I think not! I have just the perfect gift for you. But it's at my house. So I'll just pop over and fetch it, and then I'll get changed, and we can have that beautiful wedding you were talking about, all right?"

"There's no need." Bluebeard held his hand out again. "Just give me the keys."

"Don't you want a present from me?" Emeline asked.

"Your presence is all I require." Bluebeard motioned for her to hurry up. "Now come along. There is much to be done."

Emeline thought that it might make him more suspicious if she continued to refuse. She nodded and pulled the keys and her phone free. She wiped them on her cardigan. "I tell you. This place is so dirty. I was up there on the south side and just dropped everything. After we're married, we'll have to give this place a good once-over, let me tell you!"

With a rusty rattle, the keys settled back in Bluebeard's broad hand.

Bluebeard scowled, his brows knitting together in dark fury. "You were in the West Wing."

So much for secrecy. Emeline's first instinct was to cower, but she forced herself to stand straight and meet his gaze. She had to play for time, come up with a plan, get him off balance. False bravado was better than none. "I don't appreciate your tone."

"You went into the West Wing," Bluebeard said once again. His hands clenched over the ring of keys, his knuckles whitening. "There is blood from the chamber on these keys."

"Oh, calm your beard, Sasquatch." Emeline folded her arms. "Of course I went into the West Wing. Why wouldn't I?"

"I specifically told you not to."

"Which is why I had to. But don't worry about it. Your secret is safe."

"It was not your time yet. There is so much yet for us to experience. Was. Now it cannot be."

"Well, don't sell yourself short, darling. Corpses don't have to kill a mood."

"But I must kill you now that the secret is out."

"I promise I won't tell anyone."

"You're correct that you will tell no one. The dead can—"

"Oh, don't be so predictable." Emeline grimaced. "That's *so* overdone, even for someone like you. 'The dead tell no tales.' 'Two can keep a secret if one of them is dead.' Well, guess what? If I come back from the dead, I promise you, I'll have a lot to say, and I'll tell everyone. If you don't kill me, I'll keep quiet."

"This is beyond tragic." Bluebeard struck his hand to his forehead. "Previously, I have not been forced to kill my other wives until *after* the wedding night. That we must deny ourselves that great pleasure is the greatest heartbreak of all." He jerked the front door shut and slid its three heavy bolts into place. "You will die a virgin."

Emeline choked down the panic rising within her. "That *would* be a tragedy. So why let that happen? There are, after all, alternatives."

Bluebeard pulled a black covering from a whetstone in front of the staircase. He then removed a cutlass from the wall and began sharpening it.

"Hmmm . . ." Emeline pursed her lips and glanced back at Bluebeard. The cutlass blade whirred and sparked on the whetstone. This was bad. Incredibly bad. Time for a change of plans. "Listen, before you kill me, I need to get my soul in order. Can you give me ten minutes?"

"You must not leave the château or attempt to escape, or I will be forced to punish you further."

"Well . . . dying is more than enough punishment for me. I'll see you shortly." Emeline bolted up the stairs, into one of the unlocked rooms, and practically tore her phone from her pocket. As the screen flicked on, the picture Anna had sent was downloaded, along with the message **Here's someone I think you'd like saying yes to. Would you like to meet him at noon on the other side of the bridge?** The picture was of a charming-looking guitarist with curly brown hair and dark gray eyes. He had a strawberry mark on his left cheek. Stupid phone.

Emeline texted back. **Get police to Grete's Woods five miles from Walter County Line. Old château fair distance from main road after old Victorian bridge turnoff. Emergency. Killer with blue beard. Not joking.** The little white icon flashed and flashed, loading and loading but never sending.

"Come on!" Emeline smacked her phone against her hand.

The message still sat there, the circle running around and around. There wasn't enough signal to make a call either. She was going to have to get higher. Maybe if she reached the roof.

Emeline opened her Emergency Dial app and punched in 911. The voice messaging service clicked on and calmly asked her to state her emergency and leave the GPS on her phone turned on until help arrived.

"Yes," Emeline said, drawing in a steadying breath. She couldn't rush this. It wouldn't do any good if her message was garbled. "I'm in Grete's Woods about five miles from the Walter County line. It's an old château in the middle of the forest about half a mile from the old Victorian bridge turnoff." She paced back and forth across the stained wood floor. "I need emergency assistance. There are thirteen dead bodies here, and I think that the murderer is about to kill me too! The GPS is on, but the trees are obscuring the signal, I think—please come immediately!"

She pressed 9 to end. The automated voice assured her that

as soon as a sufficient signal was restored her message would be delivered.

The door slammed open, punching the wall with a sickening thud. Bluebeard stood in the opening. He was framed in cold silver light, the freshly sharpened cutlass in his right hand.

"What are you doing?" he demanded.

"Hey! I still have five minutes!" Emeline said sharply. She jabbed her finger at him. "Get out of here."

"You're trying to escape, but you'll find that you have no signal here." Bluebeard grinned wickedly.

He then closed the door and pulled a large wooden block from the wall. It struck the floor, bloodstained and cracked.

"Now come. It is your time."

Emeline stared at the glinting cutlass and the bloodstained chopping block.

"Kneel. I will be swift," Bluebeard said.

"Hold on. Hold on." Emeline lifted her hand, darting another glance at her phone. "I don't suppose you'd be willing to tell me why it is that you're doing this." Perhaps if she got him monologuing, the messages could finish sending.

Bluebeard did not blink as he stared at her, his eyes grim. "You lost that right when you betrayed me."

"Your standard of betrayal is very low, isn't it?"

"Your time is finished, treacherous woman. Now kneel."

"You know . . . I think I'm going to risk a heftier punishment— and run for my life!" Emeline darted across the room to the door. It didn't matter if it was just a closet. It had to be safer. She jerked the door shut behind her.

It was a closet. A tiny closet. Thin shafts of light peered

through the ceiling and cracks in the wall. Up above, a great opening yawned between large beams that supported another floor.

The door jarred, and the knob twisted.

"Little maiden, let me in!" Bluebeard shouted.

"Yeah, not by the hair of my chinny-chin-chin, you freak!" Emeline jammed a fallen board into the hinges. Pulling herself into the rafters, she clambered upward.

Down below, a few more blows shattered the door. Bluebeard tore it apart. "Get back here!"

Emeline scurried along through the beams, pushing through cobwebs and dust bunnies, startling mice and lizards that scattered in every direction. She caught a glimpse of the landing through the slats. Swinging around, she dropped through. The hole wasn't as large as she thought. Rotten wood, plaster, and wallpaper rained down on her.

Staggering up, she steadied herself on the banister. Then she ran to the top of the staircase. There were two more doors here on the north side, but that was it. The first one was locked. So was the second. Wherever the door to that other tower was, she couldn't see it.

The door below slammed open again. "I'll pluck out your eyes, cut out your tongue, and slice off your ears!"

"If you stuffed my mouth with garlic, you could keep me from coming back as a vampire," Emeline said, drawing herself up to her full height.

Bluebeard slowed his pace as he advanced up the stairs, cutlass extended. "You have nowhere else to run."

Emeline pushed on one of the doors. "I've killed giants, you know. And if you kill me, then my curse will fall upon you." She struck a dramatic pose and pointed. "Eye of newt and toe of dog," she started, kicking the door with each syllable as if it was part of the incantation. "Double toil and stubble, cauldron roil, cauldron bubble—"

Bluebeard laughed coldly. "Is that the best you've got? I fear no curse. Do you know why?"

"Nope." Emeline spun about and kicked the weakening door one last time. The knob crashed through the rotten wood, and the door swung open.

Running inside, she slammed the door shut and turned to find herself in a shabbily furnished bedroom. She set her shoulder to a nearby dresser and shoved it against the door, along with a rotting armchair. The dusty vanity strewn with cobwebs proved more difficult. But she dragged the mirror over and shoved it between the door and the dresser.

When Bluebeard hit the door, the mirror cracked.

"Hey, you'd better be careful about that!" Emeline shouted. "If you break that mirror, you aren't going to find out if you're the fairest of them all." She caught sight of a cutlass on the wall. Racing over, she seized it and wiped the cobwebs away. "Of course, you'll also get seven years' bad luck. Not sure which one you'll hate more."

"Open this door at once!" he commanded.

"Give me one good reason why I should." Emeline slid over next to the window, the glass of which was dry and cracked.

"If you open this door, I will swear my love to you and embrace you one last time. Indeed . . ." His voice softened. "If you open this door right now, I will even kiss you."

Busy scooting a chair to the window, Emeline paused. What sort of freak was he? "Oh, true love's kiss? Well, who can say no to that? Half a second. I'll have to break the mirror in front of the door to let you in." A few swift cracks with the cutlass's leather hilt left an opening wide enough in the window for her to escape.

No sound came from the hall.

Emeline stuffed down fears that he had guessed her plans and was waiting on the other side of the window. This was her only chance. She clambered out onto the roof.

As she had seen from the ground, the roof was in abysmal condition. Holes gaped at intervals, and the shingles were well worn in the best spots. Large globs of mold and fungus grew in thick patches. Fortunately, the roof wasn't a straight shot down on either side. It had sections where it was flat, others where it was seamed with tiles, and even more intervals where dormers and garrets jutted out. Emeline eased to the edge and peered over. It was more than a thirty-foot drop.

Glass shattered, and Bluebeard leaped out through a dormer. Steadying himself on the roof, he brandished his blade, madness glinting in his eyes and sunlight glistening in his beard. "I should have known better than to trust you."

Emeline whipped around. "I'm armed now. So back off, or I'll run you through."

"I fear nothing you can do, because in an age long ago I was cursed by sun and moon and stars to never have a marriage that lasted more than three cycles of the sun."

Emeline backed away. She held her own blade in a defensive position. If only she had known that that fencing class in college would have proved more practical than volleyball. "Have you ever considered that *you* might be the reason none of your relationships work out?"

"If it wasn't I who killed them, it would be something else far more horrific."

"Maybe you should stop getting married, then," Emeline said.

Bluebeard drew closer. "I am compelled to do so. And because of your treachery, I will neither kiss you nor speak sweet words to you as the life drains from your body."

"I'm devastated," Emeline said. The sound of an engine cut her off.

A bright-pink Range Rover barreled down the path, kicking up pine needles and dirt in a steady stream. It screeched to a stop in front of the château. Anna leaped out, the engine and lights still on. She waved her arms. "Emeline! Emeline! Are you all right?"

"There's a crazy man with a blue beard trying to chop my head off—this is what happens when you say yes to the universe, Anna! There are crazy people in the universe!"

Turning, Emeline brought the cutlass up in time to counter Bluebeard's blow. It sent painful vibrations all the way through her arm. She leaped out of his path.

"I'm so sorry. I'm so, so sorry!" Anna wailed.

"Come back," Bluebeard bellowed as he circled the chimney. "Your time has come, vile woman!" He then pointed his blade at Anna. "And as for you, interfering wench, you're next. Married or no, I'll cut off both your heads."

"Ahhh!" Anna screamed, covering her mouth.

"Anna, you're utterly useless. Did you call the police?" Emeline demanded.

"Emeline, look out!" Anna pointed, her hand shaking.

It wasn't necessary. Emeline could clearly see the blade slicing straight at her head. She wobbled and staggered to one side before sliding to one of the dormers. Flinging her arm up, she seized a handhold and struggled up. "Tell me you did something!"

"I told Silas— Watch out! Oh, Emeline!" Anna shrieked.

"Oh, lovely. Maybe he can cater my death. I'd kill for a glass of lemonade. Or maybe some crab puffs!" Emeline ducked again.

Bluebeard came in hard and fast. The shingles splintered and cracked under his feet, setting him only slightly off balance. Emeline ducked behind the chimney and ran to the other side. None of the trees were close enough to the roof for her to climb down.

"I'll go make sure the cops find us!" Anna shouted. "Stay alive!"

"I plan to." Emeline darted to the edge. One of the shingles crumbled. She staggered back, falling. Her cutlass spun out of her grasp and spiraled down to the ground. The slippery, muddy shingles flattened beneath her, causing her to fall over. With a frightened shriek, she dug her nails into the roof.

Bluebeard advanced, chuckling cruelly.

Finding a loose shingle, Emeline wrenched it free and threw it into his face.

With a sharp yelp, he fell back. Emeline stood just as Bluebeard got back to his feet. He growled at her, flecks of wood and mold clinging to his once-immaculate suit.

Emeline's mind spun with panic. There was one possibility left. On the other side of the roof stood a tall pine tree. It was a good several feet away from the château, but maybe if—

Bluebeard swung the cutlass again. Ducking, Emeline squatted, then ran. Her feet slid and her balance wavered.

"Get back here!" Bluebeard roared.

It was all sliding and dodging and flashing blades. But somehow she made it over the top, slid down the edge, and leaped out. For one incredible moment, she was floating through the air. Then, *boom!* Pine needles, branches, and clinging, gripping, and falling.

Somehow her knees hooked onto a branch and she stopped. By instinct, she seized the branches and twisted herself upright. For what felt like an eternity, she hung there, breathing in deep gasps of cool spring air.

"Emeline! Look out!" Anna's voice sounded nearby. How had she gotten back? Sirens wailed and bright lights spiraled through the firs.

Relief flooded her. The police. Emeline released a pained breath, but as she looked up she saw Bluebeard crash into the branches above. Somehow he made it while still holding his cutlass. His weight shook the whole tree.

"You will never escape me," he growled, leaping down to the next branch. "Your blood must yet stain my blade."

Emeline twisted around and dropped. Bluebeard followed. All she could see was blue, pine, and silver as she fell hand over hand in the most controlled manner possible. She tore through the last branches, landed on the soft soil, and seized her fallen cutlass.

Bluebeard dropped nearby in a flurry of needles and pinecones. He waved his cutlass over his head. "Run all you like, but you'll never—"

A silver pie plate sliced through the air and struck him in the head. For a moment, he staggered. Then he collapsed.

Apple pie and cinnamon sugar crumbles spilled all over the ground.

Emeline looked over her shoulder, surprised. "Silas?"

Silas ran up alongside her, another pie at the ready. Raspberry, from the smell of it.

"Are you all right?" he asked.

"Um . . . yeah, all things considered. What are you doing here?" Emeline didn't know what else to say. The police officers descended upon Bluebeard.

"I heard you were in trouble, so I came as fast as I could," Silas said.

"Oh, Emeline! I'm so sorry." Anna flung her arms around her neck and burst into tears. "I had no idea. I don't know what happened to Peter, but this is *not* what I had planned!"

"Oof!" Emeline groaned. She patted Anna awkwardly on the back. "It's fine. I'm fine. He's under arrest. It'll all be fine."

"I feel so bad," Anna said.

"Well, now we know the universe hates me," Emeline said.

"Maybe next ti—" Anna started.

Silas tapped her on the shoulder. "Actually, Anna, would

you mind putting this in the truck for me?" He offered her the oven mitt and the still-warm raspberry pie.

"Sure." Anna wiped the tears away.

Silas waited until Anna was out of earshot. "I'm glad you're all right, Emeline. I would've really been sad if anything had happened to you."

"Thanks." Emeline smiled. Her cheeks warmed. He was being awfully sweet.

"I don't think I could have catered your funeral. I'd have been too upset."

"That makes two of us."

"It would have been hard for me to cater your wedding too."

"Oh?" Emeline raised an eyebrow.

Just then she heard a disoriented growl and looked over to see Bluebeard being loaded into a squad car. As the cops drove off, the last thing Emeline saw of him was that great head with all that cobalt-blue hair lolling about, muttering incomprehensible words.

Emeline lifted her hands in a slight wave, smirking. "Bye-bye, Bluebeard. Please forget to write." She lowered her hand, relieved. It was a little hard to take all this in.

Of course, there was still what Silas had said. Was it just her imagination, or had he . . .

"Cupcake?" She hadn't realized Silas had left, but looking over, she saw him returning from his truck and holding up a small silver container shaped like a clam. Several vanilla cupcakes topped with sea foam–green frosting sat inside. Each one had little pearls and aquatic designs etched on its smooth top.

"Cupcakes? That's your answer to this?" Emeline set her hands on her hips in mock frustration. "I find it hard to believe that all the trauma, all the terror, could possibly be solved by one cupcake."

"Well . . ." Silas shrugged, smiling. "Maybe not one. But perhaps two. Or maybe three. That's why I brought three dozen. To be on the safe side."

"Plus two pies. I never knew pies could be used as weapons."

"They're better-ranged weapons than cupcakes. The cupcakes are for eating."

"Hmmm." Emeline bit into the frosting. It tasted faintly of pistachios. "Delicious."

"Thanks . . ." Silas braced his thumbs on the ties of his thick blue apron. "So . . ."

"So . . ." Emeline studied him. "Do you think I could catch a ride with you back to civilization?"

"Absolutely. Let me clear off the passenger seat." Silas headed toward the truck.

Anna tapped Emeline on the shoulder. "This might not be a good time," she whispered. "But I think Silas might have a little crush—"

Emeline shoved the rest of the cupcake in Anna's mouth. "I noticed. Now off you go."

Spinning around, Emeline clasped her hands behind her back and walked to Silas's catering truck. It smelled heavenly. "You know, this is really nice. When I was younger, I used to think baking would be a fun hobby until I realized how much work it was."

"Yeah, it's great." Silas lifted another tray of cupcakes and then moved them to the back. "Everyone's gotta have a hobby."

"True. I think I'll plan on avoiding men whose hobbies include being creepy and killing their brides."

Silas laughed. "Personally, I collect antique oil lamps."

"Hmm . . . that sounds like a reasonably safe hobby." Emeline arched an eyebrow.

"Reasonably." Silas winked. "Of course . . . if you're still interested in exploring new things, I'd be more than happy to show you a whole new world."

"I don't know. I might be done trying new things. It doesn't seem to have worked out so well." Emeline smiled.

"Either way . . ." Silas rubbed the back of his neck, grinning impishly. "I like being part of your world."

"Nicely played. Are you going to give me a ride or not?" Emeline tried to suppress a smile. It was impossible.

Silas stepped away from the passenger door and bowed. "Be my guest."

The cool breeze played with the loose tendrils of hair on her forehead, pressing away the scents of death and decay. As she fastened her seatbelt, she looked at him, her heart beating faster. "You told me before that there was something I was missing that was right in front of me. I don't suppose you'd like to tell me what that was?"

"Well . . ." Silas's cheeks turned bright red. He shifted the truck into gear. "I was thinking . . . um . . . me."

Emeline's smile grew. "So . . . you collect antique oil lamps and your shop is full of Oriental rugs. Any chance one of them could take us for a ride?"

"If not, we could always find another adventure," Silas said.

"Well, onward then!" Emeline pointed out the windshield at the sky. "Second star to the right and straight on till morning."

"That's the spirit." Silas revved the engine, and they lurched forward down the road.

Emeline settled into the seat happily. If she'd known what was in front of her the whole time was this wonderful, she'd have said "yes" a long time ago.

Home-School Hair

christine owen

CHAPTER ONE
Something and Someone

*T*HERE WAS A BOY . . .

Isn't there always a boy? Check yourself. Go on, really check. Is there a boy? For you? Someone you've snuck glances at, someone you've thought about, noticed new clothes on, watched eating, thought about texting, wanted to kiss—a boy. There is always a boy, dabbling at the edge of our consciousnesses, teasing us collectively with that way his hair falls, or how he looks in the rain, the way he's all gritty after sports. There is always a boy.

My boy was named Tyler. Well, that's using the term "my" pretty loosely. It was more like "there's-this-guy-who-comes-to-the-coffee-shop-I-work-at-every-day-and-never-notices-me." But yeah, we'll go with "my."

And that's where my story starts: the day he finally did notice me.

I'd just been mopping the bathrooms. Of course I had. The manager hadn't mentioned, while interviewing me in the pristine mocha-colored establishment, backlit by stainless-steel accoutrements, that I'd be on bathroom-cleaning duty for *months* after being hired. But I was chalking it up to adventure, to the new Zoe.

I'd finally convinced my mother, combating her overprotectiveness, that I should do something now that I'd finished homeschooling and before I started college (something besides Netflix and texting *Star Wars* quotes to my shady online friends). Still, she'd only reluctantly consented to my getting a job on the first floor of our downtown apartment tower. It was a coffee shop that served the thoroughfare traffic of Chicago's businessmen and commuting students. And, seeing as how I was technically still in our building, she hadn't had much to argue against.

So I smelled like cleaner (and that was the best smell—undercurrents of other things too, I'm sure), with my long hair pulled up into a ginormous braided bun. I mean, we're talking huge. A bun the size of a basketball—no joke.

But he stopped me in the hall, my Lysol fragrance filling the tight space, and pointed a finger at me. At me. With heart hitching in palpitations, I dared to hope. It—it was . . . He was speaking to me! He was moving his mouth! Oh, those lips, oh, that perfectly trimmed stubble . . .

I pushed my bangs over with my hand, not realizing I still had the yellow cleaning gloves on. And they were wet. *Eww.*

"Excuse me? Do you work here?" he asked, beautiful eyebrows perfectly arched in inquiry.

No, I just happen to wear a green apron and clean poop off every surface I find. I'm like an excrement fairy, just flitting about among the bathrooms of the world, leaving a glitter-sprinkled porcelain wake behind me.

"Yes." I swallowed awkwardly. "Yes I do. Work here. I work here, that is. That's me. I'm Zoe. Hi."

Nailed it.

"Um, do you know who's supposed to be . . . ?" He motioned behind him to the empty counter.

Ah! Lucy, our very pregnant shift supervisor, was nowhere in sight.

Rushing behind the counter, I almost slipped. Not that the line of disgruntled coffee-less customers shooting withering glares in my general direction would have cared. Chewing gum with a fervor, our drive-through guy, Frank, took car orders via headset and motioned frantically for me to work the register.

"Lucy's in labor," he hissed through gritted teeth and a fake smile.

Taking a breath, I flashed a grin at Tyler, the first in line.

"Hi again," I said, turning back to him. "What can I get started for you?"

Professional . . . be professional . . . Don't look down at his slightly fitted buttoned shirt, crisp and blue and soft all at the same time. The way his leather coat was slung casually across his shoulders in lopsided fashion as if he didn't care either way—jacket or no jacket, whatever. His dark hair, slight sideburns, glasses. He was a young Clark Kent. Clarification—he was Captain America disguised as Clark Kent (which was somehow hotter).

"Maybe, uh . . ." He studied the menu and then looked over at me.

Why was he having trouble ordering? He got the same thing every single day.

"Could you . . . Would you mind just . . ." He looked pointedly at my hands. The gloves.

"I am *so* sorry! Ah! I never do this, you know, the register and all." Ripping the offending garments off, I threw them to the ground, where they landed with a wet-sounding plop. I quickly washed my hands in the drink sink.

"The usual latte?" I said, and wrote "Tyler" on the cup.

Wow, stalk much, Zoe?

"It's Tyler."

"Oh, yeah." I pretended to keep writing. "Thanks."

"Rough day?" Smiling slowly, he seemed not to care about the line of people behind him.

"It's getting better." Returning the smile back at those ocean-blue eyes, I held his gaze for longer than normal, barely believing what I was saying. Was I flirting? Were we having a moment here? Would this be how our story started? The one we'd tell at our wedding, to our kids, to our grandkids? To their children? And their children's children? I mean, I'm assuming life-prolonging drugs will be available by then. That's only reasonable. Oh, and jet packs.

"Are you Amish?" He waited at the second counter. Placing the carefully made drink in front of him, my hand faltered. Amish? With my face registering surprise, he rushed to clarify.

"I mean—it's just the hair, sorry." He reddened a tad, which made my knees weak; it was that cute.

"Oh. Yeah. I have long hair. I'm not Amish, just . . ." I struggled to explain my upbringing in one word: Vegan. Bookish. Sheltered. Boring.

Friendless.

Only child with a micromanaging mother . . . "Home-schooled."

"Ah." His face cleared. "That explains it." He motioned to my head. "Home-school hair. I knew there was something."

I smiled and nodded in a daze as he turned and left. He knew there was something? What's that supposed to mean?

Oh, Tyler. You were so perfect until you talked.

I guess there was something, though. Wasn't there always Something? With everybody? Everybody has their Somethings. Their Someones and their Somethings.

My mom had cut my hair only one time. She told the story now and then—I wish I could say that it was after a few glasses of scotch with a cigarette hanging out the side of her mouth—but no, it was only when she'd gotten soused on black coffee, on a sugar high from her calcium chews. And she'd always start the same way: "Oh, Zoe, I regret ever taking scissors to that hair of yours."

Then she'd stare at me, stroking my almost knee-length yellow locks until I inched away. And in those seemingly strange moments, I knew that she was thinking about him. My dad. Because I was too. I could still hear him. I could still feel the vibration of his rumbly voice against the back of my head during story time when I was a child. How he'd do characters' voices for me in falsetto.

And after the infamously butchered hair, when I'd gone to him crying over my ragged ends, he'd held me tightly. So tightly. With strong arms and dog tag clinking. And he'd looked up to my mom; I'd felt his chin shift as he did, roughness rubbing against my cheek. He'd looked up to her and said, "Let's let Zoe's hair grow until I get back." And I'd nodded in agreement through my tears, soaking his dusty green ARMY-emblazoned shirt as he whispered, "Hair always grows, Princess. Hair always grows."

But it had been ten years since he'd left. They'd delivered a flag.

And he wasn't coming back.

So my hair was still growing.

CHAPTER TWO

A Superhero from the Fifties

TAKING THE ELEVATOR down to the first floor still felt strange. All the buttons, the seemingly infinite choices. And the people coming and going with strange packages indicative of their trips. Sometimes I just rode it for a while, up and down, making designs with the lights.

Without my dad, my mom had had something of a breakdown. I was young, so I don't remember specifics exactly. Just a lot of lying on the couch, crying. Things being thrown and broken. My aunt and uncle spending time with me, their eyes laden with sorrowful pity. And after the metaphorical smoke had cleared, my mom was . . . changed. Of course she was. She couldn't not be. But she didn't really ever bounce back.

She never left the tower again. Never. In ten years.

And that means I didn't either.

Yeah, yeah, yeah, I know what you're thinking. I know those labels. That box. But that wasn't her; she wasn't a Certain Way with a Certain Disease, Post Traumatic this and Agora that. To me, she was just . . . gone, I guess. Part of her was with my dad. And that was kind of okay with me. I wanted her to miss him, partly because my ability to was waning. I just didn't have enough memories anymore. Yet it still felt selfish to go on with our lives as if nothing had happened.

She worked from home, we had groceries delivered, I was homeschooled. At first people were understanding of her . . . situation. But after a year, and then two, we got looks. We got calls. The concern was gone from the voices, replaced by anger. *Snap out of it*, they seemed to say. *Other people can get through this, why can't you?* But. I don't know. She just couldn't. She still determinedly cooked vegan for us, avoided sugar like the plague, and crocheted, painted, and ordered books to read all the time. But she didn't laugh as loudly as I remembered. We didn't fly kites or have picnics or play softball or whatever it was that normal families did. But I thought she was still a good mom.

Until my job. Until the world was a kaleidoscope of all the things I'd missed—businessmen and dyed/pierced college students and soy low-fat extra-caramel macchiatos. I'd bluffed my way through most of it, not understanding pop culture references. (Who exactly was One Direction? And why did they make everybody so frenzied?) Cleaning the bathrooms had helped me transition well. I'd been able to focus on a mindless task and slowly became initiated into the ways of others. The quick jokes, how everything was sarcastically the opposite, the constant barrage of slang, the dirty innuendos. It never ceased.

The exhilaration of the elevator ride was fading, though. I felt like every other commuter, dragging my body, bleary-eyed, into the shop when my shift started. Work today was slow, and soon the customers filtered out. Frank went around cleaning various contraptions as closing time approached.

"Oh, Lucy had her baby." His voice came dully from halfway inside the espresso machine, echoing off shiny copper surfaces.

I grunted in response. I hadn't known Lucy very long and was secretly relieved to escape her unending labor topics. I'd heard enough traumatizing things to last me a lifetime, some of which had been titled: When Epidurals Don't Work, Vacuum Assistance, Uncontrollable Pushing By-Products, and C-Section Scars. Oh, and the constant, recurring Labor Feels Like Being Burned Alive. That one was fun.

She'd come up behind me as I refilled a machine or made whipped cream and whisper, "Burned alive, Zoe. Burned aliiiive!" Shoot, I'd almost lose my skittles. And I wasn't even the one pregnant here!

I served a few customers—an older man and woman who stage-whispered that it was their date night—and then I saw him.

Tyler. At this hour? Nervously checking my hair, I adjusted my silky black blouse, though it remained hidden behind the company apron.

He strode in and jutted his chin sharply at me. Perfect hair, slightly mussed from the day. A green coat this time. And jeans. Dark jeans. I was a sucker for dark jeans.

"Hey, Home-School Hair."

He had a nickname for me?! I died from excitement, forced resurrection for propriety's sake, and then died again as he winked at me before placing his order. Filling it numbly, I barely remembered to smile. Tyler just winked at me. *Like . . . wow. Who does that?* He's like a superhero . . . from the fifties! My brain was molasses. Counting his change like a three-year-old, I got it wrong multiple times and dissolved into one-sided laughter.

Frank looked at me strangely.

"Are you okay? What's your obsession with Golden Boy?" Frank's beard and mustache twitched as he talked. A hipster from Minnesota (I think?), he was in grad school for . . . something. I'd never really paid much attention.

"Golden Boy?" I scoffed as if nicknames were repulsively juvenile things, never mind my earlier behavior.

Frank joined me at the side counter, arms crossed, as I shamelessly peeked to take in the sights. He mimed looking at Tyler and then going faint, fanning himself girlishly. Collapsing, he clutched his heart silently and then laughed at his own lame joke.

"Stop iiiit," I whined softly.

"I don't know, Zo, he doesn't seem right for you." He eyed me and then looked back at Tyler, scrunching up his nose in distaste.

"'Zo'? Really, Frank? Really? My name isn't short enough already?" I rolled my eyes.

"What? Do you prefer 'Home-School Hair'?" Tugging on my

hair, he went to do more cleaning with an I-give-up *pfft*. I took the opportunity to clean too, sweeping by Tyler.

"Hey," he said, looking at my broom with another smile. Wow, his eyes were crazy attractive when he smiled; they lit his whole face up like a . . . beaming beacon. Or was it "like a beacon, beaming"? *Hmm.*

Weird how beacon sounds almost like bacon.

I heard him laugh. "I think that part is probably clean by now."

I groaned inwardly, mortified. How long had I been standing here like an idiot, sweeping the same spot and staring at him?! *Please, God. If there ever was a miracle needed, open the ground and swallow me now.*

"Yeah. I like to be . . . thorough." I rushed to move, sweeping elsewhere as he laughed.

"You're funny, Home-School Hair."

Funny? I didn't want to be funny! Funny was one step removed from *weird*. And I'd been called weird. Many times. By strangers in online chat rooms. By other students in group home-school projects over Skype. By relatives. By the takeout guy at the Chinese place across the street when I asked if they delivered thirty feet away.

Finishing the cleaning halfheartedly, I retreated back behind the counter to lick my wounds. Tyler, getting up to leave, walked past the register to the door.

But then he stopped, running his fingers through his hair . . . Did he forget something?

"Hey, Home School. What are you up to tonight?"

CHAPTER THREE

Navy Swimsuit

I'VE NEVER UNDERSTOOD the phrase "out-of-body experience" before. But I sure as heck did now. Tyler— the Tyler—my Tyler—had asked me casually, like I did things often, what I was doing tonight. What I was doing?! My first thought was the truth—heading home to watch *The Biggest Loser* with my mom, followed by *Say Yes to the Dress* (they seemed to go together somehow), while we ate homemade veggie burgers washed down with prickly pear kombucha. All in all, kind of a perfect night.

But I caught myself just in time with a noncommittal "Nothing."

And then it was a daze. I seemed to watch him from afar as he mentioned the penthouse apartment in our tower, asking if I knew it. That they had a pool. If I wanted to come. That there'd be a few other friends there too. And I'd nodded and said "Sure, sure" a few times, shaking like jelly inside. And then he'd left. I'd turned to Frank and hadn't needed to ask. "Go!" he'd said with a quirky smile. "Get out of here."

And before I knew it, I was trying to find my swimsuit while simultaneously convincing my mom not to worry.

She sat on the edge of my down comforter–topped bed, dressed in her usual "somewhere in between dressy and pajama" clothes. "It's just that I don't know this boy, Zoe! I don't know anything about him!"

"I know, Mom. But I really want to go. I've never been invited to anything before."

Where is it? Digging among my seldom-frequented clothes, I frowned. I mean, I could swim, like if I had to. But we didn't go often. There was a tiny public pool in the tower that was usually filled with overweight older men holding beers. Not to mention the fact that in Chicago it was only hot enough to be usable for a couple of months.

"And it's in the tower! I won't be far!" I hadn't known Tyler lived in our high-rise, but it explained the early-morning coffee almost every day before what I assumed to be his college classes.

She sighed.

"I guess I can't argue with that. I just— You and . . . and boys. I can't wrap my head around it. I'd still like to meet him."

You could meet him anytime, Mom. Anytime. If you just left our apartment. Just leave. What's the big deal? Why is the world so scary? And why have you projected your fears onto me? My inward comments grew callous as my frustration built.

"You can meet him after this. If it goes well. I'll bring him by another time, okay?"

Victory! My trusty navy one-piece acquired, I hastily put it on.

"Okay, okay. Just stay out of trouble. And come back before midnight." She gave me a swat as I left, calling out more instructions. But I barely heard. Grabbing my monster swim cap and goggles, I threw on a white T-shirt, running for the elevator like my life depended on it. Maybe it did. The life I hadn't begun to live yet depended on me taking action.

Well, universe, this is me, Zoe, taking action.

The elevator doors closed with a deep *thunk,* and I pressed the button for the top floor. A screen prompted me to enter a code and I did, surprising myself that I remembered it through my Tyler-induced fog. My heart beat out of my chest. The goggles creaked ominously around my neck, and suddenly my breath quickened with a shot of adrenaline: *A towel! I've completely forgotten a towel!*

But just then the doors dinged open, and there was no turning back.

I took a step into the plush apartment at the end of the hall. It looked deserted. "Hello?" I called, but no one answered.

Everything was white and gray and silver. There were long, low couches and a huge flat-screen above the fireplace. Expensive-looking framed art and modern sculptures plastered the walls and tables around me. I thought back to our living room—the well-worn gingham couch and old laptop where we watched Hulu. Maybe this was a mistake.

As I turned to go, French doors I hadn't noticed opened off to the side, and sounds of young voices cascaded out in a rush.

"Hey! Home School!" Tyler called to me, barely recognizable with only swim shorts on and a drink in his hand. He sounded boisterous, in his element. Whispering something, a couple of girls giggled, glancing in my direction.

Oh. I smiled weakly, noting their perfectly made-up faces and neon-colored bikinis. Their see-through lacy cover-ups that were more lingerie than pool-worthy. And heels. Goodness. They were wearing heels. Apparently "swimming with friends" was code for "Victoria's Secret Fashion Show next to a pool."

"Did you even wear a suit under that potato sack?" one of the girls muttered in my direction.

"Look at her swim cap," another one remarked. (I'll admit it was rather remarkable. My mom and I had fashioned it out of a couple of rubber caps; when I swam, I rolled my hair into Princess Leia–styled balls and capped each one . . . The effect was pretty alien. But actually kind of cool, like a crazy brain deformity.)

Ignoring them, I looked around for Tyler. He was over by a wall, pushing buttons on a remote and garnering oohs and aahs over the pool lights changing. His eyes lit up as he chatted with several girls. What happened to him heading in my direction? I guess he'd lost interest. The snooty girls walked past me with more whispering.

This was definitely a mistake.

I walked back through the beautiful cream furniture and impressive paintings out to the elevator again and pressed the button. Trying not to cry, I jabbed at it again and again. *Why is this so hard? Why do people make it so difficult?* It was like trying to grab a moving train from a standstill. Everyone had been accelerating their whole lives, while I'd been stuck on a platform, waiting. And could I come on now?

Not likely. Not truly. I could pretend I was the same, but I'd never—

"Zoe! Wait!"

The elevator opened just as I heard the voice. He knows my name?! That was an improvement, right?! I was starting to cringe at "Home School," just waiting for it to become "Homie" and then "Ho." Not the most desirable of nickname progressions.

Tyler rushed to me, shirtless, trunks dripping water on the tile floor. He was skinnier than he'd looked before.

"Look. Don't go, okay? I don't know what those girls said to you, but . . ." He lifted my chin a tad so I was looking at him. "Just don't go yet, okay?"

For the first time I didn't swoon at the slightest attention, despite his touch and half-nakedness. But then he widened his hand and slid it to my cheek, slowly stroking along my jaw before pulling back. Goose bumps poked up on every surface of my body in an instant, and I laughed quietly. Was he going to kiss me? Would this be my first kiss?

But he only grinned. "Should we try again?" He held the apartment door open and ushered me inside.

"Lexi! Lex!" Tyler yelled as soon as we entered, and one of the guys directed him to the pool. A girl was doing flips from the diving board, to cheers and whistles from a group of admirers. She sauntered over to us, her tiny yellow bikini fit to perfection. A dozen earrings hung off one ear and also adorned her nose. Tattoos ran the lengths of both her arms. Of course. He had a girlfriend. And she was magnificent.

"Hey." She, this Lexi girl, looked me over with scrutiny.

"Could you find something for her? Something more . . . appropriate?" Tyler rubbed his neck, apparently feeling the awkwardness as much as I did. *Heeeeey, this girl looks like she's ready for a junior high swim meet . . . but she came to the lingerie swim prom . . .*

Lexi laughed and grabbed my hand, pulling me back into the apartment. She led me down a hall and into a gorgeous room. Posters were plastered on the walls, and paper stars and

Christmas lights hung haphazardly among them. The effect was a technicolor glow on every conceivable surface. Opening a tall side dresser, I peeked over her shoulder as she rustled through an entire drawer—*drawer!*—of swimsuits.

"Hmmmm . . ." She held up a few pieces to me, frowning at my chest.

"You might be a different size, but I think this should work." She slammed a turquoise and gold mash of swimsuit into my hand and motioned me to the bathroom. Peeling off my goggles, cap, and huge shirt, I squinted in disbelief at the tiny triangles of fabric I was supposed to be entirely clothed in.

"I'm Tyler's sister, by the way." She spoke through the door, and I exhaled in relief. ". . . So are you his girlfriend?"

I froze as the question echoed against the elegant fixtures. "Uh, no. I'm Zoe. I just work at the coffee shop downstairs."

I slid the bottom on and then struggled to tie the top. Finally, it seemed like every string was at least tied to another, and I warily looked into the mirror. Gasping in horror, I crossed my arms, trying to cover myself. Was I missing part of the suit somewhere? The middle? The back? The sides?

"Uhh, Lexi? Do you have anything more . . . conservative?" My underwear covered more than this spiderweb clothing. I peered out the door, unsure.

"Woah! Zoe! What are you talking about? You look great!" She adjusted a few of the strings, untying and then tying them again.

"See, it forms a pattern in the front." I looked down and nodded, relieved that at least there was the illusion of more coverage now.

"I have a cover-up if you're not comfortable." She held out a completely see-through golden mesh dress and we both erupted in laughter at the irony.

"It's ridiculous!" I gasped, holding it up to the bathroom light.

Lexi wiped tears from her eyes. "There are matching shoes too!"

We'd started up cackling again when there was a loud knock at the door.

It was Tyler. He glanced to his sister and then at me. We were winded from laughing, and I didn't think to stop smiling. Hugely. Genuinely. Without a care in the world. Standing there in what could only generously be termed swimwear.

His mouth dropped open and he dropped the glass he'd been holding, shattering it on the tile floor.

CHAPTER FOUR

Jazz Hands

*L*EXI SCREAMED.

"Get out! She's not ready yet!" And she pushed the door closed again.

My laughter quickly ceased. "Oh, man, Tyler just saw me seminaked . . ." I could barely process it. Did I just say that out loud? And even more important . . .

Was he in favor or opposed? I didn't have the worst figure in the world, but I *was* pasty white like uncooked dough.

Lexi snorted and slapped my shoulder. "Zoe! You're wearing a very normal swimsuit! You're not naked in the slightest!"

Her laughter was contagious and I joined in some more.

Once we quieted down, she found me a more opaque black cover-up and smeared gloss on my lips and mascara on my lashes. She undid my twin utilitarian braids and fishtail-braided one long one with a murmur of "Oh my, so much hair." And then, biting her lip, she evaluated her handiwork and nodded.

"You're done," she proclaimed.

Deep pulses of some kind of drum music suddenly started shaking things in her room.

"Oh good, music! Let's dance!" Squealing, Lexi rushed down the hall, dragging me behind her. We grew closer to the source of the vibrations.

Dance? Dance?!?! Oh no. *No, no, no, no. No.* So much, no. Dancing I could do, sure—like a proper waltz and things. Even the Macarena I'd practiced for hours. But move my body strangely to beats of foreign music, all while trying to look sexy and cool and totally fine with it? *Nooooo.* That did not happen. Give me a *Glee*-like chorus line perhaps, or a *High School Musical* burst of singing, even Shirley Temple tap-dancing with curls bouncing and jazz hands, but at least tell me the steps!

Lexi—my rock, my sort of friend, my accomplice in making fun of gaudy swimwear—deserted me immediately. And I was left to watch as a dozen boys and girls pushed furniture around and writhed and jumped and laughed and danced. Oh, how they danced. Some danced while yelling things to each other; others, couples, danced sensually off to the side as if they were the only two people in the room. And still others were showing off genuinely awesome moves as small circles formed around them to watch.

This wasn't supposed to be happening! I wished I had a contract for what Tyler had originally said when inviting me. I feel like I remember "a couple of friends" and "hanging out by the pool." Stick to the script, people! No dancing!

Tyler was among the circles watching his friends spin and contort strangely on the floor. Huge applause went up every so often, but I couldn't figure out what part of the performance elicited it. I joined shyly, thinking that I could at least clap for the dancers.

Tyler raised his eyes to mine and made his way to me in the mess of people. In the background some guys had started a fire in the fireplace and it crackled and popped cheerfully, smelling like coziness.

"Hey, Home School! Pretty great, huh?"

I nodded over the music.

"Wanna dance?" he yelled practically into my ear, and I shook my head fiercely and nonverbally got across that I was a horrible dancer.

"You're cute," he said, looking me up and down.

Ah! No take-backs! I felt like yelling. *He said it! Tyler said I was cute!*

He took hold of my hand and started leading me away. *Yes, yes, yes, yes.* Anything but dancing. I followed him to the elevator, where he stopped.

"Wanna get ice with me?"

My running smile at the thought of being alone with him froze. Great, he's on drugs! I really know how to pick 'em.

"What's . . . ice, exactly?" I returned cautiously, hearing my mom's words in my head and trying to think of a reason why I needed to go home.

He laughed. "You know, frozen water that makes drinks cold?" He grabbed my hand again—I could get used to that—and we jumped on the elevator together. Relief flooded my body. Ice I could do. I was like a pro at ice.

"You know, Zoe . . ." He angled me against the shiny metal wall. "I'm not a bad guy . . ." I felt the coolness of the elevator seep through my lacy cover-up, making me shiver. Bringing his hands up to my face, he cupped it like a large bowl of soup. Then, as he leaned in with those perfect lips that smelled slightly of alcohol, suddenly I knew: he's going to kiss me. He's going to kiss me but I don't want him to. Not like this.

I wanted . . . well, everything, you know? All of it. The fairy tale. The prince, the rescue, the love, the wandering, the finding, the protecting, the ending, and then the kiss. I knew it was from reading too many happily-ever-after books or watching *The Princess Bride* too often (heck, even *Star Wars* had cliché love stories), but that's how I felt.

My skin crawled as he got closer.

"Sorry . . ." I murmured, and turned away so he came in contact with my cheek instead.

"It's not that I—I mean, I really do—" I stumbled to explain, feeling I owed him that at least.

Tyler looked at me, his eyes trying to say something. He looked sick. Like, really sick. Oh no, what if he's one of those hot guys with super-low self-esteem (do those exist?), and I've just crushed his spirit forever?

And then the elevator doors dinged open, and Tyler—this gorgeous man of mystery, my knight in shining armor, my Prince Charming—threw up on my feet.

CHAPTER FIVE

Puke Toes

I INSTANTLY LEARNED that there is nothing more disgusting than throw-up on bare feet. More exactly, between your toes. I'd imagine that if it were on your hands, you might scream and run to a sink, shaking it off wildly as you go. If it was on your body, you'd go to the shower, ripping off the offending clothing along the way. But your feet, and slightly sprayed up your legs? Try using those to walk now, making acrid steps and literally embodying the word "squelch" as you searched for a place with water to get clean in. Running? Not so much. More like a back-of-the-heel hobble.

But there was nowhere to wash my feet, and now Tyler was curled up in the elevator, whispering things about the Cubs' Curse.

Should I go home? But where would I leave him?

"It was the goat, Zoe. The goat that cursed us," he slurred, going from smooth talker about to kiss me to . . . this mess.

Oh, Tyler. I'd wanted you to be so much more. Placing my pool cover-up over his shivering, bundled form, I stroked his perfect hair a couple of times.

The coffee shop. It was bound to be closed now, but some-times Frank or Lucy stayed late to count money. Hobbling over to the glass doors, I pounded on them until—yes!—Frank rounded the corner inside, looking confused.

He unclicked the lock.

"Um. I have puke on my toes."

He nodded somberly, like that was to be expected, and dragged Tyler in.

Frank carried me to the bathroom (I was not about to mess up the very floors he'd just cleaned), and I used him as a brace to wash one foot and then the other. His head was turned away the whole time; he was probably disgusted at the trails of semi-liquid puke runoff I was creating.

"Sheesh, Zoe! Where are your clothes? I can't even look at you!" He coughed and glanced up at me, meeting my gaze in the mirror.

I sighed.

"I know. I look horrible." I slathered the pink liquid soap and washed my legs as high as I could. Finally. Puke smell gone!

"Horrible?" He laughed. "Uh, no. You look insanely gor-geous. That's the—er, problem."

Insanely gorgeous? I'd never been called more than "cute," and that was only an hour ago! I immediately reddened in self-consciousness. Here I was in some scanty bathing suit, washing my legs with . . . Frank. Who called me gorgeous. Hmmm. Not how I had imagined the night going.

Extricating my leg awkwardly from the height of the sink, I fell back against him. Pausing to catch our balance, I was suddenly very much aware of his hands on my bare side, and against my back. His mustache twitched in a smile and he righted me, letting go.

"Got it?" he said softly.

"Mm-hm," I agreed, feeling dizzy. And I couldn't help looking up at him, biting my lip. Frank? I'd never really noticed before, but his brown eyes seemed to see inside me. They were intense and . . . real. More real than I'd ever seen, somehow. It must be a Minnesota thing. And, strangely, I couldn't look away. I didn't want to.

"Hey, you," he whispered, sliding his hands around me again, this time by choice instead of merely catching my fall. It felt . . . empowering to be wanted in that second. To be owned by his palms at my waist. All thoughts of Tyler, passed out in the shop beyond, faded.

"Hi . . ." I managed to croak from some ball of pure nervousness deep inside.

What was going on? Was it a full moon? Was he a vampire to bend me to such wiles? Wait. Werewolf. He had the hair for it. We held the half hug, half touch for a minute (actually a fairly long time if no words are spoken). His hand provided the only action, fingers slowly pacing up and down my side, as if in indecisiveness.

"So . . ." he started.

"So . . ." I repeated. It seemed pretty apparent that we both excelled at small talk.

"Did you know that your mom calls me every day?" He smiled, and we finally had a track. Yes. Mom being crazy. I could talk about that for hours. If I could only focus on something besides my side being touched in such a tingly way . . . How is it that conversations always became impossible the instant there was mutual attraction?

"Oh she does, huh? Do you gab?" I twirled my hair with one finger and jutted out my hip in an impression of those girls I'd seen with Tyler.

He laughed.

"Nah. She's just checking that you got to work okay." He leaned in until I could feel his breath on my cheek. His hand finally settled, making a decision.

"Zoe . . ." And then he cut himself off with a low cough and pulled back.

I sighed as his hands left my side, my back, all in reverse of their delicious closeness. My arms were cold and lonely where his touch had been, and then I realized the purpose of men: those tiny moments when your arms weren't cold anymore.

Frank rubbed the heels of his hands against his eyes.

"What am I doing . . . You're like seventeen, right?" he muttered, looking away from me. No, no, beautiful eyes, don't leave me! I'd only just started to notice them!

"Nineteen. But, um. Yeah." Should I go home?

"Okay. Nineteen. So we're still in the bathroom then, huh?"

"It would appear that we are." I tried to be enthralled by the paper towel dispenser and to not think about my lack of clothes or how much I wished he'd throw caution and whatever else to the wind and kiss me.

Where do we go from here? And then the fire alarm went off.

CHAPTER SIX

Zoe, Zoe, Let Down Your Hair

*D*O YOU THINK it's a drill?" My voice wavered with nervousness. In all the years we'd lived in the tower there had never been one.

"We should go," Frank said.

People were already filling up the atrium of the first floor, but reluctant to go outside into the night. Some even banged on the storefront glass and indicated we should open the shop for the event.

A trashy-sounding song suddenly burst from Tyler's phone, and we didn't think much of it until it came again and again. Finally I went to answer it, slipping it from his hunched-over breast pocket and feeling a little sleazy at having a passed-out-drunk . . . Date? Friend? Acquaintance?

"Hello?" I answered.

"Tyler? Zoe? You guys have to help us! There—there's a fire, and—" It was Lexi. I heard screaming in the background and someone else yelling. The phone clicked off.

My face must have told the story, because Frank instantly grabbed my hand and we took off running. We fought past the ever-growing throngs of people and caught an elevator as it emptied out.

"Let's see how far we can get." Frank pushed the penthouse button and I entered the code. The tomblike silence felt strange after all the people in the lobby, and I still felt the ghost of Lexi's call haunting me.

"Do you think we—" My eyes started to water. If Lexi was hurt, my first girlfriend in maybe ever, I'd . . .

"Zoe. You stay in the elevator when we get there." Frank lightly put an arm in front of me like I was about to jump out of a moving vehicle then and there.

"No way, I—"

"Zoe. Seriously. You have to stay safe. Your mom couldn't handle it if . . ." He squeezed my arm reassuringly.

The doors opened, and we smelled smoke immediately. Frank took off his shirt and bunched it up over his face. Stepping out, he pressed the lobby button for me. But the doors didn't close. There was a slight beep, and then the elevator lights faded to black, powering off.

"You'll have to take the stairs!" he shouted through his makeshift mask, and then ran into the large apartment.

Why had I not noticed before how hot Frank is shirtless? Tyler had been nice looking if skinny in that emo new-age way, but Frank was built like a man . . . like a . . . a woodsman.

Okay. Now is not the time, Zoe.

I followed after Frank once he was inside, not heeding his commands (he was sweet, but come on, I was going to help).

The apartment was in flames. Truly. I'd never seen something burn like this. Like a bonfire, but inside, consuming millions of dollars' worth of paintings and electronics and couches and rugs. It had started in the fireplace; I dimly remembered the happy little fire from the party, but now it was a vengeful monster. Flames licked over everything in sight, spreading downward through the floor as much as horizontally. *Oh no—the floor* . . . I felt the boards creak below me and I tread cautiously.

"Lexi?" I called. The place looked deserted; that at least was a good sign. "Frank?"

No response to either. There was a gaping hole where the fire was eating away at the kitchen, and I was drawn with morbid fascination to look.

"Zoe? Help!" The voice was faint, but I could tell it was Lexi's. I crawled on my hands and knees to stay lower than the billowing smoke; my lungs burned already. I peered down into the hole in the floor. She was trapped against some kind of framework—the supports between levels.

"Zoe! Thank God! I've broken my leg or something!" she yelled up to me, her knee twisted at an unnatural angle.

"Zoe!" Frank found me then, pulling a large guy's body behind him.

"I found him in one of the rooms! Let's get out of here!" he yelled through his shirt, grabbing my arm.

"Not yet! My friend is trapped down here!"

The fire around us hit a gas line or something and there was this huge boom, like a mini–atom bomb explosion. Frank threw himself over me an instant before we were yanked back in the pressure wave. We slammed against the wall, leaving dents. Screaming. So much screaming. Why wouldn't somebody stop screaming? Then I realized it was me and I stopped, shaking.

"Come with me, Zoe. Leave it to the professionals." He picked up my entire body, kicking and screaming, and forcibly took me out of the penthouse.

"This is not your choice!" I yelled. "The elevators are down! They'll have to climb a hundred floors of stairs to get her!"

I hit his back with balled-up fists as hard as I could, weeping. Thrashing as roughly as possible, I evaded his grasp and fell to the ground, only to find strong arms holding me back again once I got up.

"You can't leave her to die, Frank! You can't!" Tears streaked through the smoky residue on my face, and I wiped them away fiercely, spreading snot and soot across my visage.

He studied me, as serious as I'd ever seen him.

"Zoe, sometimes people . . ." Frank started, but I sternly shook my head, lips pressed together, wishing away years upon years of people telling me just that. I recognized the tone. I knew the "Sometimes things happen, Zoe; sometimes people die" speech.

"Please." I was begging. It was about my dad. It was about my mom. It was about Lexi. It was about me. *Please, Frank.*

"We'll try once, okay? If it doesn't work, we leave her," he said, raising his eyebrows for a confirmation.

"Yes! Yes! Once! I promise!"

We ran back inside. The smoke was black this time, and I couldn't hear Lexi. My eyes watered instantly as we crawled inches above the ground. There was little to no more breathable air, and I hacked with each ragged breath.

"Lexi! I'm here!" She looked up weakly and smiled. What could I use to reach her? A chair? An umbrella? I didn't see anything in sight.

Frank tapped my head and smiled wryly.

"Zoe, Zoe, let down your hair." His eyes were squinting from smoke but held mine for a second. One time. One try. Then we leave her. I nodded. Lying down, he held my braid close to my scalp and threw the rest down to her. *Please be long enough. Please.* I'd never wanted anything more in all my life.

And then I felt the tug. Frank held my hair near my scalp so Lexi's weight wouldn't pull it out, and when she got close he pulled her up himself.

We stumbled out of the apartment just as another explosion sounded behind us. Firefighters burst from the stairwell, out of breath. They entered the apartment and dragged the other guy out, the one we'd left. Others gave us oxygen and helped Lexi start down the stairs. I wanted to be relieved, but some tenseness held me back.

"It's electrical—already spread down to multiple floors," I heard the closest firefighter radio in. "Make sure the Evac Team gets everybody out."

Oh no . . . *Mom.*

CHAPTER SEVEN
Cinderella and *Grease*

FRANK, MY MOM. She *won't* leave the building," I said with mounting dread. We had collapsed, sitting on the floor to recover, oxygen masks in hand. Expansive glass surrounded us, showcasing the top-floor view.

What had they said? Electrical? Does that mean it could reach my mom?

"I know." He coughed deeply, wiping away pale pink blood flecks from the corners of his mouth.

It would almost have been romantic, sitting by the window at the top of the building. My last trip out was when I was almost ten. And after that . . . all I had were the windows looking down at the garden and the glittering lights of the city holding the promise of the future. I'd always imagined that one day I'd leave the tower. That one day Mom would "get better"—whatever that meant; people always said it. But one day I'd just walk outside, and it would be like a musical. Like *Rodgers & Hammerstein's Cinderella*, in the preparation for the ball. I'd walk along and twirl, and a child would hand me a flower. Then I'd pass under a balloon archway being raised for some special event, followed by a handsome stranger smiling and kissing my hand. Women with long silks would arrive in a miniature parade, and I'd lose the man and be searching, but in cadence with the music, in a happy way. And I'd find him in a candy shop, where we'd eat chocolates and drink milk shakes and then somehow it would turn to *Grease* and we'd live happily ever after.

"Uh, excuse me, sir?" I went to the nearest fireman. "My mom is on level forty-five; do you know if she's okay?" He radioed in something garbled and then listened to an equally garbled reply. "Yes, miss. They've cleared every floor up to fifty. She'll be outside with the rest." The firefighter went back to help, and I dejectedly trudged back to Frank.

"What's the matter? The guy said she was fine." He held my hand.

"No, she wouldn't have let them take her out. And we would have seen her down there."

Frank looked at me with a knowing expression. I must have seemed panicked, because he just squeezed my hand and said, "Here we go again . . ."

And we took off down the stairs.

⸎

AFTER MORE THAN FIFTY flights of stairs, we were jittery and sweaty. My legs shook like they were made of rubber, and we couldn't stop coughing. Finally, I banged on my apartment door. It looked so unassuming, so unchanged by the night's monumental events.

"Mom?" There was no sight or smell of fire yet, thank goodness. Our little apartment looked as cozy as ever—sunny yellow paint in the quaint kitchen, family pictures in wooden frames down the hall.

Remnants of my mom's veggie burgers sat uncared for on the counter. She would have put those away. "Mom?"

"Mrs.— Zoe's mom?" Frank joined in.

Hearing weeping, I ran into my mom's room.

"You're okay! Thank heavens!" Mom rushed out of her closet and embraced me with viselike hands, reaching around me to wipe at her tears. Who knew the woman could be this strong? It must be all the Pilates DVDs.

"Mrs.— Ah, we should go . . ." Frank tried to sound official but succeeded only in shocking my mom, who hadn't noticed him yet.

"A boy? You brought a boy? Is this the boy?" She made eyes at me suggestively, and I groaned.

"Mom," I spoke through gritted teeth, "this is Frank. I work with him."

She clapped her hands together and squealed like a schoolgirl. "Frank! I know Frank!"

He smiled and tipped an imaginary cap in acknowledgment.

"Mom. There's a fire. We have to get you out, like now." I hissed at her but she waved me away, enthralled with meeting someone new.

"So, Zoe . . . do you *like* like him?" she whispered, obnoxiously ignoring me.

Seriously, when did my mom turn into a teenager?

Then she glanced at me, doing a double take. "And what in the world are you wearing?!"

"Don't change the subject. We have to get out of here!" I coughed with my own escalating volume.

"I'm just trying to meet—" she started, but I cut her off.

"No. Don't. You're stalling. But we saw where it started. And there's a real fire. A huge one. It's in the walls, coming here." Starting to tear up, I took her hand, feeling her stiffen. *She won't leave. She won't. Not even for this.* I pulled her arm but she smiled quietly, sitting back on the bed.

"You—you know I can't go, Zoe." Her voice rose barely above a whisper, and she glanced to Frank, embarrassed.

"Mom, please!" I was crying. Taking her hands, I rubbed her palms in frustration, in helplessness. She continued to mutter things, her eyes moving wildly.

I pressed my forehead to hers.

"Please, look at me." Her eyes finally fixed, desperate, onto mine, clutching and not letting go.

"We're going to walk out now. We're going to do this to-gether." I took a breath and noticed Frank closing the bedroom door in a puff of smoke, sealing in the already-expanding fumes.

"How are you this strong, Zoe?" she whimpered.

"You made me this way, Mom. We're gonna be strong together."

"**STEP. ONE.** Step. Two. Step. Three. Step. Four . . ."

With each step, with each floor, we counted. She prayed. Frank followed behind us. In this way, we made it to the front door and—as she squeezed her eyes shut—out the door and down the many flights of stairs.

The lobby had been cleared, and we stopped by the main doors.

"I can't—I can't—I can't—I can't—" Her tears were streaming now, unhindered by thoughts of embarrassment. Frank held the door open and people outside yelled for us to walk out.

"Why not, Mom?" I asked, pressing my forehead back against hers. She looked at me.

"Because . . ." Her voice caught with tears, stopping and then continuing from watery emotion. "He's dead . . . out there." She stopped to cry and then finished, wailing, "If I don't go, he won't be dead. It won't be as real."

I'd never seen her cry like this before. It made me so uneasy that someone so strong—my own mother, who'd done so much for me—was so helpless. I didn't know what I should do.

So I cried. We cried together, shaking. The two women loved so much by the man who had left us.

"I miss him too, Mom. Every day."

Frank embraced both of us and gently moved our two frozen bodies out through the doorway. We let him.

Maybe that's all it was. The Letting. Maybe, when you're not strong enough to take the step, when nothing in you can do it, and when there's nothing left to muster up, there can be only the Letting left. And, if you're lucky, really lucky, then a prince will come along at the right time, not because he's stronger or better, but simply because he's there. And he's taken that step before. He's not patronizing or higher, but he's forged on. And to rest in someone's forging step is a great thing.

We were outside.

The cool air rushed. Sounds of cars and sirens. People milled around in pajamas, looking at us strangely. But our crying, our despair, faded. Suddenly, Mom laughed. I hiccuped. Until we both were lurching out huge guffaws, causing quite a scene. Relief flooded in with the laughter.

Frank joined in, hacking as he coughed, still sheltering us both with his arms. Part of him probably thought we'd run back inside at the first opportunity. Finally, he let us go.

"Thank you, Frank," I said, with tears still drying and an exuberant smile perched crazily on my face. We were free. Somehow. And I hadn't even known I was trapped.

"Please. You've really got to wear something, Zoe." He wiggled his eyebrows, wrapped his jacket around my bikini-clad body, and then pulled me in, kissing me to wild applause.

Epilogue

ARE YOU SURE?"

"Are you ready?"

"You don't have to do this, love."

"I know. But I want to." I nodded at the man behind me and then at Frank and my mom, who each held one of my hands. Even Tyler and Lexi had shown up for the event—my first friends.

The professional worked the scissors hard against my thick rope until I felt the whoosh of freedom and a bare neck.

I was supposed to let my hair grow until my daddy came home. Until he came back to us. And, well, he had. He was home. And we were too. The "going on" part of living—that's where we'd found him.

Hair always grows, Princess. Hair always grows.

My Love God Went to Hawaii and All I Got Was This Lousy Papaya

debra goelz

*I*T IS A TRUTH universally acknowledged that parents in possession of a kingdom must have a capable heir if they're ever going to retire. Sadly, Weston, the only child of mattress magnates Gerald and Victoria Fitzgerald, had a great many skills, mostly related to hosting lavish luaus with well-toned grass-skirted dancers wearing colorful leis, but none having to do with running a business.

Every weekday morning promptly at eight, Gerald and Victoria drove to the office in their Lamborghini, drifted into the designated spot labeled "Park Here at Your Own Risk," and took the elevator to their second-floor office, overlooking the showroom of Bull's-Eye Mattress Kingdom's flagship store in Waikiki, which had been in the family for three generations.

The Fitzgeralds' office held three identical desks side by side that faced a one-way window overlooking their glittering showroom, where rows of chandeliers hung from the forty-foot ceiling—each mattress elevated on its own pedestal.

Strewn across two of the three desks were dozens of glossy travel brochures offering the promise of adventure in a vast landscape. An assortment of mermaid collectibles adorned the unoccupied desk.

"I like the river rafting in Zambia," said Victoria. After an hour, they'd whittled it down to ten options.

"We could do that on our way to Antarctica for the Ice Marathon," agreed Gerald.

"Still not sure about that one," said Victoria. "Sounds cold."

"After thirty years of warm, I'm ready for some cold. But this coffee. Ugh." He grimaced and set the Bull's-Eye cup on the desk.

"It does that when you forget to drink."

Victoria traced the photo of the young couple trekking across the frozen landscape, holding hands, the sun low behind them. Each click of the second hand on the Bull's-Eye clock was a reminder that Weston had not yet arrived to work.

She sighed. "Where is he?"

Almost in answer to her question, something stirred from within the playhouse in the children's department at the far end of the showroom. The Fitzgeralds provided the house, along with boxes of toys and books and pretend stores with pretend cash registers, to entertain young shoppers while their parents were encouraged to spend actual money. A form, vaguely Weston-shaped, emerged—rumpled, wearing several smashed leis wrapped around its neck.

"Not again," said Victoria, sighing in exasperation.

"Weston," Gerald yelled over the loudspeaker.

Weston smiled and waved at the office window. "Be right there," he mouthed, limping toward the men's restroom.

"This ends now," said Victoria.

"You're going to kill your own son?" said Gerald. They hardly ever talked about their old life as hit people ("hit men" being a sexist term).

"Of course not," said Victoria, her trigger hand clenching. "We'd still be minus an heir. There's only one solution. He must marry a highly competent woman with a business degree."

"Brilliant plan, my queen."

"The problem is, Weston is twenty-seven and still can't be bothered dating a woman more than once. God forbid he'd have to remember her name. We'll have to find someone for him."

"How do you propose we find this business genius? Should we hire a headhunter? I mean the kind that finds employees, not the kind that—"

"I know what you mean, Fitzy. Hmm. We'll need someone young and impressionable but smart. Someone we can mold into the perfect wife/business manager. We'll place an ad for a management trainee."

"Brilliant, my dear."

"There'll be a test. Any potential bride must be proficient at all aspects of business—accounting, marketing, and quality control."

"You are wise, my darling."

The door opened, revealing a slightly less disheveled Weston. His hair was slicked back with water and combed. His shirt was tucked in. The leis must've been abandoned in the bathroom trash. He looked nearly presentable, though his suit was damp and he smelled like smoked pork and rum.

"Hey, Mom. Dad. Sorry I'm late. Ran into this hot mermaid at the luau."

Victoria and Gerald shared an incredulous frown and nodded their heads at each other in solidarity.

"Hey, wait." Weston wrinkled his brow. "What's up with you two? The last time you looked at me like that, you wanted to send me to military school."

"Would've done you good," Gerald grumbled.

"I was in third grade."

"My darling boy, we have a wonderful idea. If you'll have a seat, we'll go over our plan for the rest of your life."

⌒⟐⟐⌒

CUPID DESPISED THE UNDERWORLD. It smelled like brimstone and three-headed-dog breath, and there were lost souls everywhere. He hated when they flew inside his toga. They tickled, and not in a good way. He tousled a few off his golden locks, folded his hands across his lap, and admired his stunning new booties. Hades's inner sanctum was so cold, Cupid's bones froze. Hades chose to live in a dark, wintry cave with the most unflattering lighting ever. Worse than that was the poor design. Cupid imagined feng shui–ing the place. How did that nice Persephone live here? He'd have to ask her the next time they met for billiards on Mount Olympus.

The images in the lava lamp went dark. Cupid's eyes ached from the effort it took not to roll them after watching that stupid scene with humans planning the most unromantic coupling for their son—so last-millennium.

Cupid slow-clapped. "Thanks for that, Hades. Well, I'll be off. Great punishment, though. Watching that nearly killed me. Honestly, so original."

"Eros, you have displeased me for the last time," Hades boomed.

He was always cranky when Persephone wasn't around. Gods. It's been how many millennia, and the guy still can't get over it?

"Call me Cupid," said Cupid. He despised his Greek name. "Cupid" had nice, hard consonants. Much more manly. Eros was a name for a chubby, winged, baby god, not a muscular, handsome, grown-up god like himself.

Hades stared at Cupid from his elevated throne by way of reply.

"It was one little boat," Cupid said.

"It was Charon's ferry, you idiot. You sank Charon's ferry!"

"Epic party, though." Cupid recalled the finer attributes of the water nymphs who'd attended.

Hades's face flushed, and the cave vibrated.

"Come on, dude, you must have a backup boat. Besides, the old one was pretty heinous. Big important god like you must be able to magic up a new ride. Something with indoor seating? Maybe a wet bar? A motor might be nice. Charon's got to get tired . . ."

"Silence," Hades bellowed.

Cupid sat as silently as possible, because Hades's hair was flaring. The temperature in the cave rose at least several degrees.

"If you'll recall," Hades began, teeth clenched, "I told you that if you provoked me again, I would spear you to a rock with your own arrow for all eternity."

"How could I forget?"

"Hand over an arrow."

Cupid clutched his quiver of golden arrows to his chest.

Hades rolled his eyes, held out his hand, and an arrow shot through the air. He caught the shaft. Stupid telekinetic god. "I know the perfect rock. You'll have company."

"Not Prometheus. Please, no. Titans are so boring. And don't get me started on their grooming."

"Sorry, it's the only rock the gods may legally use for spearing purposes."

Cupid knelt. "Is there no other punishment?"

"Well . . ." Hades pretended to give it thought. Cupid knew Hades had something up his sleeve—er, chiton. "There is something you could do."

"Let me guess. It has something to do with that scene you made me watch in the lava lamp?"

"It does. I expect ultimate discretion in what I am about to relate."

"Of course." Cupid twisted his lips as if buttoning them.

Hades cleared his throat. "It began about twenty-one years ago. You see, Persephone and I have been married a long time."

"I'm aware. Heck, everyone's aware. Winter, duh."

"Anyway, a god gets restless after so many eons."

"I get it," said Cupid. "Marriage is like carrying the earth on your back. Or so I've been told."

"Yes, well . . ." Hades shifted in his marble chair. "Anyway, I decided to go somewhere to get a tan and watch human women in those wonderful inventions."

"Bikinis?"

"Correct. There was this woman. To say she was beautiful would be a disservice to beauty. She was more beautiful than Helen, than Hera, even than Aphrodite. Don't tell them I said that," said Hades.

"I'm not an idiot," said Cupid.

"This woman had olive skin. Raven hair. Eyes the color of the Mediterranean at daybreak. I had to have her."

"Yes . . ." Cupid leaned forward.

"So I had her. And she got pregnant. And Persephone cannot ever know."

"Could you be a little more specific about the 'having' part? It's important to my understanding."

Hades flamed.

"Okay, no specifics. Fine."

"After I discovered the pregnancy, I escaped to the Underworld. Three days after the baby's birth, Clotho stopped by. She foretold my daughter's future. She saw two possible outcomes. One—she's destined to become a demigod on her twenty-first birthday. Once this happens, Persephone will, of course, find out about my slight indiscretion and divorce me. Two—my daughter never comes into her demigod powers. She remains hidden from my wife, and I continue to be blissfully married."

"So you want me to ensure your daughter doesn't get her powers?"

"Correct."

"How?"

"Simple: she must kiss the heir to a kingdom in the last hour before her twenty-first birthday."

"That's rather specific."

"I don't make the prophecies."

"Understood. So I get this daughter of yours to kiss some guy who's an heir to a kingdom? Easy. One arrow from my quiver will take care of your problem."

"Your arrows aren't reliable. No arrows."

"Hey, I pride myself on my results. I have a full-ardor money-back guarantee."

"That may be, but we cannot risk failure. You must get her to apply for that job and help her pass the tests, so she will be able to kiss Weston Fitzgerald at the appointed hour one week hence."

"Sounds hard."

"It's that or the rock," said Hades.

"I choose the rock."

"Are you serious?"

"Nope. Besides, I have ethics."

"You don't know the meaning of the word."

"I think I know better than you, Mr. Philanderer."

"You have angered me once again. I revise my punishment. Do as I say, or I shall turn you back into a teenager and send you to repeat high school."

"You wouldn't."

"Oh yes, I would. Acne and all."

"Fine. I'll do it."

"Excellent. One week," said Hades. He raised his hand in an arc.

Cupid found himself transported to a sun-drenched beach,

wearing Hawaiian-print bathing shorts and holding a rum cocktail with a tiny umbrella in it. Cupid took a huge gulp.

Delicious. Maybe Hades wasn't entirely bad.

◦◦◦◦◦◦

THE UNDERWATER SHARK BAR AND CAFÉ boasted a glass wall overlooking the ocean and dozens of sea urchin–shaped chandeliers glowing in carnival tones. The smell of brine hung thick in the air, and the tinkling of dishware made it hard to concentrate.

Phoebe Thompson checked her watch. Six fifteen. From her perch at the end of the shellacked bar, one of the sharks out the window winked at her. Phoebe blinked, trying to reconcile a shark winking with reality. A man's shoe floated up.

She needed to get more sleep. Things never went well when she hallucinated. Her mom's shift at the Shark Bar was supposed to end fifteen minutes ago.

Phoebe needed to get home to study for her microeconomics final, but she had to drive her mom as well. Because they could afford only one car—an ancient pale yellow Fiat Spider convertible—they had to take turns shuttling each other around the island.

Her mom passed by carrying a tray of oysters on a bed of ice. "Sorry, Phoebs. The boss is making me stay late."

"It's okay, Mama," said Phoebe. The circles under her mom's eyes were darker, and strands of long black hair escaped her bun. She must be exhausted, but why beautiful, kind Inaya Thompson thought she could waitress was a mystery. Inaya was as coordinated as a drunken octopus on roller skates.

The rotund manager snuck up behind Inaya. His thick

mustache had earned him the nickname "Walrus." "Get a move on, Princess."

Phoebe cringed. She hated when people called her mom that. It was a reminder of all she'd lost. Miss Papaya Princess for twenty years. The loveliest wahine on the island. Fired because she had the audacity to get older. Phoebe glared at the manager.

"Table forty-six isn't going to serve itself." He smacked Inaya on the behind and strode to a table of important-looking customers half-hidden by a mountain of sushi.

Phoebe chose to right the serving tray as it wobbled in Inaya's hands instead of clobbering the manager. Though clobbering would have been infinitely more satisfying. Still, Phoebe couldn't ruin this opportunity for her mom. It was her sixth job in as many months.

"Thanks, Phoebs. It'll be no more than fifteen minutes. I promise."

"Sure, Mom," said Phoebe, pulling out her phone. There was a message from the job board. A summer internship could save them. If she got it, they could eat and keep the electricity running, which meant air-conditioning.

"What'll it be?" said the bartender, throwing a cocktail napkin on the bar.

"Nothing, thanks." She didn't bother to look up from her phone. "I'm waiting for Inaya." Phoebe pointed across the room to her mom, who was delivering the drink order to table forty-six. "And I'm only twenty. You're supposed to ask for ID."

"Ah, a great beauty, your mother."

"How did you know she was my . . ." Phoebe looked at the bartender for the first time. Her stomach sank, and goose bumps chased up her arms. The man had curly blond hair, turquoise eyes, smooth, sun-kissed skin, and his muscles, barely concealed by his thin Hawaiian shirt, practically begged to be touched. His lips quirked into a confident grin, as if he knew what she was thinking and was used to this reaction. She wanted to climb up on the bar and kiss him, hard.

"You okay?" he asked.

The enchantment ended. Phoebe realized her mouth was hanging open. Why was she gawking like a lovesick teenager? Phoebe knew she was never falling in love. It led only to disappointment. Abandonment. Phoebe wouldn't end up like her mother. She'd be self-sufficient. Never rely on her looks.

Head cleared, Phoebe returned to her phone, clicking on the message:

Wanted: Business school graduating senior.

Position: Management Trainee at Bull's-Eye Mattresses.

Pay: $2,000 for one-week testing period. Thereafter, $5,000 per week.

Phoebe's eyes practically bugged out of her head. Okay, so she wasn't a senior, but she had straight As, was at the top of her class, and she could pass their test.

She typed a response and hit send as a slick-looking guy sidled up to the bar and nudged her.

"Excuse me?" He was incredibly handsome—not like the bartender. But still. Light brown hair. Green eyes that were perpetually in bedroom mode. Just the right amount of devil-may-care stubble. Were the very heavens trying to distract her?

"Yes?" said Phoebe, trying not to notice his dimples or his fine suit.

"Looks like you could use a drink. Allow me . . ." He snapped his fingers.

The bartender frowned. "What can I get you?"

"Your specialty."

The bartender pulled down the top-shelf tequila, ice, limes, a fresh papaya, and two glasses. He expertly assembled the ingredients, poured the mixture into the glasses, and garnished them with a spear of fresh papaya. Phoebe cringed at the abhorrent fruit. Hanging a plastic monkey from each glass, the bartender set them in front of Mr. Fine Suit, who pushed one toward her.

"No, thanks." Phoebe waved it away. She sneezed.

"Bless you," said the bartender.

"Thanks."

"Drink up," said the man, shining his dimples at her.

"I'm allergic." She sneezed again.

"Bless you. To margaritas?"

"To papaya." It started when Phoebe's mom was fired as Miss Papaya Princess. Now looking at the fruit made her eyes itch.

"Why don't we get out of here? My Ferrari's parked out front."

"Don't think so."

He looked crestfallen.

"Have you ever been told no?"

"Not that I can remember."

"First time for everything," she said, sneezing.

"Come on." He wrapped his arm around her waist.

Phoebe picked up the margarita and tossed it in the man's

lap. He squealed. She felt like a horrible person. Why couldn't she control her anger?

"I'm sorry." She handed him a stack of cocktail napkins, and he patted his crotch. The bartender smirked. "I'll pay for the cleaning." If she skipped lunch this week, she could probably afford it.

"Oh, there's my shoe," said the man, making his way toward the window. "Sirennia?" The shoe banged silently against the glass.

Phoebe caught a glimpse of a lovely blue-green fishtail and what looked like long, gold-green hair. A mermaid? Phoebe shook her head. Her hallucinations were getting more creative. She rubbed her eyes, which now felt like ants were traipsing over them.

"I'm ready, darling," said Inaya.

"Uh, okay."

"What's wrong with Weston?" said Inaya.

"Weston?"

"Yes, the young man at the window."

"You know him?"

"He's only the most eligible bachelor on the island. Family owns Bull's-Eye Mattresses. Isn't he dreamy?"

"Uh . . ."

⚬⟡⚬

THE NEXT DAY, Phoebe drove through a torrential rainstorm to the Bull's-Eye Mattress flagship store. The rain blurred the road. Palm trees bent in the wind. Gripping the steering wheel, she concentrated on getting there alive. She had to get that job. Hopefully she wouldn't run into Weston.

She parked. By the time she got to the entrance, her thin floral dress was clinging to her every curve. She opened the door to a blast of ice-cold air-conditioning. A puddle formed beneath Phoebe. The store was like a palace, with mattresses on pedestals and sparkling chandeliers casting an almost magical light in the cavernous space. Phoebe preferred the gloom. Her mom called Phoebe a creature of the night.

"You here for the interview?" said a salesman.

"Yes, I'm looking for the office."

"Take the elevator." He pointed to an inconspicuous brushed-metal door.

The four walls inside the elevator were mirrored. She looked like a cross between a wet mop and an overwatered garden. Her auburn hair stuck to her neck. She wrung it out as the doors opened.

"Phoebe Thompson," said a Helen Mirren look-alike with a shoulder-length white bob. "I'm Victoria Fitzgerald." She held out her hand. Phoebe shook it, realizing with horror that her hand was wet and cold. Mrs. Fitzgerald wiped it on a long, camel-toned jacket that matched her pants.

"Good to meet you, Mrs. Fitzgerald."

"You must call me Victoria."

"I'm Gerald Fitzgerald," said a tall, bald-headed man. He had no eyebrows, and Phoebe fought not to stare.

"Nice to meet you." Phoebe bowed her head, not wanting to subject anyone else to her clammy hands. No Weston. What a relief.

"Tell us about yourself." Mrs. Fitzgerald indicated a chair next to a love seat on the far side of the office.

"I'm Phoebe Thompson, but you already knew that." Phoebe laughed, crossed her legs, and shifted in the seat. "I'm a marketing major at Oahu University."

"A senior?" said Mrs. Fitzgerald. Her eyes were blue, and though she seemed outwardly friendly, Phoebe felt like the woman saw every detail. Almost like she was memorizing Phoebe's face for a police sketch.

"No, I'm a junior," she said, straightening her shoulders. "But I'm a fast learner. I have straight As, and you'll be satisfied with my abilities."

"The ad called for a senior."

"Yes," said Phoebe. "But please give me a chance."

"I'm not sure," said Mrs. Fitzgerald, rubbing her chin and giving Phoebe that piercing stare. "You're only twenty."

Her stomach twisted. "I turn twenty-one in a week. I'll work harder than anyone."

"No one else has passed. Why so confident?"

"Because I'm desperate."

"And honest, apparently."

"I'm sure you'd know if someone wasn't truthful. Not that I'd lie." She held her breath.

"You intrigue me, Phoebe. I'll give you a chance. There are three tasks. The first in accounting, the second in marketing, the third in quality control. Be here tomorrow. Eight a.m. sharp."

Phoebe exhaled with relief, barely restraining herself from leaping off the sofa and hugging Mrs. Thompson. "Thank you. You won't regret this."

The elevator door pinged open. "Hey, Mom, Dad."

Weston Fitzgerald. Phoebe gulped.

"Hi, I'm Weston," he said, winking conspiratorially.

"Uh . . . Phoebe Thompson."

"A pleasure." He shook her hand. His was warm and dry, and he smelled like spearmint. She did not notice the outline of his well-toned body beneath his pristine white T-shirt.

He poured a cup of coffee and sat at the far desk, rearranging the mermaid collectibles.

Mrs. Fitzgerald shook her head. "See you tomorrow, Phoebe."

THE NEXT DAY, the Fitzgeralds plopped Phoebe into a swivel chair with a cup of dark-roast coffee and a password to access the Bull's-Eye accounting system. Her task: locate and correct a three-cent error in the bank reconciliation within the next eight hours.

The gray office had no windows, a utilitarian metal desk, a computer, and the aforementioned swivel chair. It was like a dreary cave, which Phoebe loved.

Six hours later, Phoebe folded her arms across the desk and put her head down.

She couldn't work her way through the labyrinth of Bull's-Eye Mattresses' accounting in the two hours remaining. Her head throbbed.

"I'm an idiot." Phoebe lifted her head and ground her fingers into her temples. "Why did I think I could do this stupid job? What a nightmare."

"Obviously you've never had a nightmare."

Phoebe jumped out of her chair, her heart pounding. She

crouched into a defensive position, knees bent, fists over her face, mouth set into what she prayed was a menacing grimace.

"Who are you, and how did you get in here? Wait a minute. You're the bartender from the Shark Bar." Phoebe could never have forgotten him. She picked up the only weapon she had at hand—the cup of coffee.

"Hey, put that down. This is a new shirt."

"You have three seconds to tell me who you are and what you're doing in here, or I'll . . . um . . . be forced to ruin your shirt." Even in her mind the threat sounded mealy and limp.

The man laughed. It was such a joyful sound, Phoebe bit her lip to counteract an impending smile.

"My name is, uh, Archer Calyx, and I'm your fairy godmother. I mean godfather. Godperson? I've been sent to help you." He took the coffee, sniffed, and swallowed it in one gulp.

"You're a bartender. Is your plan to mix me a drink?"

"That's more of a Dionysus thing."

"Huh?" This guy was deranged, though hearing the name of the Greek god of ritual madness and grapes sent cold prickles running up her body. "Who sent you? Why are you here?" Phoebe wondered if maybe this Archer was part of the test. Maybe the whole thing was a test of her ethics, and the error didn't exist.

"Who sent me doesn't matter. If you want to pass, I'm your guy." He set the cup back on the desk and came so close to Phoebe that she smelled the coffee on his breath.

Phoebe straightened and narrowed her eyes. "I'm fine. Go shake your daiquiris elsewhere." She shooed him toward the door.

He placed his hands gently on her shoulders. She practically melted into his body.

What sorcery was this?

Their lips moved toward one another. Phoebe had wondered for so long what a kiss felt like. But she'd vowed not to get involved with a guy until after she succeeded as a businesswoman. Her brain fuzzed, and now she couldn't remember why she made the vow. Closer. Closer. It was going to happen. She didn't even care about the job anymore. Her entire being was centered on his full lips almost touching hers. She wanted this with a desperation she felt down to her bones. It was like a magnet was pulling them toward each other.

Suddenly, her cell phone rang with the ringtone she'd set for Inaya: "Oh Mother," by Christina Aguilera.

Phoebe leapt back as if her mother were in the room, watching. "It's my mom," she said, breathing heavily, the oxygen clearing her brain.

She couldn't believe she had nearly kissed this guy, no matter how hot he was.

She slipped her phone out of her pocket and read the message.

> Fired again. I'll find another job soon.
> Looks like we'll be eating Spaghetti Loops for a while.
> Sorry hon. Love you forever—Mom

Phoebe despised Spaghetti Loop months. They had had far too many of them lately. Poor Mom. Phoebe had to pitch in more.

"Okay, Archer, show me how, but I don't want you to fix it for me."

Cupid cocked his head and seemed to be observing her as if she were a zoo specimen.

"Of course. I'd be happy to."

His fingers flew over the keyboard. Phoebe watched every stroke. When he finally got to the source, Phoebe grinned. So easy. She should've figured it out. It was probably the stress getting to her. Archer got almost to the end and rebooted the computer. "Now you do it," he said.

And she did.

CUPID SPENT THE NIGHT wandering restless and shirtless on Waikiki Beach. What was wrong with him? Why couldn't he enjoy the crashing of the surf over his toes, the sweetness of his (fifth? sixth?) piña colada, the laughter of the teenagers huddled around their bonfires, sparks of red light flying to the heavens? They were all admiring his sculpted torso, after all.

He sucked in his abs, even though he knew he was already perfection. But as the sky brightened with the oncoming dawn, his toes shriveled, his teeth crunched on sand, and goose bumps prickled up his arms. These irksome aches and pains happened when a god took human form on earth. It would be a relief to be back on Mount Olympus, where no human frailties plagued him. He fantasized about his room in Aphrodite's palace, where nubile nymphs rubbed lavender oil into his skin. He sighed. All he had to do was this one thing, and he'd be home.

Then guilt racked him. His throat closed in as he remembered Phoebe working so hard to solve the accounting problem yesterday. She made sure she understood exactly where she'd gone wrong. Maybe she could have done it herself after all?

After completing the first task, Phoebe spent hours planning the ad she'd shoot today. She reserved a studio from her university, found a photographer, wrote the copy, and cast a model.

How could this creature be a daughter of Hades? What a scoundrel that god was, betraying the sanctity of love itself by cheating on his devoted wife, then abandoning his lover and his own child?

Cupid had ethics. He was pretty sure. They must be in there somewhere. He reached inside his soul, caught a glimpse, and held on to a pink perfection of light. As he was pulling on this foreign beam, he tripped. The empty cocktail glass flew into the surf as he fell face-first into the wet sand. Gods, he loathed the gritty stuff.

Furious, he pushed himself up, sat on his heels, and fished around for what had caused him to trip. A shell. A stupid crab shell.

He picked it up, poised to throw it into the foamy sea, when it opened its little black crabby eyes and said, "What is it you think you're doing, Love God?"

"Hades." Cupid dropped the shell. It landed with a loud splat.

"Ouch." Hades unbent one of his crabby legs. "Who else were you expecting?"

"Sebastian might've been nice. He sings."

"Who?"

"Never mind. What do you want?"

"You did great work yesterday. The girl is on her way toward kissing her human."

"She *has* a name; it's Phoebe."

Hades glared at Cupid, which was impressive, considering the beady black eyes had essentially one setting—beady. "Never mind that. What are you still doing here? Today she's making the mattress movie. It will be such a success that there is no way our plan will fail."

"First of all, it's not 'our plan.' Second of all, it's an ad, not a movie. And third, well, I'm sure Phoebe can handle this one all on her own."

"It seems you're sympathizing with her. I can't have you betraying me. So as of now, you will not be able to tell anyone of our bargain. A simple spell of silence should do the trick."

A lump lodged in Cupid's throat. "Is a spell necessary?" He coughed.

"Afraid so. Now run along and be the star of the movie, ad, whatever it is."

Cupid wanted to balk, but it might be nice to lie shirtless on a mattress all day with makeup people daubing him with cosmetics. He liked the idea of impressing Phoebe with his stunning physique. Cupid exhaled, trying to sound irritated by Hades's suggestion. "Are you saying I'm so attractive that humans will want to buy these mattresses? Because that's what it sounds like."

Hades snapped a claw at Cupid's knee.

"Ouch." He pulled the claw off his leg. Blood dribbled down his shin. "Look what you've done. You've marred this body. How can I shoot the ad now? I might as well give up and return to Olympus."

"Baby." Hades waved a claw, and the injury healed. Cupid's knee returned to its original perfection.

"Look, Hades. I'm not sure about this plan. Your daughter—Phoebe, that is. She's a cool girl. She's honest and kind and self-less. You should reconsider."

Why did he say this? He wanted to be with Phoebe today. But it didn't feel right somehow to trick her into giving up her powers.

"Let me show you what will happen to you if you do not succeed, Love God."

A lava lamp rocketed from the sky, landed with a smack on the wet sand, and righted itself. The oil inside shimmered, and a tableau appeared. It showed Cupid in high school, living in a dingy cabin with other teenagers, eating pastelike cafeteria food, and sitting through a mind-numbing lecture on iambic pentameter.

"Monster," said Cupid.

⟳❖⟳

THIS PHOTO SHOOT is a disaster," Phoebe muttered under her breath, digging her fingers into her temples, where a massive headache thrummed beneath the surface. The guy in charge of lighting electrocuted himself; the wrong catering tray arrived so the only things to eat were papaya spears and yogurt pretzels; the buff model, an Econ major from her Free Market Theory class, repeatedly fell off the stack of twenty mattresses. (Phoebe had decided to go with a "Princess and the Pea" vibe for the commercial.) But the worst part was that Weston Fitzgerald kept staring at her and winking—so distracting.

"Help," cried Landen, tumbling from the mattresses. For the fourth time. Maybe he needs to stick to Econ? Or else someone was sabotaging her.

"Stop," Phoebe yelled, then sighed. "Let's take five." Phoebe looked over her notes. There were still quite a few poses to get.

"Excuse me?" said Landen, limping over, cradling his wrist.

"Yes?"

"It's my wrist."

It looked a bit swollen. Phoebe squinted, cocked her head, and it looked slightly more normal.

"I think it's sprained. I gotta go."

"What? No. You can't leave. I have to shoot this today, please. I have Advil. And bandages. And ice." Even as Phoebe entreated him, she knew she wasn't being compassionate. Her future wasn't more important than his well-being. "Uh, feel better," she said finally.

Landen grabbed a handful of yogurt pretzels with his good hand and departed. "Sorry, Phoebe. See ya round campus."

Could this day get worse? She had the studio reserved for only another hour. How would she get a replacement?

"I can take his place," said Weston, sauntering over from the black leather sofa and unbuttoning his crisp white shirt. He cupped her chin in his hand. "Don't worry, Fiona. I'll save you."

"Um . . . my name is Phoebe."

"Phoebe. Fiona. What's in a name? It's the depth of your brown eyes. The deep mahogany of your tresses. The ruby shine of your lips."

"Do those lines actually work for you?" thundered a voice from behind Phoebe.

She spun, nearly tripping over her own feet.

"Must you creep up on people?" Phoebe said, righting herself. As she looked up at Archer, her jaw unhinged, and her cheeks inflamed.

"It's a hobby of mine," he said, prowling closer.

"Where's your . . . uh . . . shirt . . ."

But Phoebe's tongue felt loose and fat. Who could blame her? Bare-chested Archer had a twelve-pack, if that was even possible. His Hawaiian-print shorts were slung low across his hips. And his face: smooth and golden with a smile that turned her insides to liquid. A god sculpted in flesh.

"Who the hell are you?" spat Weston, a little vein ticking at his temple. His Adam's apple bobbed.

"This is Archer Calyx," said Phoebe. "From the office."

"I've never seen this . . . juiced-up gym rat before."

Archer frowned and moved in so close to Weston that their pecs almost touched. "This kind of perfection does not come from artificial means," he said through gritted teeth.

A light popped overhead and shattered. Tiny shards of glass rained on Weston's head and embedded in his bare torso. Blood oozed from a hundred tiny cuts.

"Ouch," cried Weston, hopping as he tried to brush the glass away, his feet crunching into the shards on the cement floor. All this jumping only succeeded in pushing the glass deeper into his skin. "*Ouch*, I said. Did anyone hear me?"

"Mortals," muttered Archer.

"Excuse me?" said Phoebe.

"Wha—?" said Archer, spreading his arms in a pronouncement of innocence.

Phoebe shook her head at Mr. Hunky and Insane. "I'm sorry, Weston. Let me see," said Phoebe, examining his chest.

"It burns! It burns!" Weston cried, wincing.

"You poor thing," said Phoebe. She couldn't even shoot a print ad without maiming half of Waikiki. "I have a first-aid kit. Let's get you fixed up."

Archer frowned. "Don't you have a commercial to finish?"

Phoebe sighed. "Yes, but I can't let him bleed."

A gorgeous blonde floated through the door with tweezers and a low-cut nurse's uniform. Could the school have sent her? The blonde winked at Archer, then turned her attention to Weston, who was raking his eyes over her. He smiled with approval and allowed himself to be escorted back to the couch.

"Friend of yours?" said Phoebe.

"I wouldn't say friend," said Archer, dusting his hands. "Guess I'm your man." Miraculously, none of the glass had touched Archer.

Phoebe glanced at Weston and the nurse, then sighed. "All right; let's shoot."

"I *love* shooting things!" Archer chirped.

The crew took their places while Archer bounded up the ladder on the backside of the mattresses and reclined across the top. Phoebe sucked in a breath.

"Show-off," snarked Weston.

"Jealous?" Archer smirked.

From that moment on, the shoot went perfectly. Even with no editing, the images were exquisite. Fifteen minutes after Archer climbed aboard the mattresses, they were done.

Archer sat atop the mattresses, dangling his feet and grinning. The nurse had removed the glass from Weston's body. Someone had eaten all the papaya spears.

And that's when it all fell apart.

⋅⋅⋅⋅⋅⋅

CUPID REALIZED THAT AS A GOD, he should be above petty reprisals, but who was he fooling? Gods excelled at that. And what choice did he have? That Weston idiot wasn't worthy of Phoebe. How quickly he turned his interest from Phoebe to Ani, the Anigrides river nymph Cupid had summoned to be the "nurse."

Everything had been going swimmingly. Phoebe and the rest of the humans were duly impressed by his physique. That idiot Weston was cleverly sidelined with a broken light and a river nymph. The papaya spears were delicious and settled his human stomach after his night of piña colada debauchery.

Now that the shoot was complete, from his perch atop the mattresses, Cupid watched as Phoebe warmly thanked the crew for their help, giving each person a smile and a hug, then trotted over to where Weston was snuggling with Ani. The scrawny jerk had little Band-Aids decorated with tiny hearts stuck all over his chest. He looked like a plague victim, which cheered Cupid slightly. When Phoebe placed her hand on Weston's shoulder, the look he gave her was infuriating. Cupid's insides churned, and the papaya didn't seem so benign.

"Your friend will live," pronounced Ani.

Unfortunately.

"Thank you for taking such good care of Weston. My name's Phoebe." She held out her hand.

"Ani."

They shook. Phoebe turned her attention to Weston, concern in those doll-like eyes. "Can I get you anything?"

Weston scooted away from Ani, took Phoebe's hand in his, and kissed it. The rogue. Cupid's blood roiled in his veins. His fingers flexed over his invisible bow and quiver of arrows. Too bad they only caused unyielding love and not death. Yet everyone knew the pain of love could be worse than death. This gave Cupid solace.

"There is something you can do for me," said Weston. Cupid glared at him. "Um, could you maybe go get a yogurt pretzel with me?"

"Sure." Phoebe allowed him to lead her to the food table.

"I was wondering if maybe you'd like to have dinner with me tonight? Celebrate your success with the second test."

In his head, Cupid recited the lines from his favorite Cupid-centric Hallmark Valentine cards to calm himself. Usually this did the trick, but not today. He wanted to visit his wrath upon Weston.

Somehow Ani noticed his displeasure. Maybe she noticed the steam literally wafting out of his ears. She activated her considerable nymphly charms, unfastened one more button on her nurse's uniform, and joined Weston and Phoebe for pretzels.

Ani managed to draw Weston from Phoebe. Cupid had a clear shot. Somewhere in the back of his mind, he knew Hades would be furious if he shot Weston and made him fall in love with a nymph. But at the moment, Cupid didn't care. He wrested an invisible arrow from the quiver, nocked it into his bow, and shot Weston—a bull's-eye straight through his heart.

"Ouch," said Weston for the thirty millionth time today, the whiner. He clutched his heart and fell to the floor, where he landed on the glass shards that hadn't already ended up in his torso. Before Cupid could stop her, Phoebe leapt toward Weston, who looked up at her. His eyes rolled back, and as he collapsed, he breathed the words, "Phoebe, my love."

⁓⁂⁓

THE NEXT DAY, Phoebe chewed her pinkie, her mind racing, as Inaya pulled the Spider into the Bull's-Eye Mattress showroom parking lot at five to eleven. The final test was to take place when no one would be in the building, even the cleaning crew. But what was the test? Phoebe knew it had something to do with quality control, and this worried her. She was a business major, not a mattress major. What did she know about mattress quality? Every mattress in the store looked a thousand times more comfortable than her lumpy foldout sofa bed.

"You'll do great," said Inaya, kissing Phoebe's head. "I'll be back at midnight. I have a place picked out to celebrate. My baby is going to be old enough to drink."

"Mom, we should save that money for rent or food. I might not get the job."

"You will get the job. And my daughter only turns twenty-one once."

"Bye, Mom. I love you." Phoebe pushed open the heavy glass door at the entrance to the showroom.

All the chandeliers were lit, casting a dappled glow over the sea of mattresses. Mr. and Mrs. Fitzgerald, both in red jackets—

his Members Only, hers probably Chanel—beamed at her as they exited the elevator.

"You're right on time," said Mrs. Fitzgerald.

"Welcome, Phoebe." Mr. Fitzgerald nodded his bald head.

"Good to be here, and thanks for the opportunity."

"We're impressed with everything you've done so far," said Mrs. Fitzgerald.

"Thanks."

"As you know"—Mrs. Fitzgerald smoothed her hair—"Bull's-Eye Mattresses are known for their impeccable quality. We have a twenty-year guarantee. We use only the finest materials. Each mattress is handmade by experts. Every mattress that leaves our store must be perfect." She cleared her throat and glanced at her husband.

"I understand." Phoebe knew all this, having done her research. It was as if Mrs. Fitzgerald was delaying. Perhaps there was something about the test or the job she didn't want Phoebe to know.

"Excellent. So, the test is simple. Starting at eleven p.m., you'll have one hour to find the one mattress in the showroom that has a flaw." She pointed to a large digital clock mounted next to a window, which Phoebe knew was the Fitzgeralds' office. The numbers clicked from 10:57 to 10:58.

She heard a bumping sound coming from the office. "Um, how is Weston?" She looked up at the window.

Mrs. Fitzgerald flashed a glance at the office and fiddled with her pearl necklace. "He's fine. No cause for alarm. We'll be watching from upstairs. Good luck." They called the elevator.

"How will I know when I've found the faulty mattress?"

"You'll know," said Mrs. Fitzgerald. The doors closed as the digital clock clicked over to 11:00.

◦◦✧◦◦

AFTER FORTY MINUTES of lying on each mattress, starting with the twins in the children's department, making her way through the fulls, and now the queens, Phoebe had found only bed after bed of feathery perfection.

She wished Archer would show up, point to the errant mattress, remove his shirt, lie down, and invite her over for a smooch. Wait. What was she thinking? She absolutely didn't want Archer to save her, take off his shirt, or kiss her. Good thing he wasn't here rescuing her like she was some weak maiden in need of a knight.

"Did someone mention a knight?" Archer plopped across a king mattress, shirtless.

"I know I didn't say that out loud." Phoebe glanced over her shoulder at the office window.

"'Course you did," said Archer.

"How do you keep appearing?"

"I get around," said Archer, winking and patting the space next to him.

"Look, I know you think you're all irresistible, but I have to find a certain mattress, and I have about"—she glanced at the digital clock—"twenty minutes. So I'm going to have to . . . um . . . resist."

The thumping against the window intensified.

"Phoebe," said Archer in the most serious tone she'd ever heard him use.

"Yes?" She examined another mattress. Flawless.

"Why don't you and I get outta here? I know this place . . ."

"I'm busy?"

"Yes, but . . ."

Phoebe sat on the edge of the next mattress and sneezed.

"Bless you."

"Wait . . ." She lay across the bed. Sneezed again. And again. Her eyes itched. "This is it! This is the bad mattress," she said, waving at the one-way glass and pointing to the mattress.

"Great. Let's go," said Archer.

A crash echoed through the room. Weston had smashed through the window and was tumbling onto a king-size mattress beneath.

"Weston," Phoebe cried, running to his aid.

"Phoebe!" He launched himself off the mattress straight at Phoebe, knocking her to the floor. She struggled beneath him.

"Get off."

"*I love you!*" he shouted.

"I. Can't. Breathe. And you're bleeding."

"I bleed for you, my love. Kiss me!"

His mouth came closer. She tried turning away, but he held her head in a viselike grip. Right before their lips touched, his weight lifted off her body, and she gulped breaths of fresh air.

Archer loomed over her, holding Weston by his sweatshirt as if he were a soiled towel. "I believe the lady said no." Tossing Weston aside, he helped Phoebe to her feet.

"Weston," shouted Mrs. Fitzgerald from the office. She pulled a hook from a tool belt hidden beneath her designer jacket, cast it out the broken window to one of the chandeliers, and zip-lined along the ceiling, falling to a mattress near Weston.

The elevator dinged. Mr. Fitzgerald.

Mrs. Fitzgerald flung her arms around her son. "Weston, honey, you okay?" Mr. Fitzgerald joined in.

"Ouch," said Weston, pulling away, examining the blood on his sweatshirt. "Mom, did you just zip-line?"

Archer smirked. "He'll be fine."

"Who are you?" Mrs. Fitzgerald blew a strand of white hair out of her eyes.

"Friend of Phoebe's."

"Huh?" said Phoebe.

Mrs. Fitzgerald walked up to Archer, balled her hands into fists, and glared at him as if contemplating an agonizing punishment.

The digital clock buzzed. Midnight.

Phoebe's body jolted. Her blood ignited. Muscles contracted. She imagined her body convulsing on the floor as if she'd been hit by lightning, but no one reacted. As quickly as it came on, the energy surge subsided, though her heart hammered and her fingers and toes tingled. She stood in the same spot she'd occupied before the shock.

"Congratulations, Phoebe," said Mrs. Fitzgerald. Obviously she hadn't noticed anything unusual. "You succeeded. With five minutes to spare."

"Uh, thanks," said Phoebe. "You know, anyone without severe allergies would never have found it."

"We weren't looking for 'anyone,'" said Mrs. Fitzgerald. "We were looking for someone special. Like *you!*"

"Okay," said Phoebe, unconvinced. The Fitzgeralds were a

bit crazy. Then she realized she'd gotten the job. Never again would she and her mom have to eat Spaghetti Loops. "I mean, thank you. I look forward to working for Bull's-Eye Mattresses."

"There's one thing we haven't mentioned," said Mrs. Fitzgerald.

"It's not even significant," said Mr. Fitzgerald, who became quite interested in playing with the zipper on his Members Only jacket.

"Yes?"

"Well, part of the deal is that you have to marry Weston."

"*What?*" said Phoebe and Cupid simultaneously.

"We need an heir. He's not quite up to the task."

Weston grimaced. "That's just . . . embarrassing."

"We'll arrange a flight tomorrow to Las Vegas," said Mr. Fitzgerald.

Phoebe folded her arms across her chest. "I'm not getting married."

"I'm afraid you are," said Mrs. Fitzgerald.

The front door opened, and Inaya stepped inside. "Phoebe. I'm here."

"Mom, no. Get out of here."

Mrs. Fitzgerald grabbed Inaya with one arm. "I think you better cooperate, Phoebe. It'd be a shame if something happened to your mom," she said, drawing a rope from her tool belt.

"Leave her alone," said Phoebe, wishing she, Archer, and Inaya were somewhere safe.

No sooner had the thought formed in her head than the three of them were sitting side by side atop a twenty-foot pile of mattresses. "What's going on?" Fear rippled along her neck, and her palms were slick with sweat. She closed her eyes, knowing it would disappear when she opened them. She'd seen a lot of weird things in her life, but this had to top them all. She raised her eyelids, but the hallucination persisted.

"What the hell?" said Mrs. Fitzgerald from far below.

"Calm down, dear. I'm sure there's an explanation," said Mr. Fitzgerald.

"I'm asleep, right?" said Phoebe.

Archer and Inaya exchanged a glance.

"You two acquainted?" she asked.

"I don't know what Eros is doing here, but he knows your dad."

"What are you talking about? My dad? Eros?"

"I prefer Cupid," said Archer.

"Like *the* Cupid? I thought he was a fat baby with wings."

Archer frowned. "I grew up. Like everyone. What is it with people being hung up on me being a baby? Uh-oh."

The Fitzgeralds froze like statues. The floor undulated. Chandeliers swayed. The temperature climbed as patches of fire singed the floor models. "There's your father now," said Inaya.

"Eros," thundered a voice from beneath the room. "You have failed me for the last time. The girl was not to come into her powers. Prepare for high school."

"Hades?" said Inaya, jumping gracefully off the mattresses. She planted her hands on her hips. "Is that you, you no-good, lying, cheating, cave dweller?"

"Uh." His voice was less thunderous.

"Coward," said Inaya. "I can't believe I fell for you." Inaya had never been more angry, powerful, or beautiful.

The room stilled. The temperature dropped.

"Thank the gods," breathed Cupid, wiping his brow. "He's gone."

"Yeah, he's good at that," said Inaya.

"MY DAD IS HADES?" Even confusion looked beautiful on Phoebe. Cupid scooted closer. She smelled like Valentine's Day—of roses and chocolate.

"I need space," she said, elbowing Archer. "Ow. You're hard as a marble countertop." She rubbed her elbow.

"Thank you," said Archer. "It's not as good as my god body." Cupid cleared his throat. The tightness that had been there since Hades invoked the spell of silence had disappeared.

"You're a *god*?" Phoebe rolled her eyes. "What an ego."

"Well, you're a goddess."

"I'll bet you say that to all the girls."

"It's true. Your dad is Hades. So technically you're a demi-goddess. And now that you're twenty-one, and you didn't kiss Weston, you've got your powers. Hades had sent me here to make sure you passed the tests so you'd kiss 'the heir to the kingdom' and stay human, but I fell in love with you, so that plan went kaput. Now we can run away and get married and live happily ever after. As soon as I finish high school. Again."

"How dare you decide what I'm going to do with my life? Whether or not I'll be a goddess. You're more insane than the Fitzgeralds. By the way, why haven't they moved since that earthquake and disembodied voice stopped by?"

"Hades froze them."

"That's horrible. Unfreeze them."

"I can't. I'm in human form. Remember? I'm pretty sure you can, though. Now, back to us. Will you wait for me to graduate?"

"Why would I be with someone who lied to me? Tricked me?"

There was only one thing left to do. He kissed Phoebe, invoking his entire soul.

She tasted as good as she smelled. He pulled her next to his prone body, and they melted together. He touched every part of her body within reach. She moaned. Or maybe that was him. When he'd finished kissing her senseless, he pulled back to gaze into her eyes. "That's why."

"I don't know if a kiss is enough of an inducement. Even if it was better than anything I've felt in my life. But I am not the kind of girl . . . goddess . . . whatever, to live my life for a man. God. Whatever. How long did you say you'd be in high school?"

Cupid grinned. "I'll let you know." And he kissed her again.

⁂

"PHOEBE, WE SHOULD PROBABLY go celebrate your birthday. Maybe you should wake up these people."

"Okay, Mom." Phoebe wished she and Cupid to the floor. It worked. Awesome.

She wished the Fitzgeralds unfrozen.

"What's going on?" said Mr. Fitzgerald.

"Phoebe, my love," said Weston.

This was the last thing she needed. A lovesick mattress heir. She wished Weston would stop being in love with her.

Weston's eyes cleared and he shook his head.

"Let's get on with the wedding plans," said Mr. Fitzgerald.

"The Mrs. and I need time to pack. So much gear for the Antarctic."

"Look, you two," said Phoebe. "I won the contest fair and square. I have the job. You can't change the rules. And guess what? Weston doesn't want to marry me. If you want to go on vacation, be my guests. As a matter of fact . . ." She waved her arms. The Fitzgeralds were outfitted in parkas and snow pants. Boots and plenty of fleece. "Have a great trip." She wished them to Antarctica. "Good-bye, Weston," she said, teleporting him to the spot outside the Shark Bar where he'd lusted after the mermaid.

"Cupid, where can I send you?"

"Mount Olympus would be nice."

"Sure. Will you be okay?"

"Yeah. I'll see you in a few years." He kissed her lightly on the lips. Her body arched into his, and she kissed him hard. "I'm really hating your dad a lot right now."

"Bye, Cupid." She wished him away, surprised at how hard it was to let him go.

"Let's go celebrate your birthday," said Inaya.

"Mom, why didn't you tell me my dad is Hades?"

"I didn't want you growing up thinking you were destined to be evil."

"How could I grow up like that when I have you for a mom?"

"I love you, Phoebe."

Hugging her mom, Phoebe teleported them to the closest bar, where they toasted her twenty-first birthday.

The next day, she teleported into the Bull's-Eye Mattresses office, made a cup of strong coffee, put her feet up on the desk, and surveyed her kingdom.

Awake

jesse sprague

Rose

THOUGH GARBLED BY DISTANCE, a voice pierced the shroud over Rose's mind. The darkness around her practically constrained her limbs and froze her lips. Without the ability to speak or move, all Rose could do was listen.

She shoved aside the comforting nothing and strained to comprehend the heated words. *Crane's* heated words. The anger in her husband's voice bit, burning off layers of haziness until the sound rang through her.

"I *refuse* to believe there's no solution," Crane said.

Beneath the rage of his tone was something that hurt her—a deep weariness. If her hands hadn't weighed so much, she would have lifted them to comfort him, smooth his wild curls.

"I'm sorry, Crane," another man said. His voice had the crackle that came with advanced age. "You have enough medical training to understand what these signs mean. You've read her vitals. I can't refute anything the doctors have told you. Refusing the truth won't help you or Rose."

Rose stretched out mentally, pressing against limbs as responsive as stone. Pounding against her eyelids—steel shutters to her lonely world. If only she could find a crack, a single weak point, and could move! She could rush to Crane, tell him death came for everyone in their turn, that she loved him and had never blamed him.

"I have done everything the doctors asked." Crane's voice was closer now. "*Everything*. I won't accept she's getting worse, that—"

"I think you need to prepare yourself for the inevitable. Her brain is shutting down. It's not what I want to say, but it's true. This must be very hard for you, but she's already weakening. From the readings, within a few weeks, even if she wakes up, she won't be your wife anymore."

The voices faded until they were no more than a buzz.

⟡

CRANE HAD ALWAYS SAID she was his heart, but now all Rose could be was a weight around his neck, a grief that wouldn't fade so long as her stupid body insisted on remaining alive.

If stopping her lungs from drawing air were possible, Rose would have. Crane should be able to continue with his life. In spite of the despair cloaking her, she had memories to live on. Would Crane allow himself that comfort? He'd always blamed himself for her disappointments.

His voice, even in its absence, hummed in the background

as days passed and brought back swelling memories of their life together.

She recalled their honeymoon. He'd taken her five miles from town to a bed-and-breakfast for a long weekend. It rained the whole trip—a freezing rain with a biting wind. They'd lain under a floral comforter together, and she'd told him about all the wonderful vacation spots in her travel magazines—places they'd go someday. It wasn't until years later, when she found Crane studying her vacation notebooks, that she realized he had no idea how perfect that time was for her. He'd thought he'd failed her.

Sure, she liked to daydream of distant locales and five-star hotels that cost more than he made in a month, but a day in the rain with him beat any exotic location without him. Crane was her real dream. He was a warm, steady home filled with love. If only she'd been able to make him see.

Crane's voice filtered in . . . "Rose, it's not ready."

She imagined his soft palm, the skin dry from too much hand sanitizer.

"What else can I do?" he asked.

Tears burned inside her, unspent, clogging the emptiness with words that frothed behind her unresponsive lips.

"If I'd just come home an hour sooner that day, you would be fine. I cannot give up now . . . this was the point of it all—you. Always you, Rose. The machine isn't ready to be tested. The dispersal of energy is wrong; the fluctuations must be less extreme in the final distribution."

As Crane moved, something crashed, shattered. Unseen, glass shards flew all over the room, a room she was trapped in but had never seen.

Crane had moved to this house in what had seemed like a bribe to Rose's spirit. She'd begged him for years to move to Able's Hollow. The university had a reputation for accommodating research scientists. He could teach and work on his projects. But he'd refused.

Rose smiled at the memory, though her lips never twitched.

"Able's Hollow?" Crane had said, his foppish curls falling over his glasses as they walked through the woods surrounding their house. Ahead of them was a small wooden bridge.

"I've looked at the statistics," Rose had said. "Temperate weather—so neither too cold for me in the winter, nor too hot for you in the summer. It's only an hour from your folks, and less than two from mine . . ."

But he'd frowned. "No, Rose."

"Can you really be so superstitious?"

"My brother still calls me the family's Ichabod. Ichabod Crane, a teacher and intellectual—"

"I've read 'The Legend of Sleepy Hollow,'" she said. Really, she hadn't; she had seen the movie. "A town's name is a stupid thing to inhibit us. The university *here* won't let you do anything. Six times this week you've mentioned you need a new position. We could be happy there."

"We are happy here." Crane stepped up onto the bridge, gazing across the stream to where a patch of wild strawberries beckoned them.

"I'd be happier on the other side of the bridge." Rose dropped his hand and ran over the wooden boards.

Berries filled her memory. They had been the sweetest she

ever tasted, often taken from his fingers or lips while the water gurgled at their trespass.

In the distance she heard Crane's machine turn on—a low whir and several clacks. Those noises didn't belong in the memory; they belonged to the cold world following Rose's accident. The stream faded, as did the ghost taste of berries. A clatter of metal on metal.

"I love you so much, Rose. This needle should do it. This will integrate the necessary compound into your system. My life for yours. It should be enough, but there are so many errors. I can't get the one-to-one ratio I need. And the variation . . . I'm not sure what will happen anymore, but we can't wait. The process takes six days." He sighed, a desperate sound. "Six days never seemed so long. Just hold on . . ."

Her consciousness dimmed, was pulled from her. Time passed without her comprehension. It might have been days or weeks. In the emptiness something pricked her arm, shooting rivers of ice with jets of heat through her. The dark boiled, bubbled, and swallowed her.

And then a wave of light hit her. And her eyelids fluttered. Rose stirred inside herself. The dark stripped away, leaving her naked. The back of her heel slammed into a hard surface as she kicked out, and ripples traveled up her body, like a reverberation through gelatin. She lay on her back in a shallow tub, and above her the gray ceiling came into focus.

Rose sat up, her mouth hanging open, flapping as she struggled for air. Color assailed her eyes. Red and green flashed, and all around her a gooey, blue liquid glowed. A few wires snaked through the blue, fixing themselves to her pale flesh.

Half-formed words fell from her—five years of thoughts and desires clashing for release from lips that had not moved in just as long.

Her body shook, causing the gel to quiver. Light reflected from its surface, dazzling her eyes.

"Crane?" she croaked, her first sensible utterance.

In the bed of gel, she was naked and her arms were crossed over her bare chest. She blinked and squinted, trying to make sense of the jumble of machinery around her. Metal panels dotted with lights, displays, and buttons lined three of the room's four walls and linked to a central panel on her left. She shoved herself to her feet and forced her legs to hold her.

Just on the other side of the control panel, Crane lay in a similar construct to hers, only his was empty of the blue gel and no wires were affixed to him.

Rose stumbled out of the tub, her legs buckling under her. With arms that were equally weak, she pulled herself over to Crane and grabbed his hand. No response. What had he said about the machine?

She slapped her forehead, but the jarring brought no insight. He'd told her about most of it, in terms only other scientists would understand. All she knew was that the gel conducted energy without having to convert the form of the energy.

"Crane," she repeated, with more force. She shook his shoulders, and his head lolled to the side.

Not so much as a facial twitch. She leaned into the tub, pressing her torso to him and her lips against his. He had to wake up. She wouldn't let him sacrifice himself. The subtle rise and fall of his chest told her he wasn't dead, but she knew all too well that a coma wasn't really life. She had to undo it. Only he'd never said anything about reversing the project if it went awry.

Was this what he'd intended?

Tears trickled down Rose's cheeks. She kissed her husband again, tasting the salt of her own tears on his lips, but no other change.

"My life isn't worth yours. It never was. Please, how do I undo this?"

She sobbed until her throat was raw and the cold of the lab had numbed her bare flesh. Her legs wobbled, threatening to give at each tentative step as she walked to a table near the doorway. A sundress, covered in flowers, a pair of white sandals, a cardigan, and her makeup bag had been arranged across the surface. She dressed, not touching the bag. In fact, a flush crept up her cheeks just from seeing it there.

Every day, Crane had done her makeup for her. She knew this not because she had felt his touch but because, on occasion, he'd talked about it—like the time her favorite lipstick color was discontinued and he'd been on the verge of crying as he told her the news.

A series of lights over the lab door lit as she approached. When the final one went green the sealed lab door opened soundlessly to reveal a basement room, containing a few pieces of artwork from their previous home and a washer-dryer unit. In the doorway her head spun, and a heavy weariness descended. Her muscles had resisted her since her first movement from the tub, but now her mind faltered, refusing to keep command over her recalcitrant body. The few steps toward the stairs left her vision fading out in bursts.

This was no place to collapse. Not with Crane in the other room. So she turned, gathered her strength, and stumbled back to the doorway. A burst of energy hit her at the threshold, and she paused, gripping the door frame.

Maybe she could make it to Crane. That way if he woke, he would not be alone. But as she entered the room, her strength returned. With growing horror, she stared at the blue goo and the dangling cords. The shots he'd given her must keep her connected to the machine. Even without the bath and wires attached to her, she was still feeding off Crane.

Realization hit. "I can't leave this room."

The door slid automatically shut behind her as she stumbled into the room. Instead of going to Crane, Rose moved over to the machine. There was a large flashing display with rhythmically altering numbers. A timer. Rose closed her eyes and pressed her fingers to the side of her head.

Had Crane said something about this? He couldn't have intended her to remain in here forever, so it stood to reason the process wasn't complete. Could the numbers indicate the time left until her changes finalized? Rose sighed; despite escaping the heavy fatigue she'd experienced outside the lab, she was still tired. Answers were more likely to come after a proper rest.

She returned to Crane and knelt on the linoleum floor. With her head resting on his chest, she drifted off into a light, fitful sleep. Dreams haunted her, scattered memories—twisted and torn. Memories of working the beauty pageant circuit, the cold, judging stares, and her mother's vocal disappointment when she lost, mixed with ones of Crane's fingers massaging her shoulders as she curled against him to watch TV.

A crash from upstairs startled Rose from the whirling dreams, so unlike the emptiness of her coma. She trembled and clutched at Crane's hand. What sounded like hundreds of men marched overhead. The thudding footfalls hit, and resounded like the steps of giants.

After shaking the remaining veil of sleep from her mind, Rose forced her exhausted muscles the few feet over to the light switch and flipped it off, leaving her in a darkness that flickered with neon flashes from the machine. A low-wattage row of lights turned on, painting a pathway through the chamber.

She hobbled back to Crane. "Is this place hidden?"

She struggled to remember what the lab door had looked like from the outside. She was reasonably sure the door was camouflaged on the basement side, but still her stomach clenched with nerves.

Muffled voices filtered through the walls. Why were people in the house? Why now, after all these years? It didn't make sense.

In the faint light, Rose caught her reflection on the mirrored surface of the control panel. The face there ripped a gasp from her throat. She hadn't expected the healthy, youthful face of her beauty-queen days. But the skinny wraith she saw shocked her—how could she have lost so much weight? She'd never been so dreadfully thin. Mascara dotingly applied by Crane ran in streaks over her face, and a slight lip stain was the only color on her ghostly flesh. Her cheeks were hollow and high enough to make a model proud. At thirty, when her accident put her in a coma, she'd been happily putting on weight— an extra fifteen pounds meant she could eat like everyone else, and she and Crane both got fewer insulting comments about trophy wives and beauty-and-the-beast pairings. Those fifteen pounds had more than fled while she was asleep.

Rose bit her knuckles and looked away. The crashing upstairs continued . . . until they finally descended to her level. Noises of a rough search came from outside the lab door. Someone was banging around the washer and dryer.

She sobbed a little. Whoever those people were, they didn't sound friendly. If Crane had enemies, he'd never mentioned it, but she couldn't risk it. Not with him in this condition.

Another person pounded down the unseen stairs to the basement. Briefly, all went quiet. Rose shoved her fist further between her teeth.

"Anything down here?" barked a crisp male voice.

There came a reply, but the wall made it unintelligible. Rose closed her eyes, preparing for the worst.

Then there was a hammering of footsteps up the stairs. For a little while longer they swept the house, but soon all fell silent.

Rose wept. Alone in a tomb, she waited.

❧

A FEW HOURS PASSED and then footsteps sounded above again. No crashes this time, just slow, methodical taps.

"What's happening, Crane? What do I do?" Rose's hands twisted in his shirt, but no matter how hard she searched, he gave no visible response.

Someone came down, slower than the previous group. Rose stood, her legs gummy but functional. Perhaps the person was not a friend, but what other choice remained? Sit in the lab until Crane died of dehydration? No. She had to do something.

"I can't be alone in here. I need help," she explained to her sleeping husband. She moved to the door, pushed the button there, and let it slide open.

Alex

ALEX VALERA DROVE into Able's Hollow in the quiet stasis before dawn. All was calm, like the world itself slept. The timing fit the assignment, and he smiled at the dim glow on the horizon, wishing his old partner was there to be annoyed at his shenanigans.

Wrappers from the gas station burritos sat in the passenger seat. He'd rolled down the window, but the steady howl didn't give him the distraction of human interaction. As soon as he arrived in town, he'd send Gina an inane text—it would relieve the worry swirling inside him.

He'd played around with calling the town Sleepy Hollow. In fact, he'd called Gina at home to tell her his next assignment was in "Sleepy Hollow." Baby Anna had been crying in the background, and it should have cued him that Gina was in no mood. She snapped at him more now that she was a mother than when she'd been his partner.

"Don't be ridiculous," she'd said.

"Headless horsemen would be too fantastical even for me, Gina. But there are a heck of a lot of sleeping people." He smiled as the word "heck" came naturally from his mouth. Eleven months with a child had gutted his vocabulary and set him up with a whole new set of "swell" words.

"Sleepy Hollow was the name of the town, not the people's condition." Gina sighed. "Get some good food in you on the drive, you hear?"

He had been smart enough not to ask her to define "good." But as he pulled into Able's Hollow in the eerie light, he wished there was something other than burritos and coffee in his stomach. His gut flip-flopped as he reached the roadblock and flashed his FBI contractor's credentials. The queasy lurching intensified as he drove onto the empty streets.

The first curved outline etched on the sidewalk might have been mistaken for hopscotch squares from a distance. It wasn't. The markings didn't denote a child's game but the outline of a human form. More white body tracings dotted the road as he drove. They covered everything.

He pulled up to the hospital—a small affair, lit like a lone star. Even from the edge of the parking lot, filled with abandoned cars. He saw the bodies on stretchers, spilling from the hospital's halls.

This assignment was going to get nasty. A lot of lives were on the line.

Hopefully, the marines could airlift the residents out today—this town was incapable of providing life support for so many. He'd know more soon—and if he had any luck, before the CDC arrived to jam up the works. The future of more than five thousand people depended on a timely solution—something the government consistently bumbled. Sure, he was government-ish, but he trusted *himself*.

A whole town *didn't* just fall asleep. No outward evidence of assault or mass drug usage. Not a single case in the surrounding towns, making illness unlikely. At least, a normal illness.

Daryl Downy met him in the parking lot. Daryl had been Alex's contact within the FBI since Gina used her pregnancy to bow out of their working partnership.

Daryl opened Alex's car door. "Even for you this case is weird," he said by way of greeting.

"I can't judge yet how weird. Give me what you know so far." Alex unbuckled his seatbelt and swung his legs out, but Daryl remained in his way.

"The citizens are stable. But many, especially the younger ones, aren't doing well. Whatever happened seemed not to affect infants, so we've divided them off, but we don't have enough staff to care for them. A few neighborhoods at the outskirts of town weren't affected. The rest of the citizens are effectively asleep, not even as deep as a coma, and yet they're unwakable. We've found the point of origin. We investigated and—"

"If your next words include a sleeping princess and a loom, I'm bailing." Alex grinned extra wide to compensate for the glower on Daryl's face.

"No 'princess.' What we found was an empty home. From the house, there is a two-mile radius that encompasses the affected areas. The neighborhoods left untouched are outside the radius. We had a few houses sitting on the line in which some family members were affected while others were not."

"The owners of the house," Alex said, "what's the scoop on them?"

"Married couple. No children. The husband is a scientist employed at the local college. Hasn't been doing any research projects for the school, though, just teaching. Years back, he did some work with lab animals, transferring the energy one group got from a meal to a second group, to make *them* feel satiated."

"And his better half?"

Daryl checked his notes, leaning away from the car door long enough to flip through. "High school beauty queen. She married at twenty and co-owned a jewelry store. Five years ago a tree limb fell on her. Been in a coma ever since. Her husband signed her into home care. The most recent doctor's report said her condition was deteriorating. She was alive when this"—he motioned with his arm to the town—"happened."

"Right-o. Thanks."

"Don't thank me, Mr. Valera. If it were up to me, you wouldn't be here. Official story is chemical spill. I'd rather just go with that and let the CDC handle the victims."

"So, what are the names of this husband and wife?" Alex asked, ignoring the insult.

"Professor Crane Brier and Rose Brier."

Alex choked on a laugh. *Seriously?* His brain couldn't settle between the sleeping beauty comparison and that of Sleepy Hollow. *Crane? Briar?* "Briar?"

"B-R-I-E-R."

Didn't matter.

"Get over to the house. Check it out." Daryl stepped back from the door and folded his arms.

Alex shrugged. It wasn't like he had been excited to go into the hospital and see more misery. Starting at the house was a grand idea. He moved his legs back into the car and slammed the door shut. Daryl remained just outside.

Alex drove off to escape that look, but before pulling onto

the road, he buckled his seatbelt. As he passed by the hospital, he tried to avoid looking at the triage setup in the ambulance bay. The stakes were clear. Better to focus. Emotions were always better saved for after a job.

The vacant streets went by in a blur. Alex amused himself along the ride by stopping at the red lights. Only by the third one, his mind filled the empty crosswalk with ghost outlines of mothers with strollers and couples walking hand-in-hand. It was a relief to hit no more red lights after that.

Alex pulled up to the split-level home. The windows and drapes were closed tight. The lawn had gone to seed, and patches of yellowed grass packed against the soil. It might as well have had "Go Away" in spray paint on its siding.

He climbed out of the car and ambled up the overgrown path to the doorway. He glanced at the edges of the yard, half hoping he'd find a pumpkin patch. Though there was no one to tell the Sleepy Hollow joke to anyhow. Being able to might have lifted the depression that was settling in around him.

Most of the time he worked better alone, but there were moments he missed having Gina at his side. He still remembered the day they'd assigned her, and he got his first look—pretty face, red hair pulled into an "I don't take any shit" ponytail. The Mulder and Scully references amused him but grated on Gina; she saw them as unprofessional. The moment she got pregnant, she'd finagled a way to go back to dull office work.

He hadn't minded. Their baby was adorable.

On the doorstep, he texted a quick message to his wife. **No headless horsemen but there's a Professor Crane.** Opening the front door, he stepped inside. The light of her reply text illuminated a table coated with pictures, set up like a shrine. A few had been knocked over, and one had broken, scattering glass over the floor.

A girl named Aurora too?

So she was in a better mood, but looking at the photos, Alex didn't want to joke. His heart wasn't in the next text.

No. But Crane's last name is Brier, pronounced briar. Then as a separate text, for impact, **Her name's Rose.**

. . . Do your job.

He tucked his phone away and flipped the lights to better see the rows of pictures. Every one of them depicted the same woman—presumably Rose. Wedding snapshots from a courthouse affair sat next to professional stills of the toothy beauty. Overly made up and too chipper, she stared out with vacant eyes, not surprising for a pageant head shot. He should have told Gina the beauty-queen part.

But the more recent photos were charming, the same bright grin, less makeup but real glitter in her eyes.

He lifted the picture with the broken glass from the floor, and a frown creased his face. Rose lay in a hospital bed—for once, not smiling. Her blond hair hung limp around her wan face, and yet she retained a haunting beauty.

Alex set the image down with shaky hands, imagining his own wife's face like that. Life passed so quickly and once it was gone, no one could get it back.

And where were these two now?

The idiot outside had said there was nothing here. There was. Crane and Rose were a recipe for mad science.

Alex wandered through the house, glancing in each room

and jotting down his observations. Sparse furnishings dotted the space and everything had a light covering of dust, but there was no mess save what Daryl and his buddies left behind. No one lived in these rooms. No TV in the house, and the computer in the den looked neat and orderly.

One of the bedrooms had a smattering of medical equipment, but not the amount Alex would expect from a guy who kept a shrine to his wife. Something was off here. While Crane *might* have kept Rose in that room, Alex doubted it. The carpet to and from the room wasn't worn and all the machines looked brand-new—not a dent or a chip in sight. After five years, there should have been wear and tear.

Last was the basement—a worn path in the carpet led to the stairs. In the entire house, it was the only high-traffic area. Flipping on the light, Alex descended. The basement walls were dingy and a washer-dryer unit sat at the foot of the stairs—like a beacon of white in the room. From the tiny chinks in its paint Alex guessed this was the only appliance in the house that got regular use. A garbage can filled with takeout boxes was wedged between laundry baskets. The right wall was made of stone and cracks riddled the mortar. However, it was the tapestry on the left wall that captured his attention.

He gave a light whistle. Not a cheap piece, the ode to sleeping beauty might be handed down from generations—a wealthy man's gift. What it definitely felt like was an insight into Professor Brier's mind. Sure it was a depiction of the familiar story, but not focused on the princess waking. The beautiful maiden was absent. No, the focal point was the briar hedge—the wall that barred anyone from reaching the maiden.

The professor had been trying to wake his wife, Alex had no doubts on that front. One "sleeping" woman who couldn't wake married to a brilliant scientist, and with their being at the center of a town—*disappearing* from a town of newly comatose people—that might be explained a number of ways, he supposed. Yet, Crane's last experiment had been transferring energy from one group to another. Once his wife fell into a coma, why wouldn't he focus in on trying to fix *her*?

Alex knew in his gut this was all about waking Rose. The secret to that had to be discoverable by something here. Clearly nothing in sight, or the FBI would have found it in their run-through. If Crane hadn't been keeping Rose in a hospital or the room upstairs, where was he keeping her? All signs pointed to this basement.

Maybe a room, hidden away. The wise thing was to get the original house plans and find missing square footage. But doing that entailed pulling Daryl back in, and Alex wanted to handle the professor alone.

The time it would take for the government to move on anything might be too long for some victims.

This was a delicate business, and with so many lives involved, the FBI would never see Professor Brier as anything but a villain. Someone to be stopped. But maybe—even if he was the cause—maybe he was the only one who could stop what was happening before more people had to suffer. Which left Alex playing lone hero trying to find the mystical "wizard."

"Well," he said to himself, "ask my wife any day, I'm no prince. How do I get past the briar wall?"

"For starters, that's the wrong wall."

The soft female voice emitted from behind him, which was a blessing as the speaker didn't see Alex pale and grab at his chest or his hand slide down to the gun holstered over his hip. By the time he turned, his breathing was even.

The woman wore a flowered shift dress, which hung on her like a bag. She leaned in a door frame—a door that hadn't existed moments before. Despite the wall's support, she swayed from the effort of standing. Her skinny legs trembled. Even with the weight loss, and pale pallor. Rose Brier. Her blonde hair toppled in tangles over her shoulders, and her makeup looked as if it had seen her through a hard night of partying.

"Well," he said, "check you out. It's not every day I meet Sleeping Beauty."

Rose sighed at the joke, knuckles going white as she clung to the door frame. "And you are? Given you've broken into my home, the least you can do is introduce yourself."

"Alex, ma'am. I've been called in to investigate last night's incident."

"You're a detective?"

"Something like. I take jobs the government can't or won't handle."

She froze, studying his face until he wiped the corners of his mouth to make sure no trace of burrito lingered there.

"Come inside. You'll want to see Crane's machine."

"Not a spindle, is it?" Alex couldn't help but ask. Gina would have kicked him in the shin.

Rose glared and turned into the lab. By the time Alex reached the doorway, a halogen glow lit the room.

A giant mechanical contraption filled his vision. Dozens of

displays flashed on the wall. Two tubs took central position with a glowing podium between them. A man's body lay in one of them. Alex approached and looked in at a thin man. *Asleep.* "Shit."

He peered at the other tub and reached out to touch the inch-thick layer of blue goo.

Cords trailed from it. From the state of Rose's hair, he could tell she'd been in there, linked up. But why then wasn't Professor Brier linked as well?

Alex checked carefully over the unmoving body and the surrounding space.

"What've you and your husband been tampering with down here, Rose?"

"Why are you here?" Rose's hands balled at her sides. Her lips drew back, revealing perfect white teeth. "Do you know something about this machine?"

"You never came out of your coma, did you?" Alex asked. *Not naturally, at least.*

"No. Alex, was it? What are you doing here? I don't appreciate my questions being ignored."

It was a truism that princesses liked manners, though Alex resisted saying so.

"I'm here because last night every citizen in Able's Hollow fell into a coma. And lo and behold, I find you with this sci-fi machine and a goo-filled bathtub . . . and you're awake."

Rose stared at him, eyes wide, then bit down on her lip. A muffled sound escaped her as she moved between him and Crane. "No, no, no. How could it have affected anyone else?"

"CDC will be here in the morning to determine if it's contagious before air-lifting everyone out. There are a lot of un-conscious people out there, and I'd like to find a way to help them."

Rose's fingers folded around her husband's. She trembled, and Alex wanted to tell her that everything would be okay, but his gut told him that was a lie. This wasn't a fairy tale, and no happy ending awaited her.

"He never thought . . . It was just supposed to be him and me involved in this experiment." Rose drew in a deep, ragged breath. She looked to the side at a timer, just a flick of the eyes then she turned away.

"It isn't just the two of you."

"But the rest will wake up."

"How do you know that?" Alex pondered the timer and couldn't get past the sinking feeling that with each number that ticked away all those folks had less and less hope. There wasn't much time left. Certainly not enough to second-guess himself. Less than half an hour remained.

"I . . . Because it couldn't take a whole town to wake one person. My husband planned for this to be a one-to-one ratio—me and him. Crane assumed he wouldn't wake up. He told me so . . . but now maybe he will, since there were so many. Maybe all of them will wake up . . ."

Alex shook his head. "You don't know that. Is your life worth nearly five thousand other lives?"

"I could see Crane again . . . I just want to see my hus-band."

"We must turn the machine off before that timer stops. I can't risk all those lives."

Rose clung to her husband. "Turning it off could be more dangerous than just letting it time out. What if it kills them?"

"There are a lot of what-ifs right now. We don't have time for them. Are you going to help me?" Alex set his hand on his holstered gun. Using it on Rose . . . well, that was something to avoid. She was part of a circuit, though, and cutting her out of it just might save everyone. Even a princess wasn't worth sacrificing a whole town.

"Rose, are you going to help me?" Alex asked. So far she'd offered no resistance.

Her back was to him, and when she bent over, her long hair hung down into the tub and touched her husband. "I can figure what happens after that machine turns off. Either everyone dies and I go back into a coma or they wake up and I go back into a coma. After that, all the government types come to study Crane's invention. If we're lucky and Crane wakes up, he'll spend the rest of his life in some sort of government detention."

"This isn't a choice." Alex drew the gun but left it lowered. She didn't need to see it yet. "There's nothing wrong with those people out there, so they should wake up. But if we leave it on, we risk you taking in too much energy, and they'll all stay comatose."

"So you want me to sacrifice myself, not even knowing for sure if it will help anyone?"

"It sounds ugly, but yes. That's what I'm asking. I'm sorry."

"Do me one favor?" Rose asked.

Alex averted his eyes. "If I can."

What if it was Gina? He couldn't refuse her anything reasonable. Not this woman, whom another man had been willing to sacrifice everything for. He had to honor the value of something beloved.

"This goes above my pay grade soon," he added.

"Tell Crane it worked—before you do whatever you do with him. And that I regained consciousness. Tell him no one forced me . . . and tell him I heard him talking to me all those many years. I know how hard he tried to get me back—I know how much he loved me."

Alex nodded. "I'll give him the message."

"He talked about this project, all the things I could do when it was complete. All the places I could go . . . as if I'd want to travel anywhere without him."

"Back on point: as sorry as I am for you, thousands of people might die if we don't solve this. Do you know how to turn this thing off?"

"You should be able to power it down from the control panel here." Rose climbed into the tub where Crane lay, and Alex wished Gina was next to him. In that moment, he needed to hold her, to be sure she was still there. Rose snuggled in close beside Crane, positioning his arm around her. Did Alex have the strength to do what Rose was doing? To walk calmly into something that meant losing himself? A desire to apologize to Crane bubbled up inside him.

This sleeping beauty walked to her spindle with full knowledge. She'd never get her Prince Charming. If only Gina had been there to tease him for getting sentimental . . . but she wasn't, and he swore that when he got home, he'd make sure he didn't miss any of those precious moments. Moments Rose and

Crane would have died for. Alex would find a way to be home more, to see Anna's first steps.

For the first time, he understood why Gina had wanted that office job. Living, real living, was coming home to the ones you loved every day—being with them. His work, that wasn't life; it was his version of a coma and he wanted to be *awake*.

Rose

CRANE'S ARM FELL OVER HER, loose and unresponsive, but she could pretend he was holding her. If he'd been able to, she knew he would have. As it was, it would have to be enough having his warm breath against her neck. She would savor that sensation in her mind.

"If this works . . ." Alex said.

"If this works, I'll be back where I was before. I'll die without ever waking up again." Rose pulled Crane's arm tighter around her but even so, the trembling of her voice signaled the mounting fear that commanded her to run, run far, far away. "Crane used to talk about relative worth—how the worth of any object depends on the viewer. I know what I was worth to him . . . but I can't believe he would have sacrificed a whole town for me. I certainly won't make that sacrifice. To my view, I wouldn't be worth much if I was willing to risk all those lives. And I know he was worth more than trying to steal them for me."

Alex nodded. His eyes glistened, and he wiped at them. "I've never killed someone."

"I'm sorry."

"Me too." Alex moved up to the control panel.

"Eight-five-two-six-two is the passcode to get you in," Rose said flatly.

She snuggled Crane but found the position unsatisfying. If she could never see him again, she wanted to gaze into his face now. Memorize every line, and keep it with her until her mind went blank. She turned over on her other side and tucked her face against Crane's neck.

The panel beeped with each number Alex pressed.

"You ready?" Alex asked.

"Yes."

Rose snuggled closer against Crane and wrapped her arms around him.

"Nothing happened. It won't take the passcode," Alex said.

"What else could it be?"

"The numbers that correspond to Rose B, maybe?"

The keypad let off little beeps again, and once more nothing happened. Rose struggled for another guess at a passcode. Her eyes flicked to the timer. Not much time left now, less than a minute.

"Screw this, cover your ears, Princess," Alex said.

Rose opened her mouth to ask why when she saw the gun lift. Was he going to shoot the console? Would that work? No time to ask.

She covered her ears.

A shower of sparks erupted, accompanied by a resounding boom that echoed in the metal room, and Rose's eyes squeezed closed. Her ears rang. But even without her hearing she could feel the vibration. The rhythmic tick of a countdown commenced.

Beep.

"I love you," she whispered.

Beep.

Rose bit her lip.

Beep.

"Please go on, whatever happens. Live your life."

Beep.

She brushed her lips over Crane's—one last moment of warmth to take with her. The sound of the machine faded. With the outer hum dimming, a familiar inner fog swelled to greet her.

Darkness swarmed over her, but for just an instant, she could feel Crane's warmth against her skin. Feel his arm tighten around her. His mouth pressed to hers.

Suddenly she knew what the passcode was.

AWAKE.

It came to Rose as the deep sleep overcame her, and she fell back into the nothingness.

Truth Be Told

danielle banas

I **TOLD MY FIRST LIE** when I was five years old. It was a silly thing. I'd pulled the last pint of chocolate fudge ice cream from the freezer and stuffed my face. When my mother asked where it disappeared to, I opened my sticky, fudge-covered lips and told her I didn't know.

The lie felt like a living thing as it spilled from my mouth, a friend that arrived at the perfect moment to save me from trouble. And, like all living things, my lies tended to grow as the years progressed.

"Does this dress look nice?" *Of course.* "Did you throw a baseball through the garage window?" *Maybe, but I'll tell you otherwise.* "Why is your homework late?" *Well, you see, my house caught fire last night . . .*

I tried to stop; I really did. Like when my classmates

laughed upon discovering I liked Maddie Johnson from sixth-grade English. Instead of denying it, I shrugged and said Maddie had a lisp that made her spit in your eye every time she talked—which *was* true, though cruel of me to say. When I found out I'd made Maddie cry, I felt so horrible that I avoided her for the rest of middle school. My tactic progressed to bored indifference after that.

"Hey, Leo, do you like so-and-so?" *Ehh . . . I don't know.* "Do you want to watch that new superhero flick?" *Maybe.* "What major are you picking in college?" *Not sure.*

I wished I could say I wanted to be a photographer, but my mother didn't think that was a viable career choice. She liked marketing managers. Likely because she was one. She was so overbearing that I wouldn't put it past her to hide out in some bushes on campus, armed with binoculars and a thermos of green tea, spying on me to ensure I made it to class on time.

"Leo! I ironed your socks for you!"

And there she was. Mom. Shouting from her home office, where she multitasked every minute of every day. She folded clothes while negotiating client contracts with the same vibrant enthusiasm that normal people exuded when winning the lottery.

"Thanks, Ma." I didn't have the heart to tell her that no sane person scrubbed footwear with an iron.

"And put some pants on, Leonard."

"Ma!" I hated when she used my full name. I gestured to my legs, which were covered in my favorite pair of plaid boxer shorts. "I'm decent."

"Hardly. I told Mia you'd drive her to the library. She needs something for a homework assignment." Mom picked up her desk phone, balancing the receiver between her shoulder and her ear.

"*Steven,*" she barked. "Pull up the Wisenhower contract. They're complaining about clause four again." She turned her attention back to me. "Oh, and honey? Put on a coat. It's a bit nippy outside."

"Whatever." I grabbed the car keys and dug through the laundry basket in search of jeans and a sweater.

"And Leo? Don't let Mia pick out a vampire book. Last time she read one, she asked a boy in her class to bite her."

I grunted—my usual noncommittal response whenever Mom went off on a tirade.

"And I'm making your favorite pot roast for dinner, so don't be late." She rolled her eyes at her phone. "No, Steven, no pot roast for you. No! Clause *four,* you loon!" Her gaze swiveled to me again. I felt like I was watching a tennis match. "I'll make sure to cut up your potatoes just the way you like." I'd been capable of cutting my own food since I was four, but try telling her that. Feigning indifference was easiest. It got me out of the house, no questions asked.

Shutting Mom's door softly behind me, I went searching for my sister. She was usually relatively easy to find. At thirteen years old, Mia Clark's hobbies consisted mainly of screaming over the latest "dreamy" teen actors and screaming even louder over the latest "dreamy" teen boy bands.

"Mia's in the car," Dad said. He was kneeling in the living room, up to his elbows in couch cushions. I paused in the doorway, watching his forehead glisten with sweat as he huffed and puffed and practically tore the house apart. "Your mother hid my remote again." He tossed a cushion across the room, where it landed in the fireplace. "Baseball starts in ten"—a second cushion followed the first—"minutes!" Two pillows brought up the rear.

"Well . . ." I shrugged. "That sucks."

"Would it kill you, Leo, to care about your old man's problems for once? Pittsburgh's making it to the World Series this year, mark my words."

I reached for the front door. "Consider them marked, Dad."

"Want to watch the game when you get back?"

"Ehh . . ." I could see the hope in his eyes. (Or maybe that was just joy over finally locating the remote, lodged inside a potted plant.) "I'll pass. See you later."

As soon as I got in the car, Mia was all over me. She gripped my elbow as I backed out of the driveway, causing me to swerve and almost mow down the neighbor's cat. "Leo! Leo, we're going to the library, right?"

"Nope. We're going to hell."

"Wait, what? Because Suzie Samuels said that Mrs. Benedict changed the due date for our book report and we have to write *five pages* for Friday and I still don't have a novel picked out. I'm thinking something with fairies. Or elves. What do you think?" When I didn't reply, she lunged for my arm again. I almost ran a stop sign, and a car sitting at the intersection honked. "Leo!"

"Shhh! I'm training myself to block out the sound of your voice."

Here was the thing: I actually liked my family. I just didn't want them to know I liked them. If they knew, they would expect things from me. They would want chores completed on time, good grades in school, birthday cards, flowers on Mother's Day, a steak dinner on Father's Day—and I was afraid I wouldn't be able to measure up to their expectations. What if I bought the wrong gift or the card wasn't heartfelt enough or— *Ugh!*

Pretending not to care was safer. Having feelings was for saps.

THE LIBRARY WAS A NIGHTMARE. Mia picked up *every single book* on the shelves, smiled at the cover, read the synopsis aloud in a chipper voice that I naively assumed meant she thought the book was a winner, then frowned and wrinkled her nose and put the book down. Rinse and repeat. After she completed her ritual with book number twenty—or was it thirty?—I was ready to lock myself in the bathroom, shove my head in the toilet, and inhale.

"How about this?" Mia showed me a cover featuring a rickety house and an ominous full moon.

Mom had said no vampires. This definitely looked like a vampire book. But caring about this detail would only prolong the torture.

"It's okay, I guess."

Mia rolled her eyes, replaced the book, and then it was time to poke around the shelves some more. A minute later, she emerged with a paperback showcasing a raunchy, half-naked cowboy.

"That's fine too," I said.

"Yeah, right. Mrs. Benedict would fail me. Leo, don't you have an opinion about anything?"

"Guess not."

Liar. I had loads of opinions. I was just afraid of being told that those opinions were wrong.

Mia rounded the stacks, passing the travel and leisure section and coming to a stop in science fiction and fantasy. I stood on my tiptoes, wondering where the cookbooks were. I needed to salivate over a picture of a hamburger. Stat.

"This one?" Mia asked. "And be honest."

I leaned over her shoulder. The book looked ancient, like some kind of medieval relic. There was no photo on the cover, just a few brown stains that may or may not have been blood, as well as fine golden letters spelling out "airy Tales." I suspected the *F* had run away—and for good reason.

A shiver crept up my spine. I couldn't figure out why, but I really wished she would put the book down.

"Looks great, Mia." Another lie. "Let's go."

"Wait! I don't even know what it's about!"

"Well, read it and you'll learn." I reached for her arm and started pulling her down the aisle.

"But, but . . . Leo! Hey! You're hurting me! Just give me one second to—"

The book fell from her hands, landing open on the floor. Mia reached down to retrieve it, but I moved to stop her, struck with a sudden desire to sprint out to the car.

The tip of Mia's index finger touched the words on the page.

And time stopped.

People tend to overuse that expression: *Time stopped*. Like in movies, when the main characters lock eyes in a grocery store or whatever and then later they claim that the moment they saw each other *time stopped*. Or when a man falls asleep at the wheel and drifts into oncoming traffic and *time stopped*. Time can't stop. It can't speed up either. Time just . . . *is*. Or that's what I thought.

But in that moment, time *did* stop. It shut right down. The books disappeared. The air around me lit on fire. For a moment I couldn't see, like someone set off a flashbulb inside my pupils.

Then time did the impossible again: it sped back up. The air cleared. The heat vanished. I had this weird pins-and-needles feeling in my limbs, but Mia's hand was still there, crammed between my fingers. And the library was . . . *gone*.

I shook my head, trying to clear my fuzzy thoughts. I thought about pinching myself, but that seemed a bit extreme. And yet . . . how had we ended up downtown?

The sun was setting, throwing shadows across the familiar Pittsburgh skyline. Reflections of bridges and tall buildings glinted in the river. The water churned, splashing against the hull of the— *Hang on*. I looked down, eyes widening at the deck of a massive vessel beneath my feet, then up, taking in the skull-and-crossbones flag flying from a wooden mast high above my head. This time, I really did pinch myself. Or I tried to. Two very important things were wrong with this picture.

One, since when was there a *pirate ship* on the Ohio River?

Two, since when were my fingers made of . . . *wood*?

I wasn't on drugs, was I? I'd never taken drugs before. Well, actually, there was that teeny-weeny bit of weed after homecoming last year, but that barely counted. I took one hit, then puked in a bush. But *this* . . . this was something else.

Wooden fingers, wooden toes. I ran my tongue across my bottom lip, wincing when something pricked me. A splinter?

This was a serious LSD-level trip.

"Mia?" I squeezed her hand. "Does my face look funny to you?"

In reply, she stared at me, mouth gaping.

"We're still in the library, right?" I asked.

When she shook her head no, my stomach plummeted.

Just as she was about to speak, a pair of hands darted out, seized her shoulders, and pulled her back.

"Leo!"

"Mia!" I tried leaping after her, but my legs wouldn't cooperate. They got tangled up beneath me, and I crashed down, smacking my chin on the deck of the ship.

Mia's kidnapper laughed. He was joined by several men and women wearing knee-length leather jackets and ripped trousers. Some had teeth missing; a few pulled pistols from their belts.

"The princess is found!" The captain—judging by his stupid floppy hat—threw his hands in the air.

His crew followed suit.

"Princess!" he exclaimed.

"We're going to be rich!"

"Rich!" they echoed.

"Whoa! Hey, that's my sister! She's not a princess!" I tried to stand, but a stumpy man darted forward, pushed me back, and quickly handcuffed me to the ship's mast. "Hey! Who do you think you are?"

The captain grinned, showing off two golden teeth. "My apologies. We're often inconsiderate when treasure is involved. I'm Sal, and these"—he swept out his arms—"are the Pirates of Pittsborough!"

"You mean Pittsburgh?"

"Never heard of it. Sounds like a vile place. You'll find that Pittsborough"—he rolled his tongue around the final syllable—"is far nicer."

I struggled to wrap my head around his words. This place—Pittsborough—looked nearly identical to the city I called home. Same buildings, same three rivers. The only major differences were that here my body resembled a tree trunk, and Pitts*burgh* had the Pirates baseball team whereas Pitts*borough* just had . . . real pirates.

If my arms hadn't been restrained, I would have pinched myself again.

I glanced across the deck to Mia. She was being held in place by two women, and she was shaking. She caught my eye and mouthed, *"Help!"*

"Look, man," I told Sal. "You have to let her go. She's . . ." My brain told me to say that my sister was young, innocent, only thirteen. All logical pleas. But at the last second, my mouth did a one-eighty and spit out, "She's annoying! Mia's a pain, and I guarantee you don't want her any more than I do!"

Yikes. How did that happen? I mean, it was true, but I didn't want to confess it.

"Oh dear," said Sal. He frowned at Mia's watery eyes. "The truth hurts, yes?"

"Mia! I'm sorry! I didn't mean—" My voice got lodged in my

throat. I couldn't speak, and somehow I knew it was because to continue speaking would be to lie.

Mia gave me a dirty look. "I can be a princess," she told Sal defiantly.

"Princess!" the crew repeated, stomping their feet.

"Stop it," I said. "I don't know who you're looking for, but Mia's nowhere near royalty." *Crap.* Bring on the word vomit. "She picks her nose at the dinner table and leaves hair balls in the shower and burps the alphabet backward. Frankly, she's disgusting."

I liked my sister just fine, but that was the truth. She was gross. But I never shared my opinions regarding her habits. Indifference was easiest. Indifference didn't hurt people; it didn't make Mia cry.

"On the contrary, she looks exactly like our princess." Sal showed me a photograph of a girl with Mia's blonde hair and brown eyes. "We'll take her to the queen and she'll decide. Toodle-loo!"

The crew piled into rowboats attached to the side of the ship. Mia followed, her head held high.

I desperately called out to her.

She ignored me.

Sal and I were the last two on board. I jiggled my wrists in their restraints behind me. "Aren't you going to make me walk the plank?"

He smirked. Underneath the dark beard and matted mess of hair, he slightly resembled my father. "Sorry, wooden boy. If you jump, you'll float. An easy escape." He stroked his mustache.

Why did the evil guys always have mustaches? Hitler, my statistics teacher, this guy . . .

Sal swung his legs over the side of the ship and started his descent. "I think it would be more villainous to let you starve instead . . . although with any luck the dragons will eat you first."

"Wait, *what?*" I yelled.

Sal's honking laughter was the only reply I received.

"Hey! Your mustache belongs in a porno!" The words burst forth before I could stop them. "And your coat makes you look like a flasher. Are you wearing underwear under there?"

I tried to squash down the little voice inside of me, the one demanding the truth that no one wanted to hear. But I couldn't do it. I couldn't lie.

⚜

FOOD. I DIDN'T KNOW if my wooden body was capable of consuming it, but after being left alone for eons, it was all I could think about. I wanted it. All of it. Greasy potato chips, a foot-long hot dog, a liter of pop. I wasn't picky. By my count, it had been . . . *Hmmm, let's see . . . thirty-seven plus twenty-five, carry the one . . .* a whole *hour* since I ate last. A man could only withstand so much torture.

I thumped the back of my head against the mast, groaning at the dull thud of wood smacking wood. I'd caught a glimpse of my reflection in a puddle on the deck ten minutes earlier. My skin was covered in dark circles, like knots left behind by tree branches. My hair had grown rough and dark, like bark on a walnut tree. My skin was lighter, resembling oak, or maybe maple. Only my eyes were unchanged. Blue as the ocean, my dad always said, but nowhere near as deep.

I shifted my weight, stretching my legs. My limbs were stiff (obviously), and moving them made me feel clumsy. Like a baby learning to walk.

Wooden legs, pirates on the river, and my sister kidnapped. Could this get any worse?

My stomach growled.

Apparently, yes.

But at least the dragons hadn't eaten me . . . yet.

I scoffed. Dragons. What next? Dwarfs? Talking animals?

"Hi there!"

My head snapped up. I scanned the deck, finding nothing.

"Hey! Over here!"

I had to be hallucinating. I needed to eat something; that was it. Once I got some food in me, I could find Mia and—

"Are you stupid? Look down here!"

Feeling like an idiot, I obeyed. But the deck was empty.

Something slimy touched my hand. "Back here, you moron."

The mast bumped my head as I struggled to turn around. And there, sitting on my manacled wrists, was a fat green frog.

"Hi!"

Hallucinating. Definitely hallucinating. That thing did not just talk. My arms ached as I reached blindly behind me to capture it. Talking frog or not, I'd just found a food source.

"Whoa, buddy, I'm not a stripper. Keep your hands to yourself!"

I was mad with hunger. Seeing red. I didn't think twice when my bonds fell away. I crawled across the deck to where

I'd spied a knife and a lighter left on a barrel, but my progress was halted as the ship tilted port side, throwing me onto my stomach. The barrel wobbled precariously, and the knife fell, plunging into the river. I dove for the lighter, breathing a deep sigh of relief when it landed safely in my outstretched hand. Things were looking up. Food—and something to prepare it with.

The frog's bulbous yellow eyes blinked. "Dude, think about this. I just saved your shiny wooden ass."

Still hallucinating. Eating would fix that. I had frog's legs once when Mom went on a foreign-food binge. They weren't half-bad.

The frog jumped when I lunged. My hand-eye coordination was awful, but somehow I managed to pin one webbed foot to the deck. I clicked the lighter. The frog shied away as the flame neared its back.

It exploded.

No, not like that. Not in a mess of blood and guts or anything. But it grew. In two seconds, the frog went from a slimy green amphibian to—poof!—a not-slimy, but still green, girl.

A really cute girl. With curly red hair and yellowish, hazel eyes. But her skin was still as green as a traffic light.

Then again, my skin had turned to wood, so I didn't have room to talk. We were a match made in heaven, the green girl and I.

Until she slapped me across the face.

"That was for touching me without permission," she said. "And for not even bothering to thank me for rescuing you." She held out the rusty screw she'd used to sever the rope. "I'd give you another one for trying to eat me, but in the end you broke my curse so . . . thanks, I guess."

"Your . . . curse?"

"You're quite slow, aren't you? I gathered that." She gave me an artificially cheerful smile, like she thought I was a total dunce, and slowly enunciated, "Thank . . . you . . . for . . . help . . . ing . . . me. What . . . is . . . your . . . name?"

"Uh . . . Leo. You don't need to do that. I can understand you fine."

Green Girl shrugged and held out her hand. She wore a dirty brown smock. Her fingers and toes were webbed. "I'm Corinne. Nice to meet you, Leonard."

I cringed upon hearing my full name.

"It's Leo."

"Which would be short for Leonard, wouldn't it?"

I wanted to say no, but I found the truth pushing its way out instead.

"Yes." But the last person, besides my mother, who called me that was Billy Simmons, in kindergarten. He made fun of my name. I made fun of his butt after pulling down his pants during recess. An even trade.

My classmates never dared to call me Leonard again.

Corinne studied me, a hint of a smile on her lips. "Then Leonard it is."

I wanted to scream. I needed to distract myself.

"So . . . I broke your curse by nearly killing you?"

"Good guess, but no. I think fire is the key. Whether that be literal fire or the fiery passion of true love's first kiss." She rolled her eyes. "The wording on the curse isn't picky, apparently."

"Some curse."

She laughed. "Yeah, well, the witch who cast the spell didn't include sufficient clauses. Not that I'm complaining, but she was a total dud. She was also an unpaid intern, and you know how unreliable their work ethic can be sometimes."

"Sure . . . ?" I wondered if getting rid of my wooden feet would be as easy as chopping down a tree or something. "Listen, Corinne, you gotta help me. My sister's missing, I can't tell lies, I've turned into a tree stump—"

"*You're* cursed?"

And she thought *I* was an idiot.

"You can never be too sure," she continued. "Being wooden isn't an *automatic* guarantee, you understand. We get all kinds in Pittsborough. Hmmm . . . let's see . . ." She knelt beside me. "Hold still a sec."

If I was still human, my heart would have raced as she neared. I might have sweat a little. I would have curled my fingers into her hair, holding her close while my breath fanned out across her cheeks.

But I didn't know what I was anymore. And so there was no throbbing heart. No sweaty skin. My rough wooden fingers stayed clenched in my lap as she quickly, but firmly, pressed her mouth to mine.

Nothing happened.

"Huh." She pulled back. "Definitely no kissing clause. What did the witch get you for anyway? Vanity? Greed?"

"What?" The contrast between her bright red hair and bright green skin was awfully distracting. "No, there was no witch. I showed up like this."

"I don't follow."

Anger bubbled inside me. "I'm not from here! I'm from Pittsburgh. Not *borough* or whatever. We have sports where I'm from, not magic."

"Oh!" Her eyes widened in understanding. "You're from an alternate universe! Why didn't you say so? We've had your kind before. The last guy who passed through didn't make it out before his time was up. He's living in the Enchanted Sewickley Forest now."

My anger turned to dread. "What do you mean '*before his time was up*'?"

"Well, if past experience is any indication, you have until midnight—or, like, three hours—to return home or else you're stuck here. That clause is pretty much automatic, it seems."

Corinne said it so simply. *You're stuck here.* Just like: *Yes, I'd love fries with that.*

Three hours. I had three hours to get home.

"I can't be stuck. My sister's kidnapped, and Mom's making pot roast."

Did Mom even know we were missing? Dad was likely too busy watching baseball to notice.

"No biggie," Corinne said. "I'll help you find her. Where'd you last see her?"

"Right here! The pirates said she was a princess and they took her to the queen."

She paled. "Oh."

"*Oh?* Just *oh?* Can't you, like, take me to the castle so I can get her back?"

"The queen"—she sighed—"doesn't live in a castle. She lives in an office building. You have so much to learn."

"Well," I said, feeling pretty pathetic. The truth ached like a boulder on my chest. "I need help. What do you say?"

A strange emotion flickered in Corinne's eyes. Then, "Fine. Yes, fine. Hang on." She strutted belowdecks, tossing around a few pots and pans before returning with a cell phone.

They had cell phones here?

"I'm getting us a dragon," she said.

"A what?"

"Relax, Leonard. It's a ride-share service. I'm not *buying* a new one, duh."

⚜

A DRAGON *WAS* A RIDE-SHARE SERVICE. It was also, as Corinne neglected to mention, an *actual dragon*.

"Scared, Leonard?"

Lying was useless. "Terrified. And it's Leo."

Corinne climbed aboard the red scaly beast, scratching its neck like it was a puppy, like it didn't have teeth longer than my forearm. The dragon's wings flapped, creating a gust of wind that nearly knocked me on my butt.

"Don't worry. This guy is quite domesticated." She pulled me up behind her. "Only the wild dragons will swallow you whole."

During the trip downtown, I learned two things about riding with a dragon. First, bugs *will* fly down your throat. And second, dragons liked to talk. A lot.

"And so I says to her, I says, 'Patty.' I says, 'Patty, your breath smells like damn onions.'" Mario, our dragon, shrugged, nearly sending us flying off his back. "I thought that was a compliment. I thought that was a new toothpaste she was trying out. But then she does this. Ready? You listening back there?"

"Not particularly," I replied, flinching. Stupid truth curse. Telling a two-ton dragon you didn't care about his problems was probably a no-no in Pittsborough. But Mario didn't hear me.

"Patty breathes a fireball right in my face, singeing off my eyebrows! Can you believe it? My face is my moneymaker, you know what I'm saying?"

Corinne rubbed his shoulder. "Mario, you know how the ladies are around mating season. Hey, do you watch that new reality show? *Gnome Hunters*?"

"You bet! It's on tonight. Man, I was so happy when they kicked off Fabian last week."

"I know! He was such a drama queen!" Corinne turned around, smiling. "See, Leonard? Dragons are perfectly friendly."

But because of their size, dragons weren't allowed to enter the city, so Mario touched down across the river on Pittsborough's north shore and waved good-bye with a flick of his fifty-foot tail. Corinne waved back, grinning. I spit out a mouthful of bugs and tried to massage a kink from my neck.

"Having fun, Leonard?"

I leveled my gaze at her. "Stop calling me that. And no. Are you kidding?"

"Lighten up." She set off across the bridge into town. I followed, my stomach still growling. The sun had set and the lights in the buildings were winking on, spreading a dull glow across the streets. "Tell me more about your sister."

The truth: my new nemesis. "Mia's really annoying . . . but she's okay, I guess. The reason she's missing is because I said some hurtful things about her. I said the truth."

"Because you're cursed to?"

"Exactly! But I didn't mean for it to come out so harsh. I really do care . . ." I pressed my fingers over my mouth, willing the words to stay inside. But they shot out anyway. "I really do care about her." I groaned. "You have no idea how hard it is for me to admit that. I hate sharing how I feel about stuff. I *like* being indifferent. There's too much pressure that comes with caring, and I don't want to mess it up."

Had I really confessed that? I'd never felt so exposed. I was going to be sick.

We turned the corner onto Pencil Avenue, which I think was Penn Avenue in my version of things, and headed uptown, passing a mob of people with large pointed ears. No one looked twice at Corinne's skin or my gnarled wooden cheeks. Corinne stayed silent for a while—I was sure that meant she thought I was some kind of screwed-up loser—but then she started laughing, a crazed, high-pitched noise that stopped me dead in my wobbly wooden tracks.

"You're not dying, are you? Because I hate to admit this, but you're my only hope at the moment."

"No! I'm fine. It's just—it's just so funny! Talk about irony! Honestly, Leonard—"

"Leo."

"You hate having feelings, so you get transformed into the most emotionless thing out there—a talking block of wood!"

"I'm not a block," I said, slightly offended. "I have arms . . ."

Corinne ignored me. "And then you're forced to tell the truth about how you feel! It's just . . . wow." She wiped her eyes. "It's poetic, really."

"I hate you."

"Yes!" She gripped my shoulders, shaking me. "Hate me all you want, Leonard. It's okay to let your feelings out. That's what humans do!"

"You're awfully insightful for someone who wasn't human two hours ago."

"Never mind that." She shook her head. "Maybe you could learn something from this curse of yours. I mean, all I learned from mine was how to catch a fly on my tongue, but *you*, Leonard, you could change your life."

"Your inspirational wisdom makes me want to hurl," I said in a monotone.

Corinne harrumphed. "I guess that's a start."

We walked on, passing more citizens with pointed ears, some with whiskers on their cheeks, and a few short, wrinkly men in business suits. Corinne said they were goblins. She also said that looking them in the eye could be misconstrued as an ankle-biting challenge.

I kept my gaze trained firmly ahead.

I didn't know what we would do once we reached the queen's building. I had a feeling I couldn't politely ask for my sister back, not after she was mistaken for royalty. And especially not after I recited her list of shortcomings.

Corinne crossed the street, tugging me behind her. I tried to dodge a group of musicians on the corner, but Corinne stopped me. There was a gleam in her eyes that made my legs feel shakier than usual.

"Do you like dancing, Leonard?"

I sighed. "It's Leo. And not on these feet. Not at all, honestly." I tried to pull away, but her webbed fingers were surprisingly strong.

"Why not?"

"Because . . . because . . ." Okay, the truth was really getting old. "Because it's embarrassing. Because I don't like looking like an idiot."

Corinne nodded to the musician closest to us, a girl with blue tentacles for hair. The girl gestured to her friends, who picked up their banjos and began playing a twangy country tune. Pedestrians stopped to watch, clapping their hands in time with the beat.

Corinne tugged me closer, but my feet tripped me up and I crashed into her chest. She laughed it off. "Leonard, no one will think you look like an idiot as long as *you* don't think you look like an idiot."

"That's not necessarily true."

"Just one dance."

"But my sister—"

"We have tons of time, I promise." She twirled around, making me dizzy. "Live a little first. Feel something."

ONE DANCE TURNED INTO TWO, which turned into three, four, five. And I was shocked to find that the more time we spent on that street corner, the more fun I had. My feet were still clumsy, and my fingers couldn't grip to save my life, but something about the way Corinne spun around, looking as ridiculous as me, made it okay.

But time was running out. We had less than two hours to get Mia back, and yet whenever I mentioned this, Corinne clammed up and nervously glanced at the blinking red light atop the tallest building in the city. The queen's chambers. It was called the Steel Building in Pittsburgh, but here it was known only as the Q.

Something was up with Corinne. And my future depended on discovering what that was.

"So . . ." I began, realizing she knew much more about me than I did about her. "If I broke your curse, why are you still green?"

She skipped along the street, shrugging. "I think it's permanent. Green's my favorite color, though, so it's not a total disappointment. Orange on the other hand . . ." She laughed, but her heart wasn't in it.

"How did you even get green to begin with?"

"Long story. Oh, hey! Want some ice cream?" She took off in the direction of a nearby building, leaving me to hobble after her. I could recognize when someone was deflecting. I was a pro at it, after all.

I squinted at the sign above the parlor. "Mice Cream?"

"Yep. These guys are great. Look!"

Screaming wasn't considered very manly, but at the moment I didn't care. I screamed like a thirteen-year-old girl. I screamed like Mia at her first bubblegum-pop boy-band concert.

Three five-feet-tall white mice were staring right at me.

"We seem to have alarmed him," said the one on the left. It was wearing a putrid-yellow top hat and holding an ice cream scoop.

"Newbie," added the mouse on the right. It adjusted the lapels of a hideous glittery blue suit.

The middle mouse said nothing. It pushed a pair of horn-rimmed glasses up its nose and offered me a bowl of red ice cream.

Top Hat Mouse bowed. "Enjoy our complimentary mint chocolate chip. We added extra chips this week."

I glanced at my bowl. "Why is it red? Are there cherries in here?"

"Don't mention that," Corinne said. "They're color-blind."

I blinked. "Color-blind . . . mice?"

"Red-green color blindness mostly. Sometimes blue-yellow."

"My lady," Top Hat interrupted, "I do love your green hair. It's quite alluring."

Corinne nudged my arm and pushed a lock of red hair over her shoulder. "See? It certainly doesn't help their sense of style."

Top Hat rounded the counter, allowing me to get a closer look at him. He wore orange-and-white-striped pants and a checkered shirt. He was a bit too close for comfort. I tried not to scream again.

"You guys are the stuff of nightmares," I confessed, wincing as the truth spilled out.

"How rude!" said Top Hat. "You know, we do love to gnaw on a good block of wood."

"I'm not a block!" I said, exasperated. "I have *arms*."

But Top Hat seemed to have grown bored with me. He turned to Corinne, while his two friends retreated into a storage room.

"It has been too long, my lady." He bowed a second time, and the look of reverence in his beady red eyes freaked me the heck out.

"Indeed," Corinne said. She'd relaxed once we entered the shop, but her shoulders were tense again, eyes skittish. "Don't tell anyone you saw me here. I haven't been recognized yet."

My ears perked up. *Recognized?*

Top Hat nodded. "I will say not a word, but I would think you'd want to stay far away, my lady. Considering your history."

I elbowed myself between them. "What history?"

A red blush formed beneath Corinne's bright green cheeks. "He doesn't know what he's talking about." Her voice was deathly low. "Do you, Alberto?"

The mouse began chewing on his fingers with sharp teeth. "I know only that the queen would kill you if she saw you. She hasn't forgotten."

"*Alberto*," Corinne warned.

"No, no." I motioned for the mouse to continue. For someone who kept encouraging me to tell the truth, Corinne definitely had some secrets of her own.

"Why would the queen want to kill her?" I asked.

"She doesn't," Corinne said.

"The mouse says otherwise."

Alberto's eyes widened. With a quick bow, he scurried behind the counter. "A lover's spat! I have said too much! Please ignore me."

I stared Corinne down. For the first time since I met her, she seemed almost shy. "Why do I get the feeling you're not just some frog girl who rescued me from pirates?"

Corinne glanced out the door, peering down the street at the Q. "Because I'm not." Her eyes grew watery. "You keep telling the truth, but I haven't been honest with you. Leonard, I know the queen because . . . I'm the real princess of Pittsborough."

She snatched the remainder of my ice cream and slumped down at a table to stuff her face. "Surprise."

❧

EVERY FAMILY HAS A NUT, and Corinne's just happened to have four. First up was her fairy godmother Wilhelmina, who killed Corinne's parents—the former king and queen of Pittsborough—in an attempt to steal the crown. She trapped them inside their bedroom and set it on fire. A bit more creative than just using poison, but it didn't really wow me as far as murders were concerned.

Nuts Two and Three were Corinne's mother and father. These winners had their daughter cursed against her will in a misguided attempt to hide her so Wilhelmina couldn't kill her as well. Turns out frogs can't rule a kingdom. Go figure. With Corinne gone and no one to take over, crazy Wilhelmina got put on the throne. Which brings me to . . .

Nut Number Four: Wilhelmina's daughter, Beatrice. This nut disappeared into the Enchanted Forest to hide from her mother, which actually made her the smartest nut, but she was still an idiot solely because she was responsible for my mess. If Beatrice hadn't done a runner, Wilhelmina wouldn't be overturn-

ing Pittsborough to find her. There would be no chaos, no re-
ward money, and those pirates would have left Mia untouched.

"I can't get over that it's like there are *two* of my sister," I
told Corinne. "Beatrice is like Mia's twin. It's freaky."

"That's because this is an alternate reality," she said. We
were still sitting in Mice Cream, and Alberto was dishing out
endless free samples due to the return of Her Royal Highness
Princess Corinne. I had trouble believing she was royalty, likely
because her appetite was worse than a dude's. I'd finished stuff-
ing myself ages ago, but she was still going strong.

"Here's how it works," she explained. "In your world, Mia is
your sister, but in this world she's Wilhelmina's daughter. Or
she looks like her anyway. Just like in your world, your father is
your father, but here he might be—"

"A pirate!"

"Sure, maybe."

"No, he is!" I jumped from my seat, remembering the way the
captain's face had looked so familiar. "Sal, the pirate, he kidnapped Mia! He took his own daughter—*wow*, that's messed up."

"Not really. Sal isn't Mia's father here. If he was, he
wouldn't have taken her." She stared at the Q again, a frightened look in her eyes.

"You don't need to come with me, you know," I said.

According to Corinne, Alberto had been right: Wilhelmina
would kill her if she spotted her. Anything to keep the crown from
its rightful owner. The longer we were in town, the more reality
started to sink in. Wilhelmina knew how to use magic; supposedly she was good at it, too. Corinne could die helping me.

"Why agree to this in the first place?" I asked.

Corinne sighed. "I don't know."

"Oh, come on! If I have to tell the truth, you do too. Don't start being all wooden."

She laughed a little. "That was a poor choice of words, Leonard."

Shockingly, being called Leonard didn't bother me that time.

"Okay, you want the truth?" She pointed her spoon at me. "I decided to come along because you looked miserable on that ship. Broken." Her voice got quiet. "And I know what it's like to be cursed and want out. I thought if we found your sister . . . it might help."

"Even though you might get hurt?"

"I know Wilhelmina's quarters like the back of my webbed hands." Corinne folded her arms across her chest. "I'm a big girl, Leonard. I can take care of myself. I was under the impression you didn't like me much anyway."

"What? No way! Honestly, Corinne, for a pushy green princess you aren't so bad."

She patted my cheek, her eyes sad. "You're sweet. But you wouldn't say that if you weren't cursed."

As I followed her outside, I wondered if she was right or if I had just shared my feelings all on my own.

⚜

THIRTY-FIVE MINUTES TO MIDNIGHT.

I was in total secret-agent mode as we crept through the service entrance at the back of the Q. That is, if secret agents had feet that cramped up and caused them to stumble every two steps.

"All right, Leonard?" Corinne asked. We dodged several guards returning from a break room and ducked into a stairwell. I was panting, my hands gripping my knees, but Corinne appeared unaffected.

"I feel like my chest is about to explode," I said.

"Just hang tight. There's an elevator at the end of the hall." She pulled the door open a crack, searching for trouble. "All clear. Let's head up."

For the first time since Corinne rescued me from the pirate ship, I was filled with doubt. Mia had been furious at me the last time I saw her. I couldn't even imagine how she would react when I showed up to her rescue.

"What if she doesn't want to come back?"

"She'll come," Corinne assured me. "You don't know how overbearing Wilhelmina is. Mia's probably dying to get out of there."

I chuckled as we waited for the elevator to arrive. It was on floor forty-five and needed to come all the way to the basement. "You've never met my mother. She's the same— *Wait*. Does Wilhelmina have blond hair?"

"Yeah . . ." Corinne answered slowly.

"Brown eyes?"

"Like a chocolate bar." She paused. "Or feces."

"Does she have a deviated septum that makes her squeak when she laughs and—"

"Yes!" she said kind of gleefully, but the confirmation only made my stomach hurt.

A loud bang echoed behind us. Corinne jabbed the call button repeatedly, as if that would help us get upstairs faster.

Two women and a man in crisp white chef's attire rounded the corner at the end of the hall. They halted when they spotted us.

"Did we hire new interns?" one of them wondered aloud.

The elevator arrived and Corinne pushed me inside before the doors opened halfway. She stabbed the button for floor sixty-four. The top floor.

"I have a bad feeling about this," she said.

"No kidding! My mother's a psychotic murderer!"

She pinched the bridge of her nose. "Leonard, Wilhelmina *isn't* your mother. She just looks like her. Remember that."

The elevator shot up with an incredible speed that made my head spin. If I had my old body back, I knew my skin would be speckled with sweat. Corinne retreated into herself, probably wondering if she'd made a horrible mistake.

As I watched the numbers climb, I thought about Wilhelmina and my mother. Mia and Beatrice.

Sal and my father. I wondered who Corinne would be in my world. Would she be royalty there too? A student? A celebrity? More important, I wondered who Leo Clark was in Pittsborough, and what I would do if I met him.

⤳⟡⤵

WE REACHED THE TOP OF THE Q with a loud ding that made my teeth grind. When the doors slid apart, Corinne took the lead, pulling me down a narrow purple hallway. I quickly discovered that Wilhelmina was obsessed with the color purple. The walls, the floor, even the ceiling were painted various shades that made me feel like I was living inside a grape.

"In here!" Corinne tugged me into a closet as two guards marched by. My shoulders were pressed against the wall, and Corinne's back was to my chest. Her hair smelled like flowers and salt water.

"Is it safe?" I whispered.

She opened the door. "Define safe . . ."

The hall opened into a cavernous room, and an anxious laugh escaped my mouth at the sight before me. Wilhelmina was an evil queen, but she was also the definition of a workaholic. She lived in her office. Literally. The floor was filled with at least fifty cubicles, each one decked out to look like a different room. There was a bed and a lamp in a cubicle in the corner. A couch and television in the one adjacent. A small art gallery across the way. Not even my mother was this crazy.

"Believe it or not, it didn't always look like this," Corinne whispered. Her lip trembled. I waited for some truthful words to force my mouth open, hoping they would comfort her, but for once I remained silent. Corinne's family was gone, and nothing I could say would bring them back.

A nasal voice jerked us both to attention. Corinne nodded resolutely and we inched forward, scooting between two bedroom cubicles and a library to reach the stainless-steel refrigerator looming at the back of the floor.

They sat at a long table in front of a row of curtained windows, Mia in a swivel chair and the queen in a throne that looked comically out of place, given the rest of the decor. A guard stood beside them, texting on a cell phone. When he looked up after finishing the message, I gasped.

"What?" Corinne asked.

"That guy! That's me!"

The queen sat up straighter and Corinne pulled me down, reaching for a blanket to cover our heads. We peeked out from between the folds.

"Do you hear something, Leslie?" Wilhelmina addressed my doppelgänger.

Leslie? And I thought Leonard was bad.

"I've been alerted of intruders in the compound, Your Majesty, but I've seen nothing to indicate they're near." Then he—I mean *me*—I mean *Leslie*—did something strange. He looked at where we were hiding . . . and winked.

Wilhelmina resumed her conversation. "I'm removing your curfew, Beatrice. And I'll need to get us a dragon. Now that I have Pittsborough under my control, we can move onto New New York and perhaps the entire country." She giggled a horrible sound, making my skin crawl. I reminded myself that she wasn't my mother. Her laugh was a lie. "Sweetheart, eat your peas."

"I hate peas," said Mia. She sounded confused but appeared otherwise unharmed.

A dismissive hand was waved in her direction. "Hush, Beatrice. You love peas."

"Mom, why do you keep calling me Beatrice? That's not my name."

"Beatrice, how dare you make a joke after everything you put me through."

Leslie tried to cut in. "Your Majesty, I—"

"Not now, Leslie!"

"His name is Leo," Mia said.

Plates rattled as the queen pushed herself to her feet.

"Beatrice, your lies must stop this instant! Is a little obedience too much to ask?" Black and gold sparks crackled at the tips of her fingers. *Magic*.

"I'm not Beatrice," Mia said quietly.

Wilhelmina's eyes narrowed. Visions of Mia becoming cursed like Corinne, cursed like *me*, flashed before my eyes. I moved to stand, but Corinne beat me to it, throwing off the blanket in a whoosh.

"She's not Beatrice," Corinne said.

"You!" Wilhelmina screeched. More sparks filled her hands.

"Yes. Me. I would say it's lovely to see you, Wilhelmina, but"—she glanced at me—"I'm learning the importance of not telling lies. So here's the truth: You suck. And that throne behind you is mine."

The door at the opposite side of the office crashed open, and a dozen guards clambered through. Upon spotting Corinne, they stopped, shocked. A few rejoiced, while others seemed to prefer Wilhelmina and rushed toward Corinne in anger. I stuck out my right leg, tripping them and sending them crashing into the table. One guard recovered easily and jumped at me, but I brought my fist down on his head. (I guess wooden hands *are* good for something.)

Before I could blink, the office was upended. Wilhelmina waved her hands, creating a tornado that sent me flying and smashing through a conference room door. Chairs splintered, television sets exploded. The floor shook as the fridge tipped over, trapping two men beneath its weight.

I ducked as a body soared over me. Two bodies. Corinne and Mia huddled together, their faces streaked with blood.

The wind died down, stopping with a hiss reminiscent of a snake rearing for an attack. A tall shadow fell across the doorway.

Seeing Wilhelmina up close was terrifying. She wore the same square glasses as my mother. The same powerhouse pantsuit. But there was a coldness in her eyes that froze me solid. The floor behind her was littered with splintered wood and unconscious bodies. I wondered if Leslie was among them.

"Oh, Corinne," Wilhelmina said. "What must it be like to meet the same fate as your parents? Do send them my greetings." She cackled as the door slammed shut.

Flames sprung up, engulfing the walls.

Corinne picked up a chair, throwing it at the door. I joined her, turning the table and using it as a battering ram. But it was no use.

"She sealed it with magic!" Corinne yelled as the flames roared. I blinked smoke from my eyes.

Wooden boy, plus fire . . . equaled *ouch*.

Mia clung to me, teary-eyed. "Leo, I'm sorry! I never should have left."

"Hey. No, stop that." If this was it, if this was the last chance I had to tell her, I didn't want to say it while she was sobbing. "Mia, I can't take back what I said on the ship, but I want you to know that I do care. You're my sister, and . . . I . . ." I shrugged. "I kind of love you."

Corinne drilled her elbow into my stomach. "Okay, I *really* love you. And that's not a lie."

A buzzing energy rushed through me. My body stretched, burning as it lost its rigidity. I had nails again, skin, those little baby hairs on my arms that didn't serve much purpose except to reiterate that I was human once more.

I broke my curse.

I looked to Corinne. Her face was alight with a smile.

We broke my curse.

But . . . the building was still burning. Of course.

The floorboards cracked. Corinne screamed. Mia pulled my arm. "Leo?"

"Yeah?"

She pointed at the door, where the flames swirled faster. The air shimmered like a mirage, but the feet stepping through the inferno were undoubtedly real.

Leslie waved his arms, extinguishing the fire in a puff of smoke.

He met my eyes, grinning. I could get used to the idea of my family members having doppelgängers, but I didn't think I'd ever come to terms with the fact that I had one too. And apparently he could do magic. Some guys had all the luck.

"Nice face," Leslie said.

"Um . . . thanks?" I replied, brushing ashes from my clothes.

Leslie offered his hand to Corinne. "Long time no see, my lady. You're a lot greener than I remember."

I expected Corinne to have some witty reply, but instead she threw herself into Leslie's arms. The tender way in which they eyed each other made me wonder what type of history they'd shared. It also made me majorly awkward.

When I cleared my throat, they snapped apart.

"I have something for you." Leslie pulled a jar from inside

his coat pocket, showing us a fat brown frog resting on a leaf. There were distinct markings around its eyes in the shape of glasses, and a purple stripe down its back—the same lavender shade as Wilhelmina's pantsuit.

"You didn't!" Corinne grabbed the jar, examining it closely.

"I did," Leslie said, wiggling his fingers. A few sparks shot across the room. "The guards and I"—he nodded outside the door, where several men were stirring from the wreckage—"have been looking to get Wilhelmina off the throne for ages." He smiled at Corinne. "Now that our rightful heir has returned, we could do just that. Welcome back, Princess."

Was I mistaken, or was Corinne making googly eyes at her guard?

"Thanks, Les."

"Wait, wait, wait!" I interrupted. "You call him *Les*, but you won't call me *Leo*?"

She shrugged.

I did not understand girls.

Mia tugged my arm, drawing me out of my confusion. "Leo, are we going home?" When I glanced at my watch, my eyes bugged out. Two minutes to midnight.

"No worries," said Leslie. With a flick of his fingers, a portal opened near the ceiling. I could see fuzzy images on the other side, twisting like I was watching them from the bottom of a swimming pool. *Home.*

I turned, meeting Corinne's eyes. I hadn't necessarily enjoyed my time in Pittsborough, but there were things about it I would miss. Like the magic. And the dancing. And her.

When I told her so, she smiled warmly. "Come back and

see us again, Leonard." She reached for Leslie's hand. Something inside me felt like it was imploding.

I tried not to show my disappointment. "I promise," I told them. "And that's the truth."

TRAVELING THROUGH THE PORTAL was similar to what I imagined flying through a thunderstorm would be like. The world spun like a carousel. Lights flashed. Thunder rumbled— or maybe that was the thoughts rolling in my head. When we landed on the other side, the library was still occupied. It was midnight in Pittsborough, but in Pitts*burgh* not a single minute had passed. Mia rushed off with the book of fairy tales, determined to convince the librarian to let her keep it, while I stared at my cell phone, contemplating asking my parents if they wanted me to pick up dinner so Mom wouldn't have to cook.

They would think I'd gone crazy, but I didn't mind. I wanted to do something for them, even if it was something small. Just to show them I cared.

"Oh, sorry!"

A body bumped into me, knocking my phone to the ground. I bent to retrieve it, but my hand collided with another.

When I looked up, I couldn't contain my smile.

Her skin wasn't green, but her fingernails were. Her hair was the same vibrant red, falling in tangled curls over her shoulders. She brushed a lock from her face and looked at me like she thought I was nuts. I realized my mouth was gaping.

She gave me a timid smile. "Can I help you?"

"I . . . uh . . . I . . ." Was I drooling? "Sorry. Uh . . . excuse me."

I started to book it down the aisle, but stopped when Corinne's voice rang through my head.

Live a little, she told me. *Feel something*.

"Actually," I said, turning around, "I just wanted to say your nails look cool. Green's awesome."

"Oh." She picked at the chipped polish. "Thanks. It's my favorite. I have this weird thing when it comes to frogs, and it sort of reminds me of . . ." She shrugged, embarrassed. "Sorry. You don't care about that."

"That's not true. Frogs are awesome. A little annoying and sometimes pushy, but they're great listeners. They give good advice too."

The girl stared at me curiously, probably thinking I was making fun of her. My stomach squirmed. So much for being truthful.

After the longest moment of my life, she held out her hand. "I'm Chloe."

"Leo."

We shook. Her fingers were soft and warm. "Leo," she mused. "That wouldn't happen to be short for Leonard, would it?"

Between Earth and Sky

r. s. kovach

EVERY GOOD FAIRY TALE ends with a wedding. Because this story was starting with one, I should have known it was going to be downhill from there.

Contrary to popular opinion, I was never against my mother remarrying. Everyone just assumed I was because I'm on great terms with my dad. My parents divorced before my first birthday, but by then they'd already been together for almost two decades. They just grew apart. Or at least that's what they keep saying whenever they mention the past.

After fifteen years, Dad's still single and I thought Mom would stay that way too. She doesn't need to get married. Not for money or anything. She's been the mayor of Otter Falls for forever, so we've got enough to have a nice house, a decent car, and the rest to get by on. Now that my brothers are all out of the house, we would have finally gotten the chance to take a vacation to someplace warm. But then she announced her engagement to Johnny Kwanlin, so now they're getting my dream trip for their honeymoon instead.

Despite being a Native American, his last name used to be Smith (seriously, John Smith!), but Johnny had it legally changed to the old Tutchone name for the sacred area that's not too far from here. I think it means "water running through the canyon," and it's supposed to emphasize his connection to our shared heritage. He's a bit overboard with all of that cultural stuff, but I'm still really happy for Mom because she's with him for love. And at least she won't be alone when I go off to college in a few years.

Johnny's from the Wolf clan, while Mom's from the Crow, so it actually worked out perfectly. Being part of a traditional First Nations wedding is also pretty cool. Sure, I've been to tons as a guest, but I've never had the opportunity to participate until now.

A tribal elder does most of the talking, but there are a lot of props involved—feathers, blankets, incense—so I help with those. Some of the guests are from the city and aren't familiar with our rituals, so the elder explains things as he goes along.

I'm trying to concentrate on keeping the eagle feather steady above Mom's head, which shouldn't be too hard because I'm taller than her, but my hand is already shaking. It's not from nerves—there isn't much for me to really be worried about—but from my arm muscles complaining about having to keep the unusual pose.

I cringe, hoping no one notices. It's only been a couple of

minutes, and I know there's a whole bunch more to go because the elder is still only at the part where he's explaining the matriarchal setup of our society. Thanks to this, only the woman can initiate divorce from a man and not the other way around. I always thought that this was one of the coolest things about being First Nations.

Of course, I can only claim membership on my mother's side. I don't even really look the part because even though I inherited my coloring from my mom, my features are totally from my dad. So basically, I look like a really tan Norwegian. This has never been a problem in Otter Falls because all of the kids are a mix of something. You really can't get away from it up here in the Yukon.

It's early summer, and we're outside the community lodge. The weathermen called for afternoon rains, but so far Mother Earth's cooperating. Although the temperature is probably just in the mid-sixties, it feels higher because of the unrelenting sun. We really should have done this by the Falls, the place on the Aishihik River our town was named after, where a cool breeze can always be felt coming off the water. It carries the fresh, sweet smell of the pines through the air, inviting you to take refuge in the shade of their ancient branches.

Ah, shade! What I wouldn't give to be able to enjoy some now. I don't know whose bright idea it was to hold the ceremony in this clearing, but I'm sure not letting them plan my wedding. My wedding? What am I thinking? I must be getting heatstroke.

Luckily, the rituals come to an end and it's time for the final blessing. As the mother of the bride, Grandma Dawson gets this honor. She waddles from her chair at the edge of the surrounding circle of onlookers. Because of her age, she's the only one who got a seat, and now I see she was smart enough to have an umbrella for shade. By now, Mom is crying, but she really does look beautiful. She's dressed in an elegant animal-skin dress that's decorated with beads and shells, some of which are also woven into the braids of her raven-black hair. The blessing involves more feathers and incense, and when Grandma hugs the newly joined couple, the crowd erupts in cheers.

It's just in time because now I really feel like I'm about to faint, so instead of joining in offering congratulations, I disappear into the lodge. The Great Hall has been decorated with flowers and balloons, and about a dozen circular tables have been set up for the reception, but I head straight for the bar.

"Beer me," I instruct with an authoritative voice.

"Mira Sighansen, I know you didn't just say what I think I heard," the guy working the counter replies.

I pout. "Come on, Billy, I'm parched! Hurry up before they start coming in."

He swings a dishrag over his shoulder and crosses his arms. "You know your mother wouldn't bat an eye at throwing you in jail for underage drinking."

It's times like these when I hate living in a town of a thousand. You have to really try not to know everyone, including Billy, who I think went to school with my brother Bryce. Or was it Roland? It really doesn't matter, and my thirst takes precedence.

"Fine," I relent. Give me a lemonade. Actually, make it two."

Just then my best friend, Poppy, comes running in. She's

breathless as she interrupts without as much as a hello. "Guess who was standing next to River during the ceremony?"

"I didn't get a chance to look." I tuck the bra strap back under her tank sleeve. "Who?"

"Lulu Smith." She grimaces while drawing out the name.

"Shut the front door!" Lulu is now my cousin through Johnny, and the fact that she was trying to cozy up to the guy my best friend has been eyeing for months irritates me as much as it does Poppy. But my dad has always been against swearing, so I've learned to improvise.

Poppy's wringing her hands and pacing. "How do they know each other?"

"Beats me. I sure as heck didn't introduce them. Here, I ordered you this." I hand over the lemonade to try to calm her.

"Well, I'm going to find out." She downs the drink. "Thanks. I'll be back," she mutters, and before I can stop her, she heads into the crowd that's started trickling in.

I've known this girl since preschool, but for years I thought she was the biggest snob. Everyone always wanted to be friends with her and for the same reason, I didn't. While I busted my butt on the basketball court, she was cheering on the sidelines, effortlessly charming the crowd. Even in school, she'd get anything she wanted without seemingly doing any work. She was voted freshman class president after a short inspirational speech about how everyone should just get along, and she came in first place in the regional spelling bee with the word "inconsequential." I mean, really. Who doesn't know how to spell "inconsequential"?

Well, it turns out I didn't, because I came in second. I was so jittery from being in the final two with Poppy that I totally fumbled. But that's how we actually became friends. She was so nice to me afterward, giving me a sincere apology for taking away a victory she felt I deserved, and we ended up talking. And it turns out she's a really awesome person.

Of course she did just totally ditch me, so I'm probably going to rethink that soon. Now I have no idea how I'm going to pass the time until dinner starts. This is supposed to be the cocktail hour, and everyone's just standing around nursing their glasses and picking at the finger food while making chitchat with people they'd otherwise never talk to.

To avoid anyone coming up to me, I start wandering between the tables. Then inspiration hits me.

It took Mom weeks to come up with the seating plan for dinner, and we've been arguing about it ever since. Not only did she split up all of my siblings, but she also didn't seat me next to any of my friends. Her logic was that we should all be spread out among the other guests to represent the family at each table, but screw that. I'm going to do a little rearranging and make sure I have a good time.

I pick up a card with Poppy's name written in fancy script on it when my youngest brother, Cody, taps me on the shoulder. "Whatcha up to, sis?"

"Ssh. Help me find your brothers' settings," I whisper. "I'm going to move all of us to a table in the back."

"Hm. I didn't think you had it in you," he teases.

I swat him on the shoulder. "Shut up and grab that one! I think it's Sam's."

He laughs and picks up the card. We move from one table

to the next, working quickly to avoid suspicion. We're only missing Bryce's name when I come across an unexpected sign.

"Crapberries! I totally forgot about Dad." I realize, seeing his name card on this table.

"Didn't you hear? His rig broke down outside of Juneau yesterday, and he didn't make it back in time for the wedding."

"That sucks." I was looking forward to seeing him. He's been gone for two weeks now, and as a long-haul trucker, he'd probably have just a few days again before he's back on the road. Well, at least it's one less name to shift to our table.

"Here, put these in the empty spots, will you?" I ask my brother, but he has other ideas.

He laughs. "Do I look like event management to you? Besides, I already lost deniability with Mom if she ever asks who moved us, so you go finish your own dirty work. I think I just saw Lane with a chick I don't recognize. Excuse me."

Great. People are starting to look for their places, and I still have eight cards in my hand. I scuttle back around the hall, dropping random cards wherever I see an empty place. I finish just as the bride and groom are announced.

Slipping into my seat, I pretend nothing is amiss, but I do feel a bit guilty thinking that Mom has likely noticed the changes. Luckily, I have my brothers to distract me.

As usual, eating with them is like watching human vacuums. As soon as the first course is served, they begin literally sucking down the food. It's both gross and fascinating at the same time. Somehow they also manage to keep the conversation going. One of them is always speaking, whether retelling a story from years ago I've heard a dozen times or filling us in on what happened just last week.

"Her family's vacationing in Kluane, and they stopped at the Junction for gas. We got to talking and when I mentioned the wedding, I guess she sort of invited herself," Lane says, explaining the story of how he met his date.

"What was her name again?" I ask, sneaking a glance at the cute blonde absentmindedly twirling her spoon between her fingers two tables away.

He takes a mouthful of the bison steak. "Laura."

"I thought you just said it was Sarah," Clay corrects him.

"Eh. Close enough." He shrugs amid a chorus of laughter.

If there were such a thing as Otter Falls' most eligible bachelor, my brothers would win it in a six-way tie. In any other place, they would have been all snatched up by now. Clayton's almost thirty, while Cody and Lane just turned eighteen. Roland, Bryce, and Sam fall pretty much evenly in between. They all work on the local oil field; the twins are spending the summer as greenhorns before starting college in Anchorage. None of them want to permanently leave Otter Falls, which is exactly the opposite of what girls seem to be doing. Girls don't look back once they've made it out of here, leaving great guys single. At least until an unsuspecting tourist drives through town.

We get through dinner and the toasts with much of the same when Poppy—who'd been conspicuously absent since the first dance—grabs me from behind and grumbles in my ear. "River's taking Lulu up to the Falls, and there's no way I'm letting them go alone."

⟨⟨⟨❖⟩⟩⟩

THE FOUR OF US pile into River's beat-up Bronco and head out to the little basin just outside of town. There's a bunch of fishing stuff on the backseat between me and Poppy, but we still get a first-rate view of my new cousin's lame attempt to get the boy to notice her.

Although many people in this part of the country can claim some sort of Scandinavian ancestry, this guy seems to have gotten every recessive gene his parents had to offer. His platinum-blond hair and blue eyes make him a total anomaly, and he could get any girl he wants. River is cool, though, and he's never made a big deal out of it, which makes Lulu even more eager.

She's been yapping for the last five minutes about some new video game she knows he likes, even though he's only contributed a few "uh-huh"s and a lackluster "I guess."

I can't take it anymore, so I attempt a distraction to shut her up. "Ooh, I love this song! Can you guys turn up the radio?"

The next time Lulu has a chance to speak is when we arrive at Otter Falls. "This place is pretty cool. Do ya'll do any swimming up here?" She slams the door in my face, forcing me to get out on the other side.

"Naw, it's too rocky and shallow for that," River answers, unexpectedly offering his hand to me when I climb out from behind the driver's seat.

The warning comes too late because she's already kicked off her sparkly flats and is sticking her foot into the water. "It's damn cold too!" Lulu exclaims, turning around. Her eyes widen as she sees us touching, and I pull my hand away.

Unfazed, River grins. "Perfect for troutin'."

"So, you're a fisherman?" Lulu puts her shoes back on and idles up to him. Behind me, I can almost hear Poppy seething with rage, and I can't blame her. This girl is just too much.

"Yeah, I fish and hunt." He sticks his hands in his pockets and proudly pulls himself up to his full height, which must be six feet by now. "I'm pretty sure I've killed almost every kind of animal up around these parts."

"You got a bear too?" She pokes him in the chest. "How about a lynx?"

He blushes, and it's the cutest thing ever. "Well, that's why I said *almost* every kind."

Poppy butts in to counter her competition. "Don't forget, you said you'd teach me how to shoot the new rifle Daddy got me."

"Oh yeah? What do you got?" Lulu gets all sassy, doing this weird neck-twist thing and making her raven-black hair fly around her shoulders.

Poppy purses her lips, and I have to hold in a giggle at her earnestness. "A Winchester."

Lulu laughs. "I've been shooting those since I was ten."

My friend steps closer and puts her hands on her hips. "Well, I've been cheerleading since I was nine, and I won the regional spelling bee twice!"

I swear it's like watching two young caribou bucks fighting over a doe, just with the genders reversed. I think River has also had enough, because instead of joining in or even stopping their squabble, he ignores them and walks over to me.

That's when I notice there's something new about him. "I like the bling." I point at the silver ring on his bottom lip.

"Oh, thanks." He touches it like he'd forgotten it was even there. "I got it last week. Hurt like a bitch, though."

Before I can respond, Poppy runs over. "I could make it better."

I can't believe she just said that! How desperate can that girl act?

Lucky for her, River is either too daft to get her insinuation or he doesn't care. Actually, I think it's both, because he reaches into the bag he's been holding, pulls out a couple of bottles, and tosses me one.

"Where did you get these?" I recognize the label.

He rubs his thumb and index finger together. "I slipped Billy a twenty."

"That son of a donkey's uncle! He didn't care about me being underage, just about a payday!" I furiously unscrew the cap and take a long swig. "Blech. Did he have these sitting in the sun all day?"

"I don't mind if it's warm." Lulu grabs the bottle from me.

River isn't as cavalier, and apparently takes the temperature of his beverages seriously. After heading to the water with the remaining three beers, he sticks them between a cluster of rocks near the bottom of the waterfall.

"Nature's refrigerator," he says proudly, as if he's the first one to use the trick.

I roll my eyes and begin to turn away when a large white bird catches my attention. It's a great egret, pretty common for these parts. She's circling overhead, probably looking for a place to roost until morning. Night comes pretty late around here in the summer. It's past eleven now, and the sun is just now begin-ning to set. We'll have a few hours of darkness and then it'll be daylight again soon. The winter's just the opposite, which is why I hate it so much. Well, that and the bitter cold.

The bird finally lands at the top of the tallest waterfall, perching on a dead branch sticking up from the water. With her sleek black beak and yellow feet, she's incredibly beautiful. No wonder our people consider her a symbol of grace and patience. They're good luck too and if we were about to go on a hunt, this would be a really good sign.

I suddenly realize how quiet it is. No arguing or boasting. Not even the wind is making any noise. We're all so focused on the animal, we've forgotten about everything else.

"Man, that's a clean shot." Lulu breaks the silence from right next to me. "I wish I had my rifle here."

I don't know what comes over me, but I sure as heck don't give it a second thought.

Putting my hands against the girl's shoulders, I shove her backward into the water.

✦

THE NEXT MORNING, Mom sends me out to the nearest oil field. It's not my punishment for last night; that grounding starts as soon as I get home. No, I would've had to make this trip regardless.

Although it's Sunday, the rigs still run. They actually never stop unless they're broken, and that's why crews operate around the clock. Every idle hour on the pipeline is lost money for the community, and it's up to guys like my brothers to make sure the black gold never stops flowing.

They all took today's shift so they could have yesterday off for the wedding. So it's my job to bring them leftovers for lunch.

I'm not old enough to have a license, but out in the bush, I can get away with driving my quad bike. It's all back roads anyway, with only the occasional hiker or moose sharing the road. Mom's most worried about me running into a grizzly, but I've only seen one during the year since I've started coming out here by myself.

After a ten-minute ride, I'm almost at the path that leads straight to rig forty-nine when a deafening boom makes the whole ground shake. Stopping the bike in the middle of the road, I look at the previously cloudless sky just as it's lit up by a huge, orange fireball. For a few seconds, I can't move and stand dumbfounded as ash begins to fall around me. In an instant, day has been transformed to night with thick, black smoke filling the air.

A fit of coughing brings me back to the present. "No, no, no, no," I mumble, getting my quad moving again. This can't be happening. There's no way that explosion came from the rig. It has to be something else. Because if it was . . .

I shake my head, trying to get the increasingly bad thoughts out of my brain. There has to be a simple explanation, and everything is going to turn out fine.

There's only a few hundred feet to go, but the closer I get to the chain-link fence surrounding the compound, the more scared I become. My hands tremble on the grips as I ride through the open gate, the smoke continuing to burn my throat and sting my eyes. I stop in front of one of the administrative trailers and cut the engine, struck by how deserted everything is. It's then in the otherwise-eerie silence I hear the unmistakable sound of a rig on fire.

The steady whoosh of the oil bursting uncontrollably through a damaged pipe that's been set aflame is a sound everyone around here knows, and never wants to hear. It's the sign something has gone terribly wrong and, more often than not, is about to get even worse.

I'm quivering like a gosh-darned leaf now, and while my mind says I have to keep going, my legs are rooted to the ground. It's only a few steps around the trailer and another hundred feet back to the rig, but this is as far as I've ever been allowed. As if on cue, Monk Lewis bursts out of the building, yelling into a satellite phone as he runs past me. He's Poppy's uncle, and I don't even know if Monk's his given name or if it's just something people have always called him. It would be pretty ironic if his mother named him that, since he's already on his fourth wife, but right now, that's neither here nor there. I also can't tell who's on the other end of the conversation, but he's cursing more than anything else. Still, I'm happy to see a familiar face because it means my brothers must also be somewhere nearby, so I follow the pudgy little man in the hard hat.

"Bryce! Clay! Sam!" I shout, but as soon as I step out from behind the trailer, the heat hits me. It's like opening the oven door when you're baking cookies, but multiplied by a thousand. The chimney of black smoke that's probably visible now for miles stretches above me like a huge funnel, but the orange and red flames at its base make it even more terrifying. There are two men using a hose attached to a tanker truck, dousing the surrounding area with water, and the mist combines with the oil to fall from the sky like rain. My hair's already full of burnt pieces of goodness-knows-what, but the closer I get, the heavier the spray of sticky substance is on my skin.

"Lane! Roland! Cody!" I continue my frantic calls, still not seeing my brothers among the preciously few faces. My shoes slip on the slick surface, and I land on my butt in the mud. Wiping my eyes with the backs of my hands, I twist my neck around, but apart from the three men I've already seen, the field is empty.

"Clay! Roland! Bryce!" I scream at the top of my lungs, starting to fear the worst. A bitter taste coats my tongue, but I push myself up and run to the other side of the field.

"Sam! Cody! Lane!" I shout above the fire as it slowly melts and mangles the rig in front of me.

In the distance, I see flashing red lights approach before two hands wrap around my upper arms, pulling me away from the flames. I'm still screaming, but all I can hear is the deafening whoosh. Blinking to clear my eyes of the gunk, I catch a glimpse of something I know can't be real.

In the fire, a shape emerges. It's only a dark silhouette, but against the bright yellow, I swear it has arms and legs. When it begins to float upward, I become less certain. Then suddenly hands thrust to the side and as the wide arms flap up and down, the shadow flies into the cloud of smoke. I realize I'm screaming in terror until another similar shape follows the first. I've now lost the ability to control my breathing, and I gasp while watching a third, fourth, fifth, and finally sixth dark form impossibly fly through the flames.

My mind is spinning and my body is light, making me feel like I'm between earth and sky. Knowing there's only one way to stop my fall, I black out before impact.

When I open my eyes again, I'm lying in the back of an open ambulance with a clear view of the burning rig. Mom and Johnny are standing on the ground past my feet; she's on her cell, and he's arguing with Monk about the blowout. It must have taken them at least ten minutes to get here, so I've been out for a while. I try to sit up, but the tube attached to the oxygen mask covering my nose and mouth pulls me back.

"Whoa, there. Not so fast, kid." The EMT who's been right behind me this entire time puts his hand on my shoulder.

When he slides into view, I recognize him as my fifth-grade teacher's oldest son, Owen Bousquet. I blush, remembering what a huge crush I used to have on the guy. I haven't seen much of him since he graduated high school, but I guess he's one of the few not working in the oil biz who stuck around. Lucky for me right now too, since Otter Falls has its own ambulance and medical center thanks to this rig. There's some code or safety regulation making it necessary. Mom knows about it better than I do since she had to lobby for it.

Noticing me move, my mom ends her call and tries to climb in beside me, but Owen stops her. "Just a sec, Mayor. Let me see what we're dealing with first."

She frowns and nods in agreement, but all I want to do is give her a big hug. I open my mouth and try to tell her it's okay, but apart from a weird sound you'd expect if you stepped on a frog midcroak, nothing comes out.

"I was afraid of that." Owen takes off my oxygen mask before finding one of those metal Popsicle-stick things in a drawer. "Open wide."

My mouth tastes like I've licked a lump of coal, and it feels just as dry. When I automatically try to say "aah" the way doctors always expect you to, a sharp pain stabs my throat. I reach to my neck, but Owen's already pushing my tongue out of the way to get a better look inside my windpipe. When he finally sits back, I can tell by the serious look on his face that it's not good news.

"You should count your lucky stars, Mira," he begins, motioning to my mom—now standing alone at the open doors—so she can come over. "I don't know what you were doing so close to that fire, but apart from a singed larynx, I'd say you came out on top today."

"Should we get her to Regional Medical?" Mom is already in planning mode as she arrives at my side.

"Resting will do her much better than a four-hour car ride, and I'd rather not call an airlift in case it's needed for the others," Owen answers above my head. "I can give you some antiseptic spray that'll help with the throat pain, and if her voice isn't back in a few days—"

Hold up. What others? I raise my hand to get his attention, cutting him off midsentence before remembering I can't talk.

Turning toward Mom, I mouth the question, "*Others?*"

She pulls her lips into a thin line and swallows before taking my hand into both of hers. I know this move, and my heartbeat accelerates. This is what she did when she told me her and Dad were getting a divorce and when my dog Bucky had to be put down.

"Your brothers, Mira," she whispers. "Monk says they were all at the rig, but there's no sign of them."

That's a good thing, right? I want to ask. If there are no bodies, then there's a chance they're alive. Maybe Monk is wrong.

He naps on duty more than he's awake, and that's not the only reason Johnny got promoted to foreman before the more experienced roughneck.

Mom's teary eyes show she doesn't share in my optimism. I want to comfort her, but I suddenly remember the dark shapes I saw among the flames and begin bawling. In the end, it's Mom who has to calm me down. She explains we'll know more once the well is capped, and for now she's just thankful that I'm okay.

Getting the all-clear from Owen, I'm allowed to go home, where Poppy is already waiting.

I don't think I've ever been so happy to see that crazy girl.

Poppy and Mom help me inside—too much smoke and not enough oxygen can apparently make you really weak and tired for a while—and I camp out on the living room couch. My friend plops into the adjacent armchair before Mom leaves to take care of mayoral stuff. With the steady droll of some reality TV show peppered with Poppy's occasional commentary in the background, I quickly fall asleep.

My brain, though, refuses to rest and instead decides that I really need to relive every terrible moment from earlier. I awake with a start, my clothes sticking to me from sweat. Poppy is curled up in the chair and out like a light, so I tiptoe around her and head to the bathroom.

I almost faint when I see my reflection in the mirror. Why hasn't anyone mentioned I look like a rabid raccoon that's been dragged three miles behind a semi? After washing the soot off my face, I do the best I can with my hair by braiding it into a long rope. I really need a shower too, but I guess that can wait. Standing in the tiny bathroom, I'm suddenly feeling very locked in, so I go back through the living room and slip quietly out the front door.

Our porch faces the main road that cuts through Otter Falls, and sitting on the top step would let me get a clear view of the traffic, if there was any. We're so out of the way that the only cars that pass by are those of our nearest neighbors—a quarter of a mile in each direction—going between work and home, or an occasional state trooper making his rounds. I briefly close my eyes to let the breeze wash over me when a familiar clunking sound catches my ear. I look up again just in time to see River in his old beater rounding the nearest bend before pulling to a stop right in front of me.

If it weren't his car, I would have a hard time recognizing the boy because his usual smile is gone. He looks just as solemn as I feel. He slams the car door behind him and runs up, taking a seat right next to me.

"I heard what happened," he begins, assuming I was wondering why he showed up unannounced. "Are you okay?"

I shrug and point to my throat to explain why I can't talk, but he must have known about that too.

"Yeah, that's a bummer." He cracks a smile before unexpectedly putting an arm around me. "I'm sorry about your brothers."

I shake off his hold and widen my eyes. *What about them?* I mime, and his face turns red. "Oh no. They haven't found them yet or anything, I just meant . . . well, I hope they'll be okay too." He looks away, and while I still don't want to admit the possibility, I know eventually we'll find out either way. River is just trying to make me feel better, and I put my hand on his knee to show him I understand.

He turns back to me and gives me a hug, which apparently is my Kryptonite. As soon as the boy holds me close, I completely fall apart and begin crying again. Noticing my blubbering, he pulls away, but instead of hightailing it home like I expect, he cups my face with one hand and wipes a tear from my cheek with his thumb. I smile, thankful to have such a great friend, when he leans in and actually kisses me!

And holy guacamole, it's nice. His lips are warm and his skin smells like peppermint, and I don't even mind the silver ring tickling my mouth. Reaching up for his shirt, I scoot closer before a slamming door interrupts the moment.

We look up as Poppy storms out of my house from behind, and I don't have to feel like a fox caught in the henhouse to know she saw everything. I've betrayed her, and it makes me want to throw up. To make amends, I try to grab her arm, but she shakes it off and rushes past me. As she jumps into River's truck, I remember he's still here too. He gives me an apologetic shrug, and I suppose he has no choice but to give her a ride home, but seeing them drive away together hurts almost as much as losing my best friend's trust.

I want to scream in frustration, but I don't even have that luxury right now. I also can't will myself to go back in the house, not when Mom's still away and my brothers are still unaccounted for. My quad bike isn't in its usual spot, which means it must still be at rig forty-nine. At this point, I don't even care where I go or how I get there, so I just start walking. The rhythmic pounding of my sneakers against the soft grass and wildflowers in the meadow behind our house is oddly relaxing, and I let it slowly calm my nerves. By the time I cross a patch of pines and stop at the edge of a wide stream, my breathing is ragged, but my head is clear.

It doesn't take me long to realize where I am. After heading fifty yards up along the water's bank, I'm standing right at the spot where I gave Lulu an unexpected bath last night. The memory makes me smile, and I begin to relax. Sitting on one of the flat rocks, I pull my legs up and rest my head in my hands.

Has it been only a day since the wedding? What I wouldn't do to turn back time and have all the terrible things that have happened since then go away.

I sigh, knowing the impossibility of my wish. As if Mother Earth knew I needed a distraction right about now, a lone egret appears on the horizon. I wonder if she's the same bird we saw last night when another also comes into view. They're flying straight for the Falls, so I sit as still as I can to avoid scaring them away. I actually bite my lip when I realize there are even more than I first thought, eventually counting six large egrets.

Unlike the bird from yesterday, these animals could hardly be called majestic. Their feathers are more gray than white, covered in soot no doubt from the still-burning rig fire. The smallest one also appears to have a broken wing, and I'm just starting to back away to go get it some help *when I finally go crazy*.

It sounds harsh, but there's no other way to explain it. Plain and simple, I—Mira Sighansen—have just lost my sanity. Why? Because the six long-necked, feathered birds that had landed in the hip-deep stream twenty feet from me just turned into humans. And what's even crazier? They're not just any humans— they're my six missing brothers.

"Earth to Mira." The familiar, masculine voice comes to

me from a distance, as if the speaker is at the other end of a long tunnel.

"Yo, sis," another chimes in. The sound is much closer and there's less of an echo, making me blink in rapid succession to search for its source. When my eyes focus on the half dozen naked young men standing in the nearby basin, I know I'm still in my previous delusion.

"You're not real," I state matter-of-factly, as if it's even worth arguing with ghosts. The realization that actual sounds escape my lips doesn't strike me for another beat, when I reach to my mouth and gasp. "Oh, my dog. I can talk!"

Three body lengths away, Sam nudges Bryce. "We just turned from fricking birds right in front of her, and all she cares about is her yapper."

They all laugh, but I put my hands on my hips and pout. "Real funny, but I'd care more if you weren't a hallucination."

"Oh yeah?" Roland raises an inquisitive brow. "Could I do this if I wasn't real?" Quickly drawing his hand across the surface of the water, he splashes me.

The cold droplets land on my shirt, and the light blue fabric turns darker underneath. "Um, yeah, because I'm imagining this too."

I take a small step backward to avoid any repeats, just in case.

"Good grief, kid." Lane shakes his head, scattering water from his thick, black hair onto his shoulders. "We don't have time for this."

"Why not? You got a hot date with Laura?" I can't resist teasing, especially since he called me kid. It's bad enough my oldest brothers say it. I don't need it from one who's just two years my senior. "Or was it Sarah?"

"Listen, Mira." Clay takes over. "We're very much real, and we need your help."

I wish I could believe him, but I'm still not convinced. "All right, but how is this possible?"

A muscle twitches in his jaw and I can tell he's losing patience, but he takes a deep breath before answering. "Remember Grandma Dawson's stories? All the stuff about our tribal legends?"

I nod, recalling tales of the benevolent but trickster raven or the man-eating owl she would use to lull me to sleep when I was younger. How I never had nightmares from that, I'll never know.

"You never questioned any of those." Clay shrugs. "Why is this different?"

Because I'm not ten anymore, I think, but bite my lip to stop myself from making him any angrier. I mean if this is real, then he's already had a pretty crappy day without my added sass. Besides, even if this is crazy, it's better than their being outright *gone* forever. "Fine," I say.

"Good. Now listen carefully because we really haven't got much time." He looks over his shoulder as Cody groans; my youngest brother is cradling his limp, left arm against his body.

"You're hurt." My maternal instincts kick in and I lunge off the rock, but Sam puts up his hand to stop me.

"Whoa there, cupcake. Family or not, you need to respect some boundaries here." He points to the shallow water barely hiding them from the waist down.

"Oh." I back up as my face flushes. "Sorry. You were saying?"

"That rig shouldn't be there," Clay continues. "It can't be rebuilt, and you need to stop it."

I don't know what I was expecting him to say, but this sure as heck wasn't it. "Wh-what?" I stutter.

Moving forward, Bryce takes over. "You need to do everything you can to make sure that forty-nine isn't fixed and put back into operation."

"And how am I supposed to do that?" I look from one brother to the next, as if their solemn expressions could give me the answer I need.

"You're a smart girl." Lane smirks. "You'll figure it out."

"But why?" I ball my fists to keep my hands from shaking. "Let's say I can, which I'm pretty sure won't happen since it's like the craziest idea ever. But fine. The rig stays broken. What will that solve?"

"Just do it, Mira. It's the only way we can come back," Clay says, then turns, and the others follow suit. The way they walk off is so eerie, so final.

"Wait!" I yell to keep them from leaving. "I don't understand."

My eldest brother looks over his shoulder. "You don't have to. Just do it."

Well, thanks. That really helps. I slump back onto the rock and hang my head. Rubbing my face with my hands, I raise my gaze just as six egrets take flight, flapping their wings to climb toward the clouds and disappear from view.

⁓⊱✦⊰⁓

MY HOUSE IS STILL EMPTY by the time I get home, so I guess no one even noticed I was gone. I don't see Mom and Johnny until the next morning, when I roll out of bed and head to the breakfast table. I haven't eaten anything for almost a whole day, but I'm not hungry. As I push the increasingly soggy cereal around in my bowl, I lean my head on one hand and halfheartedly listen to the conversation around me.

My new stepdad is concerned about his job, which is totally irritating, but not at all surprising. Thankfully the fire's out and the rig is capped, but that also means the replacement parts are already on their way and can be installed starting as early as tomorrow. It'll take another few days for things to be tested and inspected, but the oil well should be back up to production levels within a week. Awesome.

Mom, on the other hand, is already planning my brothers' memorial service. She's freaking out because there are no bodies to wash, dress, or even bury, but for some reason, that still won't stop tonight's ceremonial feast we'll have in their honor. She's a stickler for tradition, I suppose. No matter how devastated she is right now, her priority is to make sure her boys' souls can be properly reborn.

If she only knew how close to the truth our tribe's myths really could be . . .

I want to save Mom from the sadness, tell her about last night at the Falls and the possibility my brothers can still be saved so she won't have to unnecessarily worry. But is it fair to give her hope when I could be wrong? I saw everything with my own eyes and had a hard time believing it until I considered all the possibilities. Even then, I was pretty much fifty-fifty about being bat-crap insane, but Cody's broken arm was the tipping point. I figured if it were all in my imagination, they would have all been healthy, right? Then again, my voice is still gone, which could be another sign that I *did* imagine everything. Ugh. Overthinking this is not helping.

Mom should be on her honeymoon, and I feel so bad for her, but all I can do is give her a quick hug before I disappear back into my room. I don't even hope for any personal visits from Poppy or River today, so I play Xbox until I hear the guests start to arrive. After pulling on some dark leggings and a loose, equally monochrome top, I open my bedroom door only to quickly shut it.

Butter my bottom and call me toast! Why's Lulu Smith standing at the end of my hallway?

I lean against the closed door and grit my teeth, figuring she's here more for running into a certain blond hottie than to pay her respects to my family. I really haven't felt like socializing with anyone today, and pretending to ignore her is definitely more than I can manage right now. Without giving it a second thought, I hurry across my room and push up the windowpane. Slipping over the ledge, I lower myself to the ground just a few feet below and count my lucky stars our house isn't two stories.

Someone has brought back my quad bike, and I consider going to the Falls with the hopes of seeing my brothers again when an even better idea hits me. Although its importance didn't click this morning, now I remember Johnny mentioning that the drill site would be basically shut down until tomorrow. He was saying something about letting all the guys have the time off since there's nothing to do after the initial cleanup. Now, as I look around the front of our house, I see many familiar trucks and realize that the usual crew who'd be at the rig right about now is set to assemble in my living room. The well is virtually unprotected.

Taking off before I have the chance to talk myself out of it, I ride to the field and quickly confirm my hunch. I'm in luck; the gates are locked and the parking lot is empty. This will give me the perfect chance to check out the premises and see if there's any way I can carry out Clayton's directives. Wait, is this crazier than even the whole swan-brothers thing? I mean, I have many skills, but industrial sabotage isn't one of them.

But they're my brothers. So after I sneak through a hole in the chain-link fence, I head straight past the trailers to the site of yesterday's explosion. My flats squish in the oily mud, making me totter along like a drunken goose. When I arrive, I see that the broken, metal frame of the rig is gone and only an empty platform remains. It's been scrubbed clean, and apart from a few dents, it looks almost good as new.

I grit my teeth as fury overtakes me. Is that it? Do they think they can just wipe away the disaster as if it were but a layer of soot? Pretend it didn't even happen? Consider my brothers dead and gone as if they were just collateral damage?

Once the new parts come in tomorrow, there will be even less evidence of the catastrophe and things will be business as usual. I can't let that happen.

Scanning the area, I notice a stray piece of metal about the size of a baseball bat half-hidden in a patch of weeds. I pick it up and march toward the rig, raise the apparatus above my head, and swing. It strikes the platform with a loud clank and bounces backward, nearly toppling me in the process. Before the next attempt, I spread my legs and take up a more stable pose. With a deep breath, I hit the rig even harder. I can tell it's not doing any damage, but at least it's making me feel better, so I continue swinging.

"Hey, kid! What the hell do ya think you're doing?" An irritated voice interrupts the metallic echoes, as a man in a blue security guard's uniform runs toward me.

Shiznits. I should have known the place wasn't completely empty.

Dropping my weapon, I start to back away but slip. This mud is really getting on my nerves, but being caught vandalizing private property takes priority, so I attempt to stand before the guy gets a good look at me.

"Mira Sighansen, is that you?" The figure squints, lowering what's either pepper spray or a TV remote control in his hand.

Dang it. I really need to move to a city with more people.

Now that anonymity is out of the question, I should probably stay on my butt and prepare to accept my fate, but instead my brain tells me to attempt running for the fence. As I look over my shoulder to scope out the path, though, approaching red-and-blue lights catch my eye.

I'm actually impressed this bumbling security guard called the cops on me until the car stops and Mom jumps out from the passenger side. My heart sinks, and I barely catch any of her half-scolding, half-relieved monologue about my disappearing and then being found like this.

When she holds out her hand to me, I realize she's waiting for some sort of answer or at the very least for me to go with her.

Still butt-deep in the muck, I retreat like a crab, and the lines on her face deepen. "Sweetheart, I know this is hard on you. It's hard for all of us. But you can't lash out like this. I wish it would help, but I promise you, it won't."

I shake my head, remembering what my brothers told me at the Falls last night. I wish I could tell Mom, but she wouldn't believe me even if I had my voice back, so I do the only thing I can. Scrambling to my feet, I run, but I slip again. My hands break my fall, but there's something under the squishy soil that digs deep into my left palm. I grunt and look at the injury as blood begins to trickle from a gash. Mom runs to me and although her attention focuses on the wound, I am more interested in its source. Pulling the object out from the mud, I can barely believe my eyes.

The triangular shape and chipped texture is unmistakable. It's an arrowhead.

And it just might be the thing I need.

I thrust the artifact into Mom's hand, which momentarily distracts her, allowing me to attack the surrounding vegetation. The nettles tear into my already injured flesh, but I can't give up now. There has to be more and even though I probably look crazy, I have nothing to lose.

When a semicircular piece of hard, red clay emerges from the weeds, Mom kneels beside me and begins to sob. The trooper still hasn't caught on and urges us to go back with him to the station to get things straightened out when dark spots appear in the sky. I don't even have to wait for them to get closer to know what to do.

Jumping up, I slip back out through the fence and follow the egrets. They're flying parallel to the rig site, and it's possible they're following the Aishihik River. When I get closer, the tree line blocks them from view, but I push on. My side hurts and I'm out of breath when I reach the embankment, yet they're still nowhere. Skipping along the rocks, I frantically search the tree-tops around me when I see something in the water itself.

At the edge of the Falls, lying scattered in the shallow stream, are six bodies. They're bruised, bloodied, and dirty, but they're all moving just enough to show they're alive.

IN THE COMING DAYS, weeks, and even months, tales form about my brothers' miraculous survival. I have to admit, some of the speculation is quite logical. The blast from the rig propelled them into the air before depositing them in the river, before the current carried their limp, naked bodies downstream to hide them from the search party. It's only Cody's broken arm—identical to the injury I'd witnessed the prior day—that convinces me there's something greater at play.

My suspicions are confirmed when a professor comes up from Whitehorse and validates my discovery of tribal relics. And because sacred land can't be used for drilling, the rig can't be re-built. Not on its current site, anyway, which was all Clay insisted.

I managed to keep my word to him, even if it was completely by accident. I guess I'm good at industrial sabotage, after all.

Things slowly begin to return to normal. As Owen predicted, my voice comes back in a few days. My family is also back together. River even asked me out on a proper date, and Poppy decided a boy isn't worth fighting over, so I have my best friend back too.

Maybe fairy tales can still have happy endings, even if they do start with the wedding.

The Friend-Zone Promposal

tammy oja

CHAPTER ONE

The Week Before Prom

MALLORY PUTS HER HAIR UP in her go-to messy bun, realizing it's the only way she can salvage being on time. Carefully she moves some of her long bangs and arranges them to cover her left eye and cheek just so. School is about to start and Trevor will be picking her up any minute. She banishes the idea of a shower and instead spritzes herself with some body spray and applies a quick layer of makeup skillfully enough that it looks like she isn't wearing any.

It's not like people are going to notice me anyway, she thinks.

As she slides on her black skinny jeans, black hoodie, and her retro Chuck Taylors to finish off her shadow-blending motif, the familiar hum of Trevor's Chevy, Black Beauty, echoes through the windows as it pulls into the driveway. Grabbing her ID and tucking it beneath her hoodie, she stops for a quick glance in the mirror to make sure her reflection doesn't look as disgusting as she feels inside.

"Mirror, mirror on the wall . . . who isn't excited for today at all? Whoops, wrong fairy tale. I am so not that princess. More like the invisible princess that wasn't."

Well, except for the *flaw*. That's never invisible.

Two friendly beeps send Mallory flying out the door, and she jumps into Black Beauty like an Olympic pole vaulter. As she pulls her seat belt across her chest, she is assaulted by the sour stench of decay.

"Trevor!! We agreed. No hockey equipment in the car. Oh, man!! How can you put that on your body? Thank goodness I skipped breakfast!"

Trevor hands over a cup of hot coffee. Cinnamon-scented steam wafts from the lid's tiny hole, and Mallory quickly lifts the cup to her nose, thankful for the reprieve.

"Thank you. You're forgiven. Barely."

He turns and flashes her his best million-dollar smile. The same one that Mallory is sure would melt the resolve of any girl he used it on. Mallory has seen it a thousand times since they were kids, although he hasn't used it on her since last year when he needed help passing algebra.

"Slept in late? Drink the coffee. I need you sharp today. I need a big favor from you, my friend." Mallory plasters on a smile, wondering what diabolical plan will get her grounded this time. Trevor has always had a knack for getting her into sticky situations, and she's had a knack for always letting him.

"What is it this time? Hack into the Pentagon database and make yourself a general?"

Trevor gives her a mercy chuckle and quickly turns it into a disappointed frown. "I'm serious. I'm desperate. And you happen to be my best friend, and only hope."

Mallory straightens her shoulders and puts on her game face. If he's pulling the best-friend card, she's going to have to perk up and pay attention.

"I want to make a promposal to the new girl, Jessica. Like a really good one. I know I wasn't planning on going, and it's only a week away, but this new girl has only been here a few months, so I've got a shot. Proposals are all the rage, Goth girl! And the best ones are planned by girls. And you're sort of a girl, so I was hoping . . ."

Mallory chokes on her coffee, making her inhale the thick, rancid odor of jock sweat and dead skin. "*Sort of a girl*? We've been over this a thousand times! I *am* a girl. Just because you've been beaten by me at like, everything, doesn't make me less of a girl!"

She plays off the insult with mock anger while she pulls a little more hair from her bun to cover her face. Hiding her birthmark is an impulse she clings to whenever any insecurities hit her.

Trevor raises his hands off the steering wheel in an "I surrender" pose and pouts. "I'm sorry, I only meant you're more of a friend than a girl—like, ugh! That's not what I wanted to say either. Just say you'll help me. *Please?* You know I'm clueless about romance and promposals and girl things."

Mallory takes another giant gulp of her coffee as an excuse for the scrunching face she knows she's making. Her hand automatically clenches into a fist and an inner yearning to smack him upside the head is slowly convincing her to give in. Still, as she's weighing her options, the buried fist remains in place. The fear of his crashing the car and killing them both wins out, for now.

He's a guy. And clueless. And it's just as much my fault for being a chicken.

Yeah, he is clueless. She has stared at, dreamed of, and drooled over him for a year now. And he still thinks she holds his feet during sit-ups because of a seventh-grade bet gone bad.

Clueless is an understatement.

But helping him take another girl to prom? That's something she doesn't think she can do. Even the thought of it makes her chest hurt.

Where are those evil flying monkeys when I need them? she thinks.

"Trev, I've always got your back. But you know, you could go classic and just ask her. It's almost too trendy now to make such a big deal of it. YouTube hits on promposal are way down."

As Beauty lurches to a stop in the school parking lot, Trevor's face lights up. He gives her a wink and a deep-pink blush travels from his neck to the tips of his ears. Mallory knows that means he's about to say something he doesn't believe. She's always told him never to play poker, because his face always betrays his emotions.

"Don't start messing with my mind today, Mal. *No one* wants classic. It's just another way to say ordinary. And Jessica doesn't like ordinary. She likes extraordinary. Which is why she's going to like me!"

Mallory rolls her eyes so drastically it gives her a stomach knot. She reaches out her still-balled fist and finally releases her fury by punching him on the shoulder.

"At least you share the same delusions! You have that going for you." Then she feels a little bad for being harsh and adds, "Relax, Trev. She won't turn you down. If she does, she's crazy."

Trevor swings around and for an instant she imagines he is about to put his arm around her. Instead he gives her bun a yank and grabs his backpack from the seat behind hers. She groans as the hair cascades down her shoulders and the messy bun takes on the look of straight-up bed head.

"No fair! Foul," she huffs, trying to swirl the caramel-colored locks back into submission.

Trevor gets out of the car, shaking his head at her. As he walks away he yells over his shoulder, "I'll meet you at lunch. We can pick your brain and come up with something perfect."

Sure, pick my brain; you've already broken my heart. Maybe you can take my kidney too and make it a trifecta of torture.

He walks left toward North House, the wing for seniors also known as the Holy Grail of hallways, where every day is a countdown to being finally done with school. The magical, mystical land where Trevor spends his days laughing with his hockey buddies and now drooling over the new transfer Jessica. The probable cheerleader, who is no doubt perfect for Trevor with her long legs and megawatt smile. Mallory hasn't met her yet, but knowing Trevor, she feels her vision is pretty solid.

As she exits the car, new bun intact, the first-period bell shrieks.

"Perfect, now I'm late. I so need a fairy godmother. Or a wizard who can rewind time." Grabbing her backpack, she does an impressive sprint toward what appears will be a very long day.

CHAPTER TWO

Wingman

AS SHE ALWAYS DOES, Mallory carries her lunch to the bench in the courtyard to watch Trevor and his hockey friends play whichever sport allows them to knock each other around the most. It keeps her away from the constant barrage of cafeteria noise and allows her to capitalize on one of her greatest roles in life: spectator.

When she pulls out her lunch bag, Trevor leaves the testosterone pack and slides next to her on the bench in the sun. Mallory glares at her friend, fully aware that he is about to wreck her day. He knocks her with his shoulder, and she punches him in the arm at full strength. Rubbing his arm in mock pain, he grins sheepishly before saying, "Stop it, you're off the hook. I figured it all out! I'm gonna rock it!"

Willing her face to maintain its normal mask of nothingness, because she knows expressing shock or heartbreak would give away her true feelings, she cocks her head and meets his twinkling green eyes. "You figured it out? Promposal?"

He sits back and crosses his legs, putting his arms behind his head with his face toward the sun. Mallory can't help but laugh when he nods and says, "Like a boss! It turns out the drama team is doing a retelling of fairy tales. The auditorium is set up to look like an enchanted castle and Kyle says he can slip me in there today after school. He's even setting me up with a Prince Charming outfit and a tiara for her. It's going to be awesome."

Remain calm, Mallory. The first rule of a crisis is to remain calm. Observe, assess, be supportive, and above all: do no harm. Fall apart later.

"Today? You're going to do it today? That's insanity. You barely know her. Maybe she's got a castle phobia! Maybe she's planning on being in England that night! *Today?*" Mallory takes a deep breath and slowly exhales. She has a million reservations about the whole promposal with a total stranger, but she can't help questioning whether she's worried for him or just plain old jealous of Jessica.

Trevor nods. "No time like the present. And thanks for the confidence. England, *really?* Where's the love, wingman?"

She gives a halfhearted "Yay!" which causes Trevor to bolt upright.

"What? It's great. And romantic. And you said she's crazy if she says no. Besides, girls love fairy tales. I totally got this. It's gonna be epic. I just need you to get Jessica to the auditorium after school, okay?"

Mallory's single bite of sandwich sticks in her throat like cement. "What? I didn't agree to get involved. The agreement was to help you come up with a promposal idea. And I say send her a pizza with 'prom?' spelled out in pepperoni and call it a day. Or better yet, just quietly ask her and avoid the ruckus."

Or, forget Jessica altogether and realize your best friend likes you, idiot.

"Come on, Mal, I need you. You're my wingman. I can't trust these blockheads for that. Please? I never ask you for anything." Before she can react, he grabs half her turkey sandwich and heads to the pack of boys playing a rough version of Frisbee in the court. She puts the remaining half-uneaten sandwich back in her bag and crosses her fingers. As she looks away from Trevor laughing with the guys and stares at her throbbing crossed fingers, she can't help but wonder what she's hoping for.

Squirrels, a pack of rabid squirrels couldn't hurt. Just one rabies-filled bite could get me off the hook.

⋆⋅☽✦☾⋅⋆

THE REST OF THE DAY Mallory can't keep her mind on class. She fluctuates between anger at herself for not telling Trevor her feelings and fear at his excitement over dating someone who isn't her. She tries to find a scenario where she comes out unscathed, and it just doesn't happen. She's doomed.

As sixth period drags by, she feels herself starting to sweat. The ticking of the clock torments her and she tries to will appendicitis to hit. Though she has a grumbling stomach from skipping lunch, she can't seem to conjure a single bout of voluntary projectile vomiting. By the time the bell rings, she's aware there's no out. No amount of pixie dust will help, no fairy godmother is going to show up and save the day. She's going to have to tell him she just can't do it. Best friend or not, she can't set up the one boy she's ever dreamed about with someone else.

Trevor stands waiting outside the door when she exits the class. His green eyes sparkle like a kid's on Christmas morning. He grabs her by the shoulders and plants a kiss on her cheek. "You are the best. You know that, right? I owe you so big! I'll do anything."

Anything? Forget the promposal. Forget asking Jessica to prom and let's pretend today never happened.

She blushes and puts her hand on her cheek to protect the

kiss. She sees his eyebrows raise and she instantly wipes it off. "Ewwww. Listen, Trevor. About the promposal . . ."

Trevor pushes her toward the outer door at breakneck speed. "She's wearing a teal skirt and a white jean jacket that's short; maybe it's a hand-me-down, I'm not sure. Her nails are pink, like cotton-candy pink, and she will be hanging with the cheerleaders, they've got practice at four, so you have to hurry. You *got* this, wingman!"

He propels her forward against her will until the cement of the front walkway is beneath her dragging sneakers. Mallory turns around in a huff, ready to blow. Until she sees his expression. He looks happy. Genuinely happy. Like, scoring-the-game-winning-goal-at-the-biggest-game-of-the-year happy. Mallory has seen the look before. Like a sunrise, it's elusive and it almost makes you do anything to catch it again. She swallows her anger, gives him a thumbs-up, and heads for the senior wing, wishing she had some ruby-red slippers to transport her away.

Wingman. I'm his wingman. The guy of my dreams has not only friend-zoned me, he's made me his flipping wingman! How do I end up in these situations?

She makes her way to the main door of the North House wing and starts scanning the crowd. She doesn't see a teal skirt and white half-jean jacket anywhere.

Well, I tried, she consoles her conscience.

Suddenly from the side door comes a gang of giggling girls. The tallest, a redhead, fits the description Trevor gave her, down to the pink-painted fingernails. Mallory goes toward the girls and ends up smack-dab in front of them, blocking their way. She stares at Jessica, and her mind goes completely blank.

Jessica makes eye contact and does a head-to-toe, scrunching up her face as if she is about to be asked for a handout. Mallory instantly wishes she hadn't found her.

"Umm, Jessica?"

The redhead frowns and her almond-brown eyes come to a slit. She glares like a viper about to strike and instinctively Mallory takes a small step backward.

"Yes?" She spits the word as if her whole day has been interrupted by a bird pooping on her shoulder.

"My name is Mallory. I'm a friend of Trevor's and he asked if you would take just a minute and meet him in the auditorium. It's important, obviously, or I wouldn't have chased you down . . ."

Mallory hates herself for feeling inferior. She should have just snubbed the girl back and walked off, but this means a lot to Trevor. Besides, being looked down on wasn't exactly a new experience for her; she could take it.

"Oh, this should be good." Jessica looks at her Barbie friends and smiles, dropping her voice to a whisper. "Trevor's the googly-eyed boy I was telling you about, girls. Let's go. This could be fun." The girls giggle and follow Jessica down the walkway like ducks following their mother.

Mallory wishes there were a back route. Trevor is about to make a huge mistake. Still, if she messes this up, he will hate her. And that's something she just can't take. She follows the girls at a distance. One small runty duck following the pack. When they get to the auditorium her eyes instantly find Kyle in the wing with his iPhone in hand and a huge smile on his face. Mallory hides in the very back and off to the side to watch the show unfold.

CHAPTER THREE

Promposal

*J*ESSICA STRUTS UP the auditorium toward the stage at full speed. The walkway and stage are draped with soft twinkling lights and it does seem almost enchanted. She pauses halfway down the aisle and Trevor swaggers out from behind the curtain. He's wearing the costume, which is about two sizes too small, holding a mini red satin pillow with a tiara on it. His face is bright red; the pillow shakes as he trembles. Mallory's heart rips when her friend's goofy grin disappears as soon as he realizes Jessica has brought a built-in audience.

Just once make me a wizard, just this once and I'll never ask again. Give me a wand, a chant, a spell, a hex, I'll even take a few bolts of lightning. Mallory's head swims with pleas to the universe to stop the show.

"Jessica, I know you're new here, and it's only a week before prom, but I was hoping you would do me the honor of being my date."

He takes it one step further and gets on his knee, pillow extended. Tiara trembling and teetering as if it wants to float into her hands.

No, Trevor! Abort! Not the knee. Don't do it. It's too much. The costume was enough.

Jessica swaggers the rest of the way up to the stage. The rest of the pack hangs back, laughing and whispering as if watching a wreck in progress. Mallory wishes she could disappear. She uses her brain to will Jessica to be nice. Trevor's entire ego is hanging by a thread. Surely Jessica is human. She could hope, at least.

Rats, plague, pestilence. A distraction of any kind would work. Run, Trevor, run.

Jessica climbs the stairs and offers Trevor her hand. She grabs the back of his head and kisses him. The pillow tilts to the side and the tiara rolls slowly across the stage. Mallory looks over and sees Kyle, iPhone pointed at center stage, capturing the magic. His smile reaches from ear to ear and he glances at Mallory and gives her the thumbs-up sign.

The floor spins. She nods back at Kyle and runs out of the auditorium silently, her vision blocked with tears. Being a wingman sucks. As much as she worries about Trevor getting hurt, she never imagined how much pain she could feel seeing him kiss someone else.

Alone in the bathroom, she washes her face, dries her hands, and punches the stall door. It swings back and forth on the hinges but the act has done nothing to relieve her pain. Curses fill her thoughts for believing in love, acting like a wimp, and ever liking Trevor. They were still, and always had been, friends. She was his wingman. Why did she believe anything else?!

Pinching her cheeks, she puts on her perfected daily happy face. "This," she tells her broken reflection in the mirror, "this is your moment to be a true best friend. You will tell Trevor how happy you are for him and tuck these feelings deep down with the rest."

She sets her mind to stone. Just like she does every day as she walks through the hallways being no one, unseen. Just like she has since second grade when Jenna C. informed her in no uncertain terms that a girl with a birthmark across her cheek would never fit in.

⁂

MALLORY FORCES HERSELF to walk back to Trevor's car. Waiting in the warm sun, she can't help but feel envious of Jessica. Right now Trevor is probably still making a complete fool of himself just to ask her to a dance. Mallory imagines herself on the dance floor in Trevor's arms.

Her dream, however, is quickly interrupted by the sound of one of the car doors slamming.

Mallory hadn't noticed Trevor coming up, but she gets in and sees his red face and slouched posture, telling her that things had not gone the way they were supposed to. She searches her mind for anything that might lighten the mood, but her heart doesn't find it that easily.

"What happened?" she asks.

He starts the car and screeches out of the parking lot. After a moment of torturous silence he slaps the dashboard, hard.

"She said no! After all that. The worrying, the stupid tiara, getting Kyle to record it, and wearing a stupid costume, she said she was 'flattered' but that she has a boyfriend at her old school—'wouldn't want to make him think I'm dating someone else,' she said. Man, this blows. I'm out. No prom for me. It's stupid anyway."

Mallory is torn between being ecstatic at not having to see him and Jessica suck face ever again, and feeling heartbreak that he's hurting. He gave it a try. Shy, quiet Trevor. Hockey player extraordinaire, best friend of an invisible princess, and always her bodyguard. He tried. She needed to help. She didn't want him suffering from a new complex that might go on for years.

Say something comforting. Cheer later. Make this easier for him.

"Her loss. She's an idiot." Mallory could have stopped there, but consoling wasn't her strong suit, and the words kept coming. "I'll go with you. You should go. It's your senior prom. You only get one. How disappointed would your mom be if she didn't get to fuss over you in a tux."

Once the words flew Mallory wished she could reel them back in.

"I'll go." *Smooth, Mallory, real smooth. What the heck are you thinking? Did you just invite yourself to prom with Trevor? Abort mission. Abort mission!* Her mind swam and silence enveloped the stench-filled air.

Trevor looked over at her. "Really, Mal? You'd do that for me? I mean, I know how much your silent-ninja status means to you. But you're right. My mom would freak if I wasn't going, and I should go—I kinda really wanted to go. It's senior prom! Screw Jessica. You and I have always had a riot, and prom is just a big party, right? Let's do it!"

Mallory smiles and nods, but inside her heart slams into her chest. Did she just volunteer as tribute for a prom gown, heels, and spending a night being one of the guys as they snort sugar and make fun of girls? What is she thinking?

At her house, she gets out of the car without a word. Her mind spinning and her heart racing. Is she seriously going to prom with Trevor? Is there a way out? An easy button? A rewind? It's four days away and she doesn't own nor have any ability to operate heels. She's going to have to consort with the enemy, her mother, who will blow the whole thing out of proportion and make it a "thing."

Heading straight to her room, she slams the door behind her. This is an emergency. She places the buds in her ears and blasts the soundtrack to *Hamilton* at maximum volume. Curse those crossed fingers!

CHAPTER FOUR

The Day Before Prom

MALLORY'S MOM PULLS HER from school at lunch. It's crunch time and she still doesn't have a thing to wear. Three days in a row they had tried several outlet stores and a bridal shop without finding anything remotely acceptable.

Today they're going on a trip to a local prom designer whom Mallory's mom had called; they had sworn they still had dresses in her size and price range. Mallory walks into the store eyes down and palms sweating. She heads directly to the clearance rack and looks for something that would blend in with a crowd. Nothing fits her idea of what a prom dress should be. Comfortable, stylish, and classically beautiful.

Her mom pulls a few dresses off the racks and Mallory sulks her way to the dressing room with a promise to be open-minded. The very first dress fits like it was made for her. Mallory stares in the mirror, and a tear falls from her eye. The dress is white with a metallic-type sheen, a small amount of beading, and the illusion of feathers ingrained in the fabric. It's floor-length but doesn't scrape when she walks. With a small heel she could totally pull it off. She twirls and frowns at herself.

She's being a total girl. This is a friend-zone date. No more, no less. She scolds her stained reflection in the tripaneled mirror.

Cool your jets, invisible princess—it's a dress, not a magic wand.

She removes the dress without showing it to her mom. She can't take the gushing and the look on her mom's face; she thinks this is a real date. On the way home they grab shoes and a bag and Mallory scours the shelves for basic coverage makeup. Tonight would be a YouTube tutorial binge. She can't seem to help the giddiness creeping in below the surface. The more she tries to stifle it, the more she imagines her and Trevor dancing arm in arm. Even if it is the friend zone, it's a fairy tale come true for a girl who lives in the shadows.

CHAPTER FIVE

Prom Day!

MALLORY HANDS HER MOM another tissue and tries to focus her vision, which is now a series of flashing circles from the thousand camera flashes that her dad has sent her way. She's finished her hair and

makeup and been in her dress for an hour. It's time for Trevor
to pick her up.

Doubt eats away at her. What if he forgets? What if he
thinks she looks horrible? What if Jessica is there and decides
she was wrong for turning him down? Her feet begin to lead her
back up the stairs, seeking the safety of her bedroom, when the
doorbell rings.

Trevor and his parents come in like a tornado, his mom
squealing and gushing with Mallory's. Together they're like a
pep squad on caffeine. Trevor groans and Mallory races down
the stairs to save him from being alone in the torment.

When she enters the room, silence settles like a blanket. All
eyes in the room settle on her and she finds it unnerving. Her
eyes scan the room and settle on Trevor, who looks amazing!
His tux is black and white, classic, with a bow tie and cummer-
bund in emerald. His face is bright red and he stands with one
foot aimed toward the door, as if ready to bolt. When he looks
her way his jaw moves its way southward.

He steps toward her and shuts his mouth only to open it
again as if trying to remember how to speak.

"Whoa, Mal. You're beautiful. I mean, you look so, well, I . . ."
Trevor stumbles with his words but his face speaks volumes.

Mallory crosses the room and holds his open hand. She's
amazed that his palm is as warm and moist as her own. He trembles as he tenderly places on her wrist the corsage he'd brought.
She smiles up at him. "Not bad for an invisible princess, aye?"

Trevor leans in and softly kisses her lips. The air fills with
electricity. She knows in that moment what a real-life fairy tale
is. This. This is it.

They pose for more pictures than should be legally permitted and finally relax in the newly cleaned, fresh-smelling Black Beauty. Trevor starts the car and pauses to tuck a curl behind Mallory's ear before planting a soft kiss on the hand he hasn't let go of since she stood at his side for the pictures. He whispers in her ear the words she had dreamt of all year.

"You've never been invisible, Mallory. You were just hiding. You aren't the invisible princess, you're the swan. I've been blind, and stupid. You've been my best friend this whole time, and I've been chasing ghosts."

Mallory closes her eyes and smiles. Fairy tales are so underrated, she thinks, but totally worth believing in.

Of Sirens and Beasts

mikaela bender

A S COACH MATSON'S WORDS SINK IN, an image of me sporting a tutu and scoring a touchdown appears in my mind. The picture isn't bidding adieu anytime soon. In an office with twelve teenage football players, silence never happens. Except now. Coach dropped the news that we'll be taking ballet.

"Why?" I'm the first to get the word out. The image in my head changes so my cleats are now ballet slippers.

"It will help with your coordination," he says, leaning back in his seat, the springs squeaking in protest of his weight. There is no way I am squeezing into tights or a unitard, and somehow forcing my size-fourteen feet into ballet slippers. Even if I wanted to, I couldn't make it happen.

His eyes zero in on me. "With the Beasts losing every game

this season, we need to try something new. Do you understand, Cal?"

I duck my head. "Yes, Coach."

Coach types something out on his phone before laying it down as a paperweight on the purple construction paper cards from his daughter. "The girls who suggested this to me said they could only take twelve of you to start with. If it goes well for the twelve of you, they'll have the rest of the team join in."

Breck shoots his hand up in the air.

"Yes?" Coach's phone lights up, and his eyes flick to the screen.

"Are we going to have to dance in a show? If so, excuse me as I go break my ankle now." Out in the hall someone knocks on the door.

Coach stands, sighing. "No. I expect you to be at every class." He opens the door, and twelve teenage girls walk into the room in single file. They face us, staring at us with green and blue eyes. Each of them has hair colored in unnaturally bright hues. Two have even bleached their hair white. This gives the impression more of a bizarre police lineup than an introduction of dance teachers to their students.

Next to me, Reed nudges my shoulder. When I look at him, he wriggles his eyebrows. I roll my eyes.

The girl on the far left steps forward. "I'm Amaryllis and these are my sisters. We're the ones who will be teaching you. Every weekday evening you'll come to our house for lessons. Your coach will text you our address."

"Your house?" Reed asks.

She smiles graciously. "That's where we typically teach."

Breck crosses his arms. "We don't have to perform in some froofy recital or something?"

Reed snorts. "Did he really just say froofy?" he whispers to me.

I nod, smirking. "We're not going to let him live that down, right?"

"Absolutely, we aren't."

Amaryllis clears her throat. Her gaze meets ours, and we mumble a quick apology.

Without an order from their sister or a word from Coach, Amaryllis's sisters exit the office, never having uttered a sound.

"We'll see you all tonight then," she says. "Wear something comfortable, unless of course you wish to wear tights." She brushes her arm across the door, closing it behind her.

What kind of conniving, half-baked scheme has Coach gotten us into?

◦৪✦৪৹

I PARK MOM'S CAR outside a two-story house that looks like it belongs in a Spanish port from a pirate movie rather than in this particular neighborhood of the Gulf town of Saint Petersburg, Florida. It's the wide variety of architecture from different time periods all mashing up against each other that makes me love this town. The houses on either side of it are pitch black. Not even a porch light glows, nor is there a car in either driveway. This is borderline creepy.

Once everyone is here, I walk up the driveway with the eleven other chosen members of my football team, the Beasts.

"Cal"—Reed steps beside me—"you ready to show us all those killer moves?"

"Moves? Dude, I haven't danced a day in my life."

Bending his tennis shoes, Reed tries to walk on them like they're those toe shoes that actual ballerinas wear. "Well, I'm going to be the best student and win over the hand of one of those very lovely sisters."

I slap him on the back, and he stumbles from his precarious position on his toes. "Good luck with that."

He shoves me back and continues on past me.

Eli, our lead quarterback, knocks on the door, and one of the sisters answers.

Her eyes move from left to right, taking us in. "Hey." She steps back to allow us to enter. "I'm Calla."

Gawking at the interior of the house, I step inside and hear her shut and lock the door.

This is the type of house one shouldn't throw a football in. "My sisters are already outside waiting," she explains.

"Outside?" Ryann raises an eyebrow. "Don't you ballerinas need special flooring?"

I never cared much for him. He came to my fifth birthday party and whined because it wasn't fair I was the only one getting presents.

She shakes her head, her white hair swaying. Yeah, white. "The air feels nice out there."

She leads us out back where her eleven sisters are lined up beside a pool that glows an eerie blue. The moon penetrates the fog, but the stars are too weak to do the same. Calla tells us to each take a partner. I step in front of the last girl, since I was in the back of the guys. Her dark hair—I can barely make out that it's red—blows lightly from the wind.

"I'm Rose." She's the third sister I've been introduced to and the third with the name of a flower.

"Cal." My arms feel awkward hanging out at my sides. She holds out her hands. "What are we doing?" I ask.

"Dancing. The reason you're here."

"I didn't realize ballet involved hand-holding."

She laughs. "Haven't you ever been to a ballet?"

I grimace. "No."

"Well." She takes my hands in hers and holds them up. My black hands contrast with her white ones like yin and yang, like the moon and the sky . . . now I'm just sounding sappy. "In partnering, these"—she squeezes my hands—"are your barre." Slowly a smile spreads across her face, appearing almost sinister. Her chest rises, and she lets out a low hum.

So do her sisters.

Rose pulls me closer and transitions her hand to my shoulder.

"The song came in that night with the tide." Their song is carried by the wind as they sing. *"No one heard it except for two drifting ships whose sailors were still sinking to the depths."*

Her and her sisters' voices are angelic.

My hand slides to her waist.

"They never cried." They step back from us. *"They gladly went under that saffron-colored moon."*

I step forward and follow her when she steps to the side.

"The song came like waves"—they all sing every line—*"rolling*

back and forth. One moment faint; the next crashing and powerful. The song was hypnotizing."

Her fingers entwine with mine, and she sends our hands up to the level of our eyes, and we spin.

"Music such as this had not been heard for centuries—not since pirates ruled the seas."

Every move is natural. Their song draws me closer. Her blue eyes glow; the only thing I see. I spin her. I'm not sure how I knew to do that. I just did.

"But no one saw the source . . ." Her hand brushes my face, and I let her guide my footsteps. *". . . for a saffron-colored moon is rumored to do such things."*

My shoes crunch the grass.

"Hiding behind clouds . . ."

Her eyes are what guide me.

"Shielding the thieves. No one shall remember the lost souls. They will be forgotten. Erased from every memory."

Screaming.

And more screaming. Of agony.

Of fear.

I jerk away from her and look toward where the screams come from—the water.

Splashing and shouts emerge from the murky blackness. The moon sheds enough light to see the water churning and tossing. I glance at my team members and immediately know a third of us are missing. Instead of rushing toward the water, we back away—cowards.

Rose tries to grab my hands, but I keep them close to me.

She looks panicked as she turns to her sister next to her and says, "It's not strong enough."

Four of the sisters surface from the water, their eyes fixated on us.

"What happened?" one of them snaps, wiping the back of her hand along her mouth.

A sister near me tries reaching toward Reed, her partner. "The bond didn't work."

Did they drown my teammates? What are these girls? Members of some cult?

The sister next to Rose looks up at the moon. "There's no more time."

I've put twenty feet or so in between me and Rose. I don't turn my back to her as I try searching for an escape route. A fence too tall to jump over surrounds the property on three sides, the water being the only side without a fence. I know none of us want to venture into the water, but what if our boys are still alive? Why would these girls kill them?

One of the four from the water licks her lips and goose bumps run up my arms. "Do it," she says.

They're going to kill us. We're eight high school football players up against twelve girls who seem more like witches than humans. The question it comes down to: is the supernatural— not sure what word to use—stronger than brute strength? I don't particularly want to find out. At least not while that experiment involves me. I dart toward the door, my shoes thudding against the pavement. They start to sing again. I stop . . . my body feeling like a marionette. Strings seem to take hold of my limbs and root into the ground.

MY EYES OPEN to a white popcorn ceiling. My head is experiencing an awe-inspiring hangover. I haven't had a hangover in a year—not since I stopped drinking. I squint. I don't remember getting in bed last night. I don't even remember leaving that mansion. The last thing I recall is pulling up to it last night.

After dressing and showering for school, I enter the kitchen and plop down on the nearest seat at the table.

"Morning, sunshine." Tongs in hand, Mom pulls a waffle from the toaster. She drops it down onto a plate with two others.

I mumble something unintelligible in response while massaging my head.

"How was the class?" She adds syrup to the side of the plate and sets it in front of me. Some of it runs off the edge, dripping onto the table.

"Good." I bite off a piece of waffle. I don't want to tell her I can't remember, or she'll think I actually do have a hangover. That or think I was drugged. She for sure couldn't stand the thought of me drinking—not after Dad was killed by a drunk driver, the reason I quit drinking. "Do you remember what time it was when I got home?"

Mom pulls down a blue-and-pink-tinted glass and fills it with orange juice. She wrinkles up her face. "I stayed up waiting for you, but I can't remember. You didn't go out with your friends after class, right?"

"No, of course not."

She takes a long sip of her juice, staring me down. "Good."

Great. I've unleashed the one thing no one should ever set free—a mom's suspicions.

⚜

I MISS THE FOOTBALL for the fifth time. As I jog across the field to retrieve it, Reed runs to catch up with me.

"What's up with you today?" he asks, and shakes his head, sweat flying off his hair. Some of the drops land on me. I flick them off.

"I don't know. It's just . . . Forget it. You don't feel weird? Nothing feels off?"

He snorts. "Yeah, but I always feel weird."

Coach Matson blows his whistle. "Five-minute water break."

Chugging back my water bottle, I spot Rose at the top of the bleachers. She lifts her hand to say hi. She can explain how I got home last night, at least what time I left. I climb up the steps and take a seat two rows below her.

She runs a hand through her hair. "You did good last night."

I open and close the stopper on my bottle. "I can't remember."

Her smile seems almost forced. "That's probably because you were half-asleep. My sisters and I had to drive you boys home. Apparently we worked you too hard. I hope you don't mind us using your cars."

"No, thank you actually. I'm sure that was an inconvenience, huh?"

Shaking her head, she scratches her cheek. "Not at all. You are coming tonight, though?"

"Yeah. Coach said he'd make us do two hundred burpees

every night for the rest of the season if we don't go. Not that we didn't enjoy the class."

I can't even remember if I enjoyed it.

She looks at me curiously. "You don't have to lie."

"I'm not."

She tilts her head to the side, her bright red hair dislodging from behind her ear. She must dye it that unnatural color. Though I have to confess it looks good on her. "You told me two minutes ago that you can't remember doing a good job last night."

"Right . . ."

She stands. "I've got to meet my sisters. I'll see you tonight, Cal."

⸙

WHEN THE EIGHT OF US show up at their front door, we smell pizza. The sister at the door grins. "Come on into the kitchen."

My little sis would die for this kitchen. I don't know what the contraptions that line the granite countertops do, or what they're called. I do know those are two ovens and two microwaves.

Their coffee machine doesn't look like a coffee machine. Buttons and levers cover it and it looks more like a robot from a sci-fi movie on TV. What happened to having a pot and filter?

On the island are three boxes of pepperoni pizza. Four of the sisters stand around the edges of the kitchen, staring at us. A better word may be glaring. I eat one piece, but it takes me a while to consume it. Having four girls seeming to judge the way we eat is a little bit intimidating.

Pulling out my phone to pretend I'm making a call, I step out into the foyer and head upstairs, wondering if I can find Rose.

"You better do better."

I freeze, thinking it's one of the sisters addressing me.

"We only have two more nights after this."

I realize the voices are coming from behind a door.

"I didn't know how hard it would be, so I didn't put enough effort into the song. Don't worry. I won't make that mistake again."

"Cal?" Rose asks from behind me.

I turn, feeling like a burglar with a stolen laptop. "I was looking for the bathroom."

"There are plenty downstairs."

I scratch the back of my head. "I got caught up in admiring your home."

She tilts her head to the side. "Thanks." She points behind her. "There's a bathroom in my room."

The best way to describe her room is that it's dull. Sure, it looks expensive, but there's nothing to suggest it isn't a guest bedroom. Even the bathroom isn't personal. I guess I was expecting pink or purple or even light blue.

She's your age, idiot. Not two. But there are no photos taped to the walls. No backpack tossed onto a wrinkled bed. Everything is tidy and cold.

Curious, I open up the sink's cabinet, half expecting it to be a mess, half expecting it to be as clean as her room. I've seen Mom's. Hers is filled with lotion and . . . other stuff. But Rose's is empty except for a few dark green towels and on the other end a small tower of toilet paper.

Poking out from underneath the bottom towel is a black frame. I pull it out, careful not to disturb the towels. Inside the frame an Asian family of four smiles at me. Definitely not Rose's family. In all likelihood it's the generic photo that always comes in frames. Though there are no labels on the photo . . . I unlatch the back and find the image is an actual photograph, not just a thin piece of paper inserted inside. The date on the back indicates it was taken five months ago. The photo could be of the last family who lived here, and they simply forgot to pack it.

I hurry up and finish in here. Walking out, I find Rose seated on her bed, her legs curled underneath her. She pats the spot beside her.

As I'm sitting down I say, "Sorry, I was looking for toilet paper."

"I didn't realize—"

"I was taking a dump." What on this sad earth did I just say to a pretty girl?

Her mouth falls open and her face reddens. That should be how I look and most definitely is.

Technically, what I told her is a lie, and it just came out. I didn't want her to think I was taking so much time because I was snooping, but couldn't I have gone with something else other than pooping? I rub the back of my head.

"I will never understand you boys." She reaches her hand out toward me, her fingers brushing my collarbone as she lifts the metal cross around my neck. "What's this?"

"My mom gave it to me when I was baptized."

She smiles, letting the necklace fall back against me softly. "Ahh . . . the Waters of Life. That's always sounded appealing to me. Tell me, have you heard of the Waters of Death?"

"You mean like the devil?"

Her hand brushes the comforter between us, smoothing it out. "Not exactly. Some say it's the Bermuda Triangle. I say it's anywhere there's an open body of water."

"I'm not following."

Her smile appears and vanishes within a second. "You aren't supposed to." She glances out her window that has the curtains pulled back. "We should head down. We'll start class soon."

I stand, the mattress creaking. "I honestly can't remember anything."

She laughs, walking to her dresser. "Do you need me to show you?" Using the dresser for balance, she turns out her feet and bends her knees, her hand and arm following her down. "Plié, remember?" She rises and bends her back so she touches her toes, her knees remaining stiff as a barre. "Port de bras. Any of this ring a bell?"

The moves definitely look familiar, and I know I've heard "plié" before but not "pour the bras."

"Right, I remember now. Long day," I say.

She nods, raising her eyebrows. "Let's go then."

I follow her outside, where her sisters and my team already await. Each of the boys stands in front of one of the girls. Four of the sisters stand off to the side. Did they not join us last night?

A hand grasps mine, and I look down at Rose holding my hand. "I guess we're late," she says as she pulls me into line and takes my other hand.

The girls begin to hum. I guess they don't have a sound system out here. Rose steps forward and steps back.

I don't budge. "This isn't ballet."

She smiles. "Isn't it?"

She and her sisters begin singing, their voices so . . . so calming. *"Maybe a deal was struck long ago between the song fish and the celestial body. A deal that allowed the moon to listen without endangerment."*

She runs her hand up my arm, her fingernails grazing my skin.

"Has not the moon controlled the sea and its creatures since that long-ago time when they both were born? Perhaps the moon turns saffron when it's weak."

Her eyes shine blue in the darkness, drawing in my attention.

"Maybe the song gives life to the moon. Maybe the moon needs life to go on."

I faintly hear grass crunching. I step toward her as she steps toward me. I twirl her.

"Singing blew on the wind that night, sweeping into the town and into homes. The people came and the people left. Not a tear was shed that night. Not a tear raised the ocean by a drop."

Screaming.

I jerk away from Rose, my eyes darting about. She reaches for me, but I avoid her touch. I count three of my team members. Four are missing. In the ocean, water splashes. An arm shoots out of the water before disappearing.

"Rose?" I look at her, my heart pounding.

She tries to grasp my hands, but I yank them away, backing toward the fence. The sisters off to the side yell at the four who are still with us.

"Why can't we just kill them now?" the sister next to Rose shouts back to the ones off to the side.

Rose takes a single step toward me. "It won't count. We

have to fix the mistake we made." Her eyes lock with mine and her mouth opens.

⚬⚬✦⚬⚬

MY HEADACHE'S BACK, and staring at the ceiling of my room doesn't do much to relieve it. My stomach churns, the feeling of disorientation overwhelming me. I try to think of what I last remember. There was pizza and an awkward conversation with Rose about poop.

I groan. Right, Rose and I talked and then went outside. After that, it's just a big black hole in my head.

I rub my forehead. I'm never going to forget that, am I? I forget everything else but that. Once I'm finished getting ready, I head into the kitchen. Taija, my twelve-year-old sister, is at the table reading and eating a breakfast sandwich.

I grab the carton of orange juice from the fridge. Shaking the carton, I feel it's almost empty, so I chug it back, which I know she hates. She doesn't notice, too engrossed in her book. I toss the carton into the trash and grab a bagel, then twist the two halves apart and drop them into the toaster.

"What are you reading?" I ask her.

"*The Twelve Dancing Princesses.* I'm supposed to finish it for book club today but forgot about it until last night."

I twist the orange tie from the bagel package around my finger. "What's happening in it?"

"Right now the guy is on his last chance to prove where the princesses go dancing at night."

"What happens if he can't prove it?"

She shrugs, flipping the page. "He's killed." She bites into her breakfast, crumbs falling on the table and her lap. "Oh, how's dance going?" she asks, her mouth full of food.

"I can't remember anything I learned."

"You're that bad? I'm not coming to your recital then."

I roll my eyes, pulling my bagel out of the toaster with tongs. "There's not going to be a recital."

"Maybe that's what they're telling you so they don't hurt your feelings."

Mom walks into the kitchen and sets her purse on the island. "Morning." She grabs the other half of the bagel out of my hand and kisses me on the cheek. "I have a meeting that's going to keep me late, so I won't be able to pick you up after football."

I stare at my bagel in her hand. "No problem. I'll just go home with Reed and then go to the practice tonight."

"You mean ballet?" my sister sings.

I grab my backpack from the front door and head outside, Mom and Taija following. I hop in the car and buckle up while Taija slides in next to me and pops in her earbuds, returning to her book.

When Mom stops at a stop sign, she adjusts her mirror, her eyes landing on me. I shift in my seat. I'm about to get a talk.

"Have you met these girls' parents?"

Oh boy. I can tell she's going to freak any second now.

"No."

"You've been over there twice. Is there no adult supervision?"

If I tell her there isn't any, she's going to lecture me along with freaking out. If I lie, I'll feel horrible, but at least she won't have to go through the trouble of performing an impromptu speech. "They're there. They just stay in their room or office." Which could be true.

"What's their last name?" The perks of having a mom who works as an assistant at a law firm—she may not be a lawyer, but she definitely picks up their interrogation tactics and brings them home.

"I don't know. I'm sure Coach does."

"You seem to know nothing about them."

I unzip my backpack and dig out my folder. I need to make sure I put my history homework in here. "The one I talk to's name is Rose."

Bingo. History homework packed.

"I just want you to be careful and make smart decisions."

I reach forward and pat her shoulder. "I know, Mom."

She places her hand on mine and gives my fingers a squeeze.

We ride in silence the rest of the way. My school is the first on her morning route so she drops me off first. As I'm getting out, she rolls down her window.

"Remember I can't pick you up today."

"Got it." I sling my backpack over my shoulder and head to the doors. Two of the boys from my team meet me before I reach them.

"How's the ballerina doing?" Camden jokes, while Tyler does an arabesque, dramatically falling onto Camden.

"It is what it is."

"Aww . . . you embarrassed?" Tyler teases. "How long is Coach going to make you four keep this up?"

"Well, if he sees improvement he's making the whole team join in. And it's just four of us?"

Camden nods. "Yeah, four, right? You're the one taking ballerina class with them. You should know."

I sigh, a headache starting to come on. "Ballet class. And I
just thought there were more of us. That's all."

"What, twelve chicks too much for you guys to handle?"

"Shut up."

As we walk to our first class, math—who schedules math at
seven thirty in the morning?—I spot Rose surrounded by six of
her sisters. If I didn't know they were her sisters, I'd say they'd
be about to gang up on her and fight.

"You can't waste any more of our time." Amaryllis runs her
hand through her own red hair and tugs at the ends. "You aren't
getting attached, are you?"

Rose doesn't answer. She simply takes a deep breath.

"You are, aren't you?" another sister asks.

"No, I'm not. Don't worry. I can handle it." She notices me
and swallows.

The sister behind her mutters, "Here come the Beasts."

"Everything good?" I ask, attempting to intervene.

The sister who muttered rolls her eyes and slinks off. The
others nod to me and leave.

Camden taps me on the shoulder. "We're going to head on
to class."

I shrug and tilt my neck, looking at Rose, who doesn't meet
my eyes. "You okay?" I ask.

"Yeah. Sisters are sometimes a bit needy."

"I know, and I just have one." I stare at the locker behind
her. "You know, I still can't remember anything of your class. I
just remember talking last night."

She brushes her hair behind her shoulder. "You drove yourself home so that's a tad bit worrying. Maybe you should see if you have a concussion."

She has a good point. I've been playing football since I was four. I've been hit on the head with just about everything more times than I can count. One time I got hit by an Ohio license plate. Long story.

"You're coming over tonight?" she asks before pressing the knuckle of her finger against her teeth.

"Of course."

She smiles, nervously biting on her skin. "It's sure to be a life-changing class."

⁂

TUCKING THE BALL UNDER HIS ARM, Reed jogs up to me, his cleats sloshing through the wet field. "Hey, Cal, does it seem like we're short?"

"I mean, I didn't want to say anything, but my neck gets sore always looking down at you."

Rolling his eyes, he laughs. "You're so funny, Calvin. No, but seriously, are we missing people?"

I look around the field and scratch my head. I notice Rose on the bleachers. "I can't think of who's missing. If we are, then they just must be sick."

"We know most everyone on this team. We'd know which ones of us are missing, right?"

"Then I guess everyone is here, and we're losing it." I run backward, spreading apart my arms. "Ball."

Reed steps back a few feet before launching the ball into the air. Looking upward, I run to catch it. The ball's about to drop into my hands, when I slip on the wet turf and crash to the ground, landing on top of my right wrist.

I feel nothing, and that's the scary part. Slowly, though, an intense pain spreads over my wrist, and I push myself up using my other arm. Reed, Camden, and Tyler rush over to me.

Bending down next to me, Tyler asks, "What was that epic fail?"

I grimace, clutching my wrist. "I think I broke it."

Camden and Tyler swear.

Reed offers his arm and pulls me up. "How are you going to be able to play?"

"Coach is going to kill me."

"I'll drive you to the clinic." Reed motions for me to start walking.

Camden jogs in front of us. "We should tell Coach first."

"He's inside and even after we track him down he'll have to fill out a form and more garbage. Let's go, Cal."

Rose joins us from her spot on the bleachers. "I'll come with you."

"Fine." Reed motions with his head to follow us. "Make sure he doesn't trip on anything else."

⚜

IN REED'S CAR I sit in the front with him while Rose sits in the back. I text Mom about what happened, using my left hand to do so. She says she'll get there as soon as she can, but her boss is being difficult, and an accident is blocking the road outside her office. Closing my eyes, I lean my head against the window, the pain becoming unbearable.

Rose begins humming, her voice soothing.

As we near the clinic, Reed asks Rose, "Can I drop you two off?" Rose agrees and Reed pulls up under the overhang.

Once inside, the man at the desk stands when he sees me clutching my wrist. "What happened?" he asks.

"I fell on it during practice. I think it's broken."

"Do you have a parent with you?"

"She's at work."

He sighs, typing on the keyboard. "Please take a seat. We'll get to you as soon as we can."

The waiting area is short on seats. The last thing I want to do is sit in a noisy, confined space with people who are sick while the pain in my arm is making me want to throw up.

Rose glances at me before shuffling through stacks of pamphlets on the counter. She starts up her humming again.

"Is there really no way someone can't take a quick X-ray?" I ask. I'm debating begging for even an ibuprofen.

"I'm sorry, but as you can see there are plenty of other people who are waiting, some far worse off than a suspected broken wrist."

I squeeze my eyes, the pain growing worse. "Do you at least have some ice?"

Rose stops humming.

"Actually"—he moves the computer mouse around—"I think we should see you now. I'll call up a nurse to take you back."

What even? "Uhh . . . thanks."

Rose makes sure the stack of papers is tidy before giving me a thumbs-up. Weird how he changed his mind like that, but hey, if it means I'll get some painkillers sooner, then I don't care.

I end up only having to get a cast around my wrist, and I'm back in the waiting room before I have much time to process anything. The pain makes everything—time and surroundings alike—blurry.

My phone buzzes in my pocket.

Mom: I'm getting in the car.

I sit down in the corner of the waiting room and set my phone on my lap. The red cast rests awkwardly on my leg. Nothing feels comfortable.

Rose sits next to me.

"I suppose you've already pieced together that I won't be going tonight," I say.

Rose frowns. "I've gathered."

I drum on my thigh. "Do you think it's weird I can't remember anything?"

"I guess so." She stares off into space.

"Mind if I take a nap? The painkillers are putting me to sleep."

"Sure."

I lean my head against the wall and close my eyes, but I have a hard time finding a comfortable position. I don't know how much time passes before a phone rings and Rose says, "I know we're running out of time . . . He cannot come tonight. Tomorrow, yes, I'll make sure it's finished."

Whatever she means by "finished," I'm not too keen on finding out.

"I'll still be there tonight," she continues. "I'm just waiting for his mom . . . I'm not." She sounds annoyed. "I know we have to make up for what we did. I'm not going to be selfish about this. I'm close to completing it." She sighs. "He's asleep. Violet, I can handle it."

I know I wasn't supposed to hear any of that.

"Calvin?!"

I crack open an eye at the sound of Mom's frantic voice. She's at the entrance, the sliding doors refusing to close because she's too near them. Her head whips side to side and her purse's contents threaten to spill out from the straps slipping down her arm. I wave to get her attention.

She shoves her way past the legs of the other occupants of the waiting room, a couple of which are broken. "Calvin, sweetie, how are you feeling?"

"It hurts, but I'm alive."

She places her cold hand on my cheek and frowns. "I know it hurts, honey."

Rose stands up and holds out her hand. "Hi, I'm Rose."

Mom shakes it, taking in Rose's bright red hair. "Ms. Finnick. Are you one of the girls teaching Cal and his team ballet?"

"Yes, ma'am."

"I'm afraid Cal will have to miss it for a while."

"I understand. I wouldn't want him to hurt himself further." When she was on the phone, it sounded like she had plans for something tomorrow, and that something seemed to be about me.

"Do you need a ride back home?" Mom asks her.

She smiles, looking regretful for having to cause any trouble. "Actually, yes. That would be amazing."

"Let me pay the bill, and then we'll be on our way."

Once we're in the car, Rose gives Mom directions to her house and says to me, "You know, Cal, you could still come tomorrow and watch."

"Yeah, I suppose so."

"I'm not sure that's a good idea." Mom's eyes flick up to the rearview mirror to look at Rose. She doesn't look thrilled with her dyed hair. "I doubt Cal will be feeling up to it."

"Right," Rose says. "I want Cal to be sure to get better."

We sit in a tight silence for a few minutes before Rose starts humming, I assume to pass the time.

I turn to Mom. "How was work?"

"Long. Especially knowing my little boy was stuck at the clinic without me." Does she have to embarrass me in front of Rose? "I think you should go tomorrow night."

I blink. "You're fine with that now?"

She nods. "Rose is right, you can still watch."

I know a few minutes ago I wasn't up for going at all, and now . . . well, now I'm okay with going.

Rose is completely silent.

⚜

LUNCH ROLLS AROUND and Rose hasn't spoken to me since I dropped her off at her house yesterday. When I said hi this morning, she ducked her head and darted into the girls' room.

Rose and her eleven sisters sit at the end of one cafeteria table. I head over to them, not yet having gotten in line. Rose swings her legs around the bench and runs off, murmuring, "Bathroom."

"Am I still supposed to come over tonight?" I ask. Rose's behavior is causing me to think I'm not welcome.

One of her sisters sets down her glass. "Of course you are." She glances at the door Rose exited through. "She's just being shy."

"We think she likes you," Amaryllis says with a smirk.

Something akin to pride swells through me and maybe a little bit of excitement. "Why are you telling me this? Aren't you supposed to keep these things a secret?"

The sister who spoke first winks at me. "It's our joy to embarrass each other."

"Right, well, I'm going to grab food."

As I get in line I wonder what I'm supposed to do with this information her sisters gave me. I pick up a slice of pizza.

Do I just go for it?

⁓❧✦❧⁓

WHEN I SHOW UP at the girls' house, my car is the only one in the driveway. No cars are parked in the street, either. I knock on the door, and Rose answers it, looking like a smile was painted on her face five days ago and hasn't been touched up since.

"How's your wrist?" Rose asks.

"Bearable."

Calla stands beside her. "Why don't you two go ahead out back?"

Rose sends her a glare but silently leads me outside. I shut the back door behind us. "Is everything all right?" I ask.

"Perfect." She sinks into a pool chair, the lights from the pool casting blue light on only half of her.

I'm here the same time I come every other night, no sooner,

no later, so where is everyone? I swear there were more than just me at the start of all this. I don't know how many there were, but Coach wouldn't have me do this alone. He may be tough and hardheaded, but he's not this cruel. "What's taking the others so long?"

"They'll be out shortly." She twirls her thumbs.

I sit down on the seat across from her. "I meant my team."

She inhales deeply. "They're sick." I'm not the only one coming to these things, then. I've really got to get my memory checked.

"What was up with you at school?" I ask.

She looks up at me. "You're full of questions tonight, aren't you? I wasn't feeling well and thought I caught something at the clinic. I didn't want to get anyone sick if I was contagious."

"You're feeling better now?"

"Yeah." She stares out at the ocean. "I'm sorry for anything that I'll do in the future."

I squint at her. "That's morbid."

She shrugs, still gazing over the water.

I hear a door open and look to my right to see her sisters coming outside but lingering by the door.

Sighing, she stands up ever so meticulously. "You ready?"

"Just us?"

With a quick, weak smile, she holds out her hand. "Yes." She pulls me to my feet and stares at me, her eyes and body not moving. I expect her to move us away from between the chairs, but she doesn't. She starts to hum, the sound drawing me in. She steps closer and wraps her arms around my neck.

The wind blows lightly, and she sways us with the wind.

"Are you sure this is ballet?"

She caresses her hand down the side of my face, her hand like ice. "Sure it is." Her fingers brush under my chin and down my neck. *"In the morning no witnesses remained—but there never were any,"* she sings.

I barely notice a tear slip down her eye or the pain in my wrist. Her feet step back and mine step forward, mirroring her movements. Faintly, I'm aware that we're moving away from the chairs.

"When people came to find those once loved, they were met with a pure white shore, untouched by human feet." She's the only one singing. Her hands remain at my neck, and mine, I find, are on her waist. *"Twelve sailors sinking to the depths were spared at the unknown cost of twelve of us. If the debt is not paid, twelve more lives go for the ones wrongfully snatched."*

My shoes and her bare feet crunch the grass. All I see are her bright blue eyes.

They're . . . they're hypnotizing.

"Yet as for the truth, only we know. And we will take it to the depths with us . . ."

Water spreads over my shoes and ankles, rising higher and higher.

". . . until the return of the saffron-colored moon."

The water is up to my shoulders.

Rose places her hand on my neck. "I'm sorry," she says before leaning toward me.

Her teeth scratch my neck.

I ROAM AROUND THE HALLS at school with a headache far more intense than any I've experienced in the past few days, or ever, really. This pain has lasted since I woke up almost seven hours ago. I can't remember anything from yesterday evening, and I'm not really sure if I remember anything from yesterday at all, for that matter. I haven't seen Rose or her sisters all day.

Before I head out, I open my locker and freeze. On the inside of my locker door are written eleven names in black marker: *Reed Williams, Marvin Monroe, Breck Eisenhower, Eli Davis, Carter Lun, Brendon Cecil, Ryann Ledbetter, Brian O'Connor, Nathan Mallot, Mark Noyes, Wes Jacobs.*

Everything starts to come back as I read the names. There were twelve of us and now there's only one . . . me. They were killed by the sisters. Somehow they bewitched us all. Every single one of us. What kind of human—or creature—could do such a thing? A witch? No. The singing, the lyrics, the ocean—they fit together like a puzzle. They were not witches. They were something far more dangerous. They were twelve beautiful sirens who lulled us with their song.

At the front of my locker is a white square of paper with a red rose lying on top of it.

Is this all from Rose? Is this her goodbye?

I pick up the note. It reads simply:

You were a beauty, and I was a beast.

Hooded

shannon klare

CHAPTER ONE

The Accident

TODAY, I HIT ROB HOOD.

It started like every day, normal and mediocre. There were tests—too many tests—and a horrible cafeteria lunch, so it was nothing out of the usual for me to quickly vacate the premises.

But in my haste, in my attempt to escape the school's redundancy, I inadvertently drove into Rob Hood.

I hit Hood with my hood. Oh, the puns.

My first instinct was to panic, because I was pretty sure he was dead, and my second instinct was to cry. I was doing both when the brunet senior pushed himself off the pavement and glared at me from the other side of the car.

I, Annie Marie Mayes, was a dead girl walking. The joys of being me.

Hood straightened his T-shirt, his movements stiff as he tossed his backpack over his shoulder and staggered to the driver's-side door. Then, his perfect face proceeded to glare at me with hazel eyes and a murderous expression.

"You could've killed me!" he hollered. "What is it? Hit-the-pedestrian-and-get-five-bucks Day? Did I miss the memo?"

"You weren't on the automated phone list," a masculine voice replied.

"Yeah?" Hood glanced at the blond male who came to a halt beside him. "Well, next time relay the info. I'm feeling slightly neglected, John."

John Little, the more reasonable of the two, put a hand on Hood's shoulder and pulled him away from my car. John was my lab partner and next-door neighbor, and he was levelheaded. This would ease the tension.

John's mouth quirked at the corners as he acknowledged his friend. "Hate to be the bearer of bad news, Rob, but you're at the top of the run-over hierarchy. If five bucks would pay for a regular pedestrian, injuring the biggest troublemaker on campus has to be worth at least twenty."

"Nice to know my worth." Hood scowled and crossed his arms. "And what happened to you taking my side on things? You're supposed to be my wingman. This isn't very wingman-ish of you."

"I am your wingman," John assured. "Just not when it comes to you threatening my easy route to an A in Anatomy and Physiology. Pick another person to yell at and I'll support you, but Annie gets a reprieve."

"Annie ran me over with a car!"

"She nudged you. Had she run you all the way over, you'd be stuck underneath the wheels and we'd be speaking with the police right now. I don't see Sheriff Nott lurking anywhere. I guess that means you lived."

Hood raked a hand through his disheveled mop of brown hair and sighed. "Fine. I'm not in the yelling mood anymore, anyway. You took all the fun out of it."

"Good. My job here is done." John tapped the top of my Mercedes and winked. "Let's give Annie the opportunity to earn some more money, shall we? She failed with you, but it's not too late to try again. There's plenty other pedestrians to run over, and I expect a thirty percent share of the profits."

"Twenty-five," I rebutted.

Hood looked from John to me, then back to John. "John, your concern for my life is amazing. Remind me not to take a vested interest in any future concussions, broken bones, or black eyes you might or might not incur."

"You lived. Quit being sensitive."

"The bruise on my left butt cheek, where she mowed into me, is what's sensitive," Hood growled in return.

He stepped away and John settled his attention on me. His expression was unreadable, though I detected seriousness somewhere beneath those light blue eyes. "Your dad will have a fit when he sees what you've done to this piece of beauty."

"It isn't the first time I've wrecked it," I pointed out.

He smiled, waved, and stepped away, headed in the same direction his friend went.

I didn't linger, either. A brief interaction with Hood, Locksley's most notorious delinquent, was more than enough to fill my daily bad-boy quota. Plus, if he changed his mind and decided to rag on me some more, John wouldn't be there to ease his irritation. I'd be a deer stuck in Rob's figurative headlights. I didn't doubt he'd run me over eagerly.

That, ladies and gentlemen, is why I exited the scene without launching into profuse apologies of the third kind. Rob wouldn't have accepted them, anyway.

He was impossible, a wild card who rarely acted presentable, and I had no desire to earn his forgiveness. Not today, at least.

Tomorrow would be different, but for today I'd leave him be.

CHAPTER TWO

Revenge

MY PARENTS ARE SNOBS.

Some might say, "Wow, harsh words," but the truth hurts.

They're the type of people you'd spot entering into some fancy place, dressed to the nines, with their noses halfway into the clouds. Then, for fear of secondhand snobbery, you'd proceed to get as far away from their general vicinity as possible. Believe me, I've watched it happen.

Fortunately, the snobby genes were ones I was pretty sure I hadn't inherited. I could've been delusional with my assumption, but either I'd been spared that hideous trait or my aunt,

Carla, had done a better job of keeping me grounded than I'd thought. Either way, I didn't share my parents' need for lofty inner circles and material objects.

Maybe I was unappreciative in that sense, the product of always getting what I wanted, but I needed their love rather than their gifts. My father didn't share my opinion. Instead of asking how my day went, he blew a gasket the second he noticed the dent Hood left in the hood.

"What did you hit?" He gawked, squatting in his tailored dress pants as he ran a hand along the front. I thought about it for a second, trying to discern how to tell him the victim was human, but he groaned and stood before I had the chance. "Never mind. I've got a charity event and don't have time to discuss it with you. I'll have your aunt call the insurance company and get a claim sorted out."

He fastened the buttons on his sports coat and stepped toward a waiting SUV, shortly followed by my mother.

She was wearing a cocktail dress and her hair was neatly secured at the base of her neck, and I knew immediately this would be another lonely night in the Mayes household. For some reason or another, every night seemed to work out that way.

"There's money on the counter," my mom commented as she passed. "Have Carla order a pizza or something, and make sure you get your homework completed. Poor grades won't get you into Princeton."

"Duly noted," I said flatly.

I watched them as they entered the vehicle. Guess tonight I would bide my time with reality television. I could camp out in the media room. I was the only one who used it, anyway.

Carla was in the foyer when I entered through the massive front doors. She was carrying a vase of flowers from one room to another, and she offered me a warm smile. "Saw the article you wrote for the *Locksley Lowdown*. Great work, as per usual."

"Thanks, Aunt Carla." While I was thankful someone had taken the time to check out my less-than-amazing attempts at journalism, I was content to sulk on my situation. I'd pick her brain about the article later—when I was full of pizza and better equipped to discuss the topic.

"Want me to go ahead and order the food?" she questioned, cutting straight through my internal rambling like she always did. When I nodded, she smiled. "Thin-crust cheese, slightly burned, with extra sauce. I'll get right on it."

"You're the best."

"I know."

She veered toward the kitchen and I continued up the stairs.

◦೭ఌV৶ఌ৹

TWENTY MINUTES LATER, we were still waiting on the pizza and I was cursing at my Trigonometry homework. Math despised me, almost as much as I despised it, so I grabbed my cell phone. There was one person in the school who could figure out a math problem like no one's business. Lucky for me, he lived next door.

"What's up?" John questioned, sounding amused as he answered the call.

"Math," I grumbled with annoyance. He chuckled and I sighed as I flipped through the pages for some decipherable answer to the problem. "It's like Mrs. Tuck finds the hardest problems in the book, then decides they'd be a great way to torture us. Will you come over and show me how to work the stupid thing? I'll pay you with pizza."

"Can't," he answered quickly. "I'm late for a date and if I don't get there in the next—I don't know—ten minutes, she's going to think I'm not interested. Rob just left. I'm sure he can swing by and help you out."

"Yeah, he'll help me out," I repeated sarcastically.

"I think he's over the whole 'I ran you over' thing."

"Sure he is." I pushed a hand through my blonde hair and blew out a sigh. "He's forgiven me and wants to be besties. That sounds exactly like him."

"Your sarcasm is annoying."

"So is your optimism." I glanced at the book again and decided any other attempts would be futile without John's help. "I could send you a picture and you could solve the problem for me," I volunteered. "I'll pay you later."

"Deal."

I grinned with relief. "Thanks, John."

"Thank me later."

He hung up and I snapped a shot of the problem. I was sending it off as someone rang the doorbell downstairs. After what felt like a millennium of waiting, my cheesy slices of goodness had arrived.

I took the stairs two at a time, elated at the prospect of pizza, but stopped in my tracks when I realized who was standing outside the door with the box in hand—Rob freaking Hood.

"Please tell me you aren't the new pizza boy," I groaned as I pulled open the door. "Because if you are, I'm preemptively complaining to the management."

"First time a girl's ever complained about me coming to their house," he mused. "Figured you'd be nicer after trying to kill me and all. Speaking of which, I think I need medical attention. My neck's sore."

He rubbed the back of his neck with his free hand and I watched wide-eyed as my pizza teetered on his forearm. This idiot was going to drop my food!

"Look," I started, retrieving the boxes before he felt compelled to toss them on the ground, "if you had any serious medical issues, you should've seen the school nurse at the time of the incident. Who's to say you didn't intentionally inflict additional harm upon yourself?"

"Like what? Throw myself down a flight of stairs?"

"Wouldn't put it past you."

I glanced around him for the real pizza guy and came up empty-handed. Rob identified my confusion and leaned against the doorway with a crooked smile. "Will was the delivery guy. Talked him into giving me the pizza for free." He *would* use his little brother as a means of worming his way into situations. I should've known the moment I saw him. "But, you can go ahead and pay me what you'd planned on paying him. You can consider it restitution."

"How do you even know that word?"

"I'm brilliant, duh." He winked and pushed himself away from the door. "Remember that the next time you decide to hit me with a car, would ya?"

"Sure thing. Who knows, maybe it'll be tomorrow."

"Funny. We'll see how well your sense of humor holds up." I knew it was a warning, but Hood pivoted and waved over his shoulder. "See you tomorrow, Annie."

I closed the door behind him, concerned at the threat, but more interested in the pizza. "Aunt Carla!" I hollered, setting the box on the counter.

"Finishing the wash," she answered. "Be there in a few."

I pulled two plates from the cabinet, put them down, and moved for the slices. When I opened the box, my jaw dropped.

Suddenly, I understood the meaning in Hood's words. The pizza, my greasy promise of happiness, was gone.

CHAPTER THREE

Theories

THE NEXT DAY, Hood was waiting for me at my locker.

It was like he was biding his time, looking for a glimpse of frustration to satiate his need for revenge, but I fiddled with the lock and did nothing more than bump him in the shoulder with the metal locker door. I could've hit him harder. Thinking about it now, I should have.

"So, how was dinner?" he inquired, straightening his posture as I pulled a book from inside. "Oh, wait. I can answer for you. It was delicious."

"You owe me a pizza," I grumbled.

"Considering you hit me with a car, we're even." His mouth

tugged upward as he peered inside my locker. Unable to poke fun at the belongings inside, he pulled his attention back to me. "Besides, I didn't eat the pizza by myself. I have a hearty appetite, but I was inclined to share." ·

"Let me guess: Will ate the rest?"

"Negative."

I rolled my eyes and shut the door. "Just know, the next time you steal from me will be your last. I already think you're the thief who's been robbing students. There's an article in the *Locksley Lowdown* if you'd like to read my justification."

"I read the article, and it had more holes than a slice of Swiss cheese."

"Fine. Why don't you tell me what I missed?"

He shook his head. "I'm not an idiot. Besides, thieves are sly. Giving you the info you missed would be stupid on my part, don't you think?"

"I know you did it, Hood."

"Think what you want." He patted the top of my head and I swatted his hand away. "We'll see how close you get to the truth."

I glared at him as he strolled down the hall. Rob Hood was an idiot if he thought I was going to let this go. The stunt he pulled with the pizza was more than enough to drive my need for justice.

The rest of my morning I spent contemplating ways to prove he was the thief. By the time lunch rolled around, my plan was almost perfected.

"Why do you look like that?" John asked, his brow furrowed as I sat in the chair across from him. When I shrugged, he took a bite of his chicken and shook his head. "As long as it doesn't involve me and won't have an effect on our A and P grade, do what you want. If I can help, let me know."

"I'll keep that in mind." I forked a bite of food into my mouth and scanned the lunchroom for Hood. When I didn't see him, I made a face. "Where's Rob?"

"He ran home to grab something. Why?"

"I had a few questions," I responded, sounding more aloof than I was. "Guess I'll ask them later." John answered me with a curious expression but I paid it no mind. This issue was between Hood and me. Bringing John into it wouldn't bode well for either of us.

"Can I ask you something?" he stated, pulling my attention away from the potatoes. "Before you answer, know I mean this in the least invasive way possible."

"Should I be worried?" He shook his head and I nodded in agreement. "Fine, ask away."

John sat forward, his fingers twined together atop the table. "Do you like him?" I did a double take at the absurd question and he let out a loud laugh. "Try not to look like I offended you beyond measure."

"I'm trying to figure out how and why you would even come to that assumption." I sat my fork down and stared at him. "Rob Hood is nothing but a troublemaker. He's annoying, awful, and between you and me, I think he's the school's resident thief."

John choked on a sip of water but I held up a hand to explain. It had to be Hood. It made total sense for him to be the culprit.

"Look at the evidence," I persisted. "Tristan Finn was the first person. His cell phone went missing during third period, the same day Rob conveniently disappeared during study hall."

"He was having stomach issues—"

"That was his alibi," I argued, "but it was a lie. He needed an excuse to exit the room and that's what he used."

John mulled it over for a minute, his lips pursed as he considered the words. "Okay, but how do you explain Richard Lyons's mysteriously missing football cleats? Rob was absent. There's no way he could've taken them."

"I think he came incognito," I rebutted.

John shot me a ludicrous expression and I went on the defensive.

"All he had to do was slip through one of the field house doors, dressed in something that covered his face. The athletics department issues hoodies. He could've tossed one on and lain low. No one would've noticed."

"A bit far-fetched, don't you think?"

I gave John a narrowed look. So much for theorizing with him. I should've known he'd take Hood's side. "And you wondered why I put the article out without letting you read it," I complained. "Had you read it beforehand, you would've pointed out all the reasons why my theories were flawed."

"I'm sorry, Annie, but you know I have a point." He gave me a sympathetic smile. "I tell you what. If it makes it better, I'll do some investigative work into the locker-room incident. I'm a team captain. I have a little clout with the guys."

"Uh-huh." I took a bite of food and chewed it slowly.

In the event he did find something, I doubted John would share it with me. He'd address the matter with Rob, fix it, then pretend it never happened. In some ways that made him a great friend. In other ways, it made him detrimental to my investigation.

That was fine. If John Little and Rob Hood wanted to make my life harder than it had to be, I would gather as much evidence as possible. Then, and only then, could I stand against the pair with my head held high and a theory that would put even the best detectives to shame.

Annie was getting down to business.

CHAPTER FOUR

Good Deeds

BEFORE HOOD, I'd never stalked a guy.

I didn't see the need in following someone with the intent to catch them wreaking havoc, but that miserable jerk took it upon himself to cause trouble and left me without any actions but to follow him. After all, I was a journalist. Being a member of the school's newspaper team pretty much obligated me to stalk.

My cold cup of coffee was nestled in the cup holder. Long gone was its warmth; the coffee had turned frigid within the first hour of my stakeout. Yes, I was that person who wasted coffee. I'm terrible, I know. Either way, I was so intent on catching him in the act that I'd neglected the caffeine.

Could I have gone in the house for more? Yes. Why didn't I? Two reasons:

One, Aunt Carla would've nominated me to help with the dishes.

Two, I wanted my trailing to be as easy as possible.

By already being in my car, I eliminated the possibility of Hood seeing me. Instead, he'd walk to his truck and pay no attention to the person who was hot on his trail. That would leave me with the simple task to drive after him and keep my eyes peeled for anything suspicious.

John's front door pulled open and I slumped into the leather seat, my blue eyes trained on the porch. Hood was carrying a bag, a duffel by the looks of it, and was talking animatedly with his friend as he crossed the lawn and headed for the truck.

I couldn't make out their words from the distance, but John headed back into the house as quick as he'd come and Hood was soon pulling his truck away from the curb. He drove slowly for a minute, as if he was preoccupied, then he sped up and disappeared into the dusk.

Once I was sure I could pull away unseen, I followed after him.

We drove through Locksley as the sky faded to a deeper blue, giving way to stars and a full moon. It was a nice night, perfect for investigating, and Hood came to a stop at a run-down building on the outskirts of town.

I recognized it immediately—everyone knew where the old school stood—and I made sure to park far enough away that my lights wouldn't be noticed. I'd have to go covert from here, but I could find out what he was doing and write a full exposé.

At least that's what I told myself.

I'd only made it halfway to his car when a hand latched onto my bicep and hauled me backward.

"Fancy seeing you here," a familiar voice chimed. "Do you

make it a habit to navigate country roads at night, or are you this crappy of a spy?"

I yanked my arm away and scowled at my nemesis. "I wouldn't have to follow you if you'd confess your guilt. You're up to no good, Hood."

"That rhymed."

"You're also annoying as ever." I placed my hands on my hips and drifted my gaze to the duffel. "What's in the bag? I'm sure it's loaded with stolen stuff."

"Has anyone ever said you're way too nosy for your own good? News flash: you are."

"Has anyone ever said you're not as cunning as you think? News flash: you *aren't*."

His brow arched at my statement, but I wasn't here to trade witticisms with him. I wanted to break this case wide open. The longer we went back and forth, the longer Hood had to formulate an escape.

"What's in the bag?" I repeated. "The missing cell phone? The stolen cleats? Oh, what about the—"

Hood tossed it at me, and I barely caught it before it hit the ground.

"It's canned food," he answered, irritated at my insinuations. "Any other allegations you'd like to throw around, or can I deliver this to the people who need it? I'm on a schedule and your meddling couldn't have come at a worse time."

"But . . . I . . . you . . ."

"I'm a nice guy? I help people who need it? Oh . . . I take pizza from the rich and deliver it to the poor?" I frowned at the last statement and he took the bag back. "In case you haven't noticed, you're judgmental. You also suck at being discreet." He turned in his place and slung the bag over his shoulder. "Wait here. If I start bringing people to the meet-up spot, they won't come anymore. They're . . . prideful."

"Who are they?"

He turned and walked backward, his tall silhouette melding with the dark. "Telling you would defeat the purpose of keeping it a secret. Wait here. We'll talk in a minute."

I huffed at his dismissal but stayed planted in my spot. If he was here to help people, I wasn't going to infringe on their privacy. That's why I stood there far longer than I should've, my eyes scanning the dark for any indication Hood was coming back.

I'd almost lost hope when I finally heard footsteps crunching along the old gravel road.

"Surprised you waited," he commented. "Thought you would've been long gone by now. I hoped for it, actually."

"I'm not going anywhere until you admit to taking the stuff from the school," I retorted. "I can be persistent. Don't make me go full journalist on you."

"Full journalist, huh? If this is an interrogation, I demand a bowl full of popcorn and tacos on standby. I like the crunchy tacos. The texture makes me giddy."

"Quit beating around the bush, Hood."

"Fine. Meet my list of demands or go without answers. The choice is yours." He winked and elbowed me as he sauntered toward my car. "We're taking yours, but I'm driving. Putting you behind a wheel is dangerous. I know firsthand."

"You're hilarious, but you're never getting my keys—" I paused as Rob twirled a set of car keys around his finger. My hand darted to my pants pocket, only to find it empty. "You little . . . you're totally the thief."

"Maybe, maybe not." He pulled open the driver's-side door and slid inside. "Get me some food and we'll weigh in on that matter. There's more than one way to define a thief."

I was gawking at him when he started the vehicle and turned on my brights. If his intent was to temporarily blind me, he was victorious. Little bubbles of light were still flashing across my vision as I fastened my seat belt.

Good deed or not, Hood was no hero. This was another prime example of his pettiness.

"Onward to taco-y places!" he declared.

"Onward to answers," I agreed.

CHAPTER FIVE

Perceptions

OKAY, HOOD. You've got your tacos. Spill the details or I'll take them back." Rob pulled the tacos closer to him, his hazel eyes wide as I pulled my phone from my pocket and sat it on the table. "I'm going to record this little . . . interview. Hope you don't mind."

"I do." He grabbed the phone and pulled off the back. "It wasn't a part of the agreement and I'm not stupid enough to go on the record about anything. I'm Rob Hood, babe. You should know better." After pulling out the battery, he slid the phone across the table and grabbed a taco. "Proceed with your first question, but I retain the right to refuse an answer."

I grumbled for a moment at his stubbornness, and at the fact that I had a phone old enough to dismantle like that, but then I sat forward and stared at him dead-on. "Did you take the stuff from the school? If so, why and where is it?"

"Whoa." He crammed a taco into his mouth and shook his head. "Someone's eager for info. Technically, I didn't steal anything, but then again stealing is a broad description of the action."

"So you were involved?"

"Not necessarily." I shot him an unamused look but he shrugged. "I answered your question. Lose the death glares, or it'll be the last answer you get. Girls are so hormonal, I swear."

I yanked a taco from the pile and his jaw dropped.

"Hey—that's a supreme!"

"Skirting the info is *supremely* annoying, Hood." I popped off the wrapper and shoved it into my mouth. Hood looked like he was two seconds from a meltdown. Good, my point had been made.

"Now," I started, trying to maintain a proper, ladylike demeanor with half a crunchy taco in my mouth. "Would you care to expand your answer? I need something that sounds less like riddles and more like facts."

"Too bad." He relaxed in his chair and smirked at me. His body language spoke volumes. "You might have won the taco war, but I've still got the advantage. Eat more of my food, and see how much I'm willing to cooperate."

I cursed him internally but chose not to repeat the mental swearing. If I pissed him off too much, I'd screw myself out of anything close to an answer. Then I'd be stuck with little to go off of and nothing to write.

Unfortunately for me, Hood seemed more content to eat than expand upon his answer.

Stupid jerk.

"Could we get quesadillas for the road?" he asked after a long pause. "I've always been a dining-while-driving kind of guy."

"If you eat in my car, my dad will have a fit," I griped. "No quesadillas, and for that matter no more driving. Give me the keys."

"Nope."

"I will pour this glass of soda on your head. Don't test me."

He blew out a long breath but kept my keys. "Tell you what, you let me drive back to my truck and I'll fill you in on the way."

"No," I maintained. "You were supposed to give me answers after I bought you food. If you think I'm agreeing to another one of your suggestions, without a sufficient guarantee you'll tell me what's going on, you're out of your mind."

"You always this hostile?" he mused.

"Only when I'm around you." He seemed flattered by the comment, and I let out an audible groan. "If you find it funny, stay your butt here. When I get back to your truck, I'll go through it and find the answers alone."

"Giving up your game plan? Not very smart, Annie."

"Just tell me what's going on."

"Curiosity killed the cat, you know?"

I slid my chair back and stood. I was beyond exasperated and filled to my daily limit of being around Rob. At this point, I would've had more success calling one of those television psychics and asking her. If nothing else, she'd be a ton more personable.

He obviously didn't understand my need to get away from him. "I still have your keys," he pointed out, halfway through my trek to the car. "It'll be hard to access, locked." I shifted, not missing the way his eyes twinkled with mischief as I stalked straight toward him. "You're more stubborn than I anticipated," he continued. "Haven't decided if that's a good thing or a bad one."

"You listen to me," I began, wagging my finger at him with all the attitude I could muster. "You didn't drag me all the way here to not hold up your end of the bargain, so cut the crap and tell me what you're up to. I know there's something, Hood. I wasn't born yesterday and anyone who's ever been around you can attest to your less-than-admirable personality traits."

"Ooh, those are fighting words. Is it my turn to emphasize your flaws?"

I was about to launch at him when a car stopped beside us and put a damper on my plans.

Yelling at someone in front of the sheriff wasn't my parents' idea of acting presentable. No matter, I'd yell at Rob later.

"Miss Mayes," Sheriff Nott greeted, his window rolled down. "Hood." His brown eyes flickered from Rob, to me, then back to Rob. "You two are out a bit late, don't you think?"

"Nope. I actually thought we'd—"

"Head home now," I added, cutting off the idiot beside me. Sheriff Nott nodded, but kept his focus on Rob.

Rob, however, kept an unwavering gaze on me. "Annie's full of crap," he commented with a smile, "but whatevs. We'll go with that if she wants." I could feel my cheeks burning with embarrassment as he grabbed my hand. "See you around, Sheriff."

"Sooner than you might like." He rolled up the window, but his comment had done what it intended—it captured Hood's attention.

"He's ancient," Hood stated as he shoved the key into the ignition. "It's a bit late, don't you think?"

The latter statement was said in the same tone the sheriff used, and I hated to admit it, but I laughed. It was hard not to.

"*Ahh*, she *does* have a sense of humor," Hood noted. "Nice to know your stuffy family hasn't deprived you of laughter."

"I thank my aunt for that every day," I said.

He paused, his hand on the gear shift as he contemplated me over the console. I couldn't figure out what was going on in his messed-up mind, but he didn't let me stew on it too long. He took my battery out of his pocket and tossed it at me instead.

"I still want answers," I reminded him as I pulled my phone out and put the battery in. "Fair is fair, and you made a promise. You can't go back on your word."

"Who says I'm a man of my word?" he countered. "Everyone writes me off as a delinquent. Delinquents rarely do anything they said they would."

"Delinquents don't feed the poor either, Hood."

There was a long silence as Rob steered us toward the outskirts of town, past the old buildings of Locksley, and onward to the old, run-down school.

It wasn't until he put the car in park that he spoke.

"People have different perceptions of thievery," he explained, unclicking the seat belt from the holder. "Some view it as malicious and ill-willed, but if a person's motives are pure, perhaps the theft was justified."

"Thievery is never justified," I argued.

"Most of the time," he added, "but sometimes the thieves are actually the good guys in disguise."

He pushed open the driver's-side door and stepped into the cool night air. "Consider it, Annie. If you still feel the same tomorrow, ask me again. I'll approach it from a different angle." Rob winked and pivoted toward me, but I was quick to exit the car.

"Will anything else go missing between now and then?" I questioned.

"Depends on the bad guys. Have a nice night."

CHAPTER SIX

Thieves

*H*OOD TOLD ME to find him if I still felt the same, but his views on thievery were a bit one-sided. That made sense if he was the thief I thought him to be, which was why I opted for a different source of info.

Richard Lyons was the unfortunate victim of my focus. He was a freshman, average looking, and had a high enough IQ to shame the entire student body. He also had a sense of humor that was underappreciated. The kid could tell a joke, but it wasn't enough to pull him from the lower end of the social hierarchy. I guess that's why my appearance at his locker raised a red flag.

His brow knit together curiously. "What did I do?"

"Nothing," I assured. "I needed to ask you a few more questions about your missing cleats. There's still loose ends to tie up and you're the best informant I have." He shifted his weight uncomfortably, but I didn't hesitate. "The day your cleats went missing, did you see anyone suspicious lurking around the locker room?"

He shook his head quickly. "The team was there, but that's it. I was one of the first ones in there, too. The cleats were gone before anyone arrived."

"And do you know anyone who would've been motivated to take your cleats?"

He shrugged as his arms came to rest across his chest. "Sometimes the upperclassmen pull pranks, but they've never stolen anything. They aim for embarrassment, not thievery."

"Which upperclassmen?"

"All of them."

I bit my lip and cast a glance around the rapidly emptying hallway. Though I suspected Rob, he was one of many seniors on the team. I needed something more substantial to point him out.

"Who else have they pranked?"

"As of right now, just Tristan Finn and me. Tristan's phone was taken, but there are rumors it was for his own good. Supposedly, a mass text was going to be sent, but that's hearsay. I don't know. No one ever gives me accurate information."

"I can relate." I released a quick breath. "Where did you hear about the text?"

"They're just rumors," he repeated.

"Nope, they're a clue."

He looked at me doubtfully but answered anyway. "Check with John Little. He was the last one to mention it, and he's less likely to get hassled about it than me." The bell rang and Richard frowned at the sound. "I've got to go, Annie. Mrs. Tuck gives detentions if you're late."

He passed by without another word, but the conversation wasn't in vain. If John had information to give, I'd get it out of him one way or another.

I trounced down the hall to Anatomy and Physiology, contemplating ways to drag the information out of him, and had almost reached class when I nearly walked into a rotund individual who rounded the corner with my principal in tow.

Sheriff Nott, out of place walking the halls of the school, paid me little mind as he continued on with his conversation. "The bait's set, Chutney. Since the thief struck the football team twice, I have no doubt he'll do it again. Mark my words, by the end of the day we'll have him booked and boarded at the juvenile detention center."

The pair of them proceeded to walk, and I hastened my pace. If John was involved with this in any way, I needed to get to the bottom of it. The sooner that happened, the better.

When I entered the classroom moments later, John lifted his attention from his textbook and shot me a look of relief. I returned it with a less-than-thrilled expression.

"I don't think she'll mark you tardy," he commented, referencing the substitute. "She had a hard enough time turning on the board. Trying to access the online roster would be way out of her realm of functioning and—"

"If you're involved with the football team's missing stuff, you'd better tell me now," I interrupted. John's lips pursed, but I forged ahead. "If you don't, I will let you and the nimwit you call a best friend get busted."

"What are you talking about?" His expression immediately shifted from defensive to concerned. "Get busted how?"

"No," I said. "You aren't getting answers until I get my own. Hood is a master of deflection, but I know you and you know you can trust me. Spill it or I refuse to help."

He mulled it over for a minute, his blue eyes studying me intently. Then, quietly, he spoke. "If I tell you, you have to keep it quiet," he whispered. "That means you bench your journalist side and approach this as a friend."

"I'm both."

He was serious, the most serious I'd ever seen him, and it was unsettling. "You can't write about this," he insisted. "If you do, the wrong people will end up with the information and it'll cause more damage than good."

"Damage how?"

He shook his head. "Not here; too many people could hear."

"Lunch?" I volunteered.

"Lunch," he agreed.

CHAPTER SEVEN

Caught

ROB'S BUSY," John stated, placing his tray on the table across from me, "but trust me when I say I speak for him too." I eyed him suspiciously, trying to figure out how and why Rob was absent. It was another check in Hood's list of suspicious actions.

"We're behind everything," he continued, low enough he was barely audible. "Congrats on your investigative skills. By the way, Rob said you tailed him last night. He wasn't doing anything bad . . ."

"He was delivering canned goods to people in need," I relayed. "Spare me the lecture. I already know he did at least one thing worthy of applause."

"He's done more than one thing," John added. I arched a brow and he nodded. "All these thefts people have been going on about weren't malicious. They were attempts to save the freshmen from unneeded humiliation."

"Save them how?"

John sat forward and let out a slow smile. "It's a yearly thing done around here, but it stays relatively under wraps. In a nutshell, the seniors pick out a handful of freshmen to prank. It's an initiation of sorts, but last year it was a bit harsher than usual and this year even more so. Rob, the thief of Locksley High as he's better known, has been keeping things from escalating."

"If a person's motives are pure, perhaps the theft was justified . . ." I replayed the words as I stared at John.

"It was better than ratting them out to the coach," he concluded. "This way, the freshmen are spared and the seniors don't get in trouble. It seemed like the lesser of two evils."

"Until one of you gets caught." I pinched the bridge of my nose and groaned. "Where is he?" I asked again, hoping for a better answer than the one John had given me before.

"The locker room."

"Then we need to find him before Sheriff Nott and Principal Chutney do."

We exited the school as quickly as we could and navigated the short trek to the field house. When we pushed through the back door, we were greeted with "John, tell me you didn't."

Hood straightened, his eyes trained on his friend as he held a jockstrap in one hand and the team's medical bag in the other. He seemed less than amused, primarily at the sight of me, and let out an exaggerated sigh.

"Have you lost your mind? She'll rat us out!"

John placed a finger to his mouth to signal Hood's silence. "Shh. They're probably here."

"Don't *shh* me!"

"Hush," I urged. Hood's eyes widened with challenge. "We need to go. It's a trap."

"What's a trap?" he countered. "The laptop they think I'm going to take, or the cameras they set up to catch me?" I scowled and he mimicked the look. "You're a few minutes late with your warning, but I've been doing this long enough to figure it out on my own. I need a few more minutes to get rid of this thing. Then I'll be on my merry way."

"They messed with the jockstrap?" John motioned toward

the white thing in Hood's hand, scoffing in disbelief. "Poor guy. He would've been sore for days."

"No kidding." Rob tossed the article of clothing over his shoulder and indicated the medical bag. "I'm taking this too. If the team notices the strap's missing, they're likely to pour the muscle cream all over his tights or jersey instead. For that matter, they might decide to pick another victim. I'd be back at this tomorrow if they did."

"You're right," John agreed. "Just hurry up and—"

The locker room door swung open and John grabbed me as Principal Chutney and Sheriff Nott stormed inside.

"Out the back door, now!"

I hurried through it and escaped as the words "Caught you in the act!" flew from the accusatory sheriff.

The next string of events I missed, primarily because the building's metal walls left me without ample means to eavesdrop, but I was front and center as Sheriff Nott and Principal Chutney paraded the pair out of the field house and toward the school.

CHAPTER EIGHT
Help

TWICE IN ONE DAY? Should I be happy or worried?"

I forced a smile as Richard watched me with a frown. He was my first stop after watching Hood and John get hauled away from the field house. If anyone could help me get them out of this, it was the freshman with the only real information I'd been able to find.

"I need your help," I answered quickly.

I rattled off what happened mere minutes before, and Richard's jaw dropped until he was staring at me, dumbfounded. "You're telling me Hood stole my cleats to help me? What planet are you living on?"

"It's the truth."

His eyes narrowed as he contemplated the idea. It was far-fetched, especially given Hood's ability to come off as a jerk, but for this to work I had to get Richard on my side. If he wouldn't believe Hood's real intentions and John's involvement in it, no one would.

"Come on," I persisted. "You're a member of the team. You can't tell me you haven't heard anything about the seniors pranking the freshmen."

"I already told you, Annie. No one tells me anything. I'm never in the loop." He sighed and pushed a hand through his curly hair, his mouth downturned at the admission.

This was it; John and Hood were officially screwed. Maybe I could find time to visit them behind bars.

I swore and moved past, trying to formulate another plan to get the pair of them out of trouble, but Richard latched onto my arm. "You're sure they were helping me?" When I nodded, he inhaled sharply. "I might or might not be able to track down another pair of cleats."

"But . . . you . . ."

"If I claim they're the ones I lost, maybe it'll get Rob and John off the hook." He darted a glance around the hallway. "I can get in, but I need you to watch my back. If I end up in the principal's office with them, I'm throwing you under the bus too."

"Fair enough."

"I know." He shifted his backpack and headed down the hall. "If we're going to strike, we need to do it while Nott and Chutney are preoccupied. You ready?"

"As ready as I'll ever be."

We hurried to the locker room I'd escaped earlier. Richard was stealth, weaving around corners and double-checking for anyone who might be lingering around, and once he was sure the coast was clear he pointed at the cameras Hood had supposedly taken care of.

"Check those. It'll be hard to claim our innocence if they've got video proof we're involved."

I beelined for one of the cameras, fidgeted with the buttons for a minute, and was sure it was off. By the time I was done, Richard had pulled open the coach's drawer and retrieved a small golden key.

"Wait here. I'll grab a pair from the storage closet. If anyone comes, and I mean anyone, you'd better figure out a way to get us out of trouble."

"I'm a journalist for a reason," I remarked. "If I wasn't good with words, I wouldn't have chosen that path."

He nodded in understanding and rushed out of the locker room. I, however, was left to stand there in the open while I waited for his return.

A few minutes later, the door creaked open and I dodged behind a locker. When Richard's head of curly brown hair passed by, I breathed a sigh of relief and stepped back into the open.

"Did you get them?" I asked.

When he held out a pair of cleats tied together by the laces, I could've hugged him.

"You, Richard Lyons, are the best freshman I know."

"Make sure you remember that."

"Believe me, I will."

CHAPTER NINE

Hooded

*Y*OU'RE LUCKY, HOOD."

"I know. Thanks for the reassurance." Rob smirked as he exited the principal's office, clearly amused with himself. Sheriff Nott, on the other hand, looked less than thrilled to be letting him go.

"I still don't buy that crap about your jockstrap," Nott grumbled, "but I can't prove it isn't yours, either."

"Interesting," Rob hummed. "It may be because I'm innocent."

"You aren't innocent. Your story is flawed, and the cleats were a lucky break. Shame they were found." He glared at Rob as he spoke. "Today you might have gotten off the hook, but I will get you. When that day comes, you can rest assured I'll be the one to haul you across town."

"Nott, your concern warms my heart."

John nudged Hood along, confusion written on his face. I,

however, stood there full of pride. The pair of them owed me for my unrivaled skills. Eventually, I would collect.

"Why are you smiling like that?" Rob asked, his gaze drifting from me to Richard. "And what is he doing here?"

"We," I answered, motioning toward Richard, "are the reason you two are out of trouble. You can thank us now, or thank us later, but you'll thank us either way."

"Feisty, feisty," Rob said, but when John landed an elbow in his side, he winced and exclaimed, "What? I meant it as a compliment!"

John ignored his friend. "Thank you both. My parents would have a conniption fit if we actually ended up with charges. Rob thanks you too. He won't say it because he's incapable of thanking anyone, but he knows you did him a solid."

"Um, Rob is standing here and fully capable of offering his own thanks," Hood complained.

John rolled his eyes, but Hood ignored him and ambled down the hall. I wasn't surprised he'd play off our involvement in his rescue. He was far too arrogant to acknowledge anyone's help.

"You're welcome too, Hood," I stated, not willing to let him get away so easy. "We saved you. You know it. We know it. You might as well admit it and get it over with."

Rob pivoted with a smile pasted to his face. "Admit what?" When I continued to look at him, he shrugged. "I do the saving, remember?"

"Right," I agreed. "You take from the rich, give to the poor, and occasionally protect the freshmen from embarrassment. Did I miss anything?"

"Nope. I'd say that's a pretty fair assessment."

"He calls it 'getting hooded,'" John commented from beside me. "We're thinking of a better name, but that's what he insists on."

"Hooded?" I repeated. "That's the best you could do?"

"It's witty," Rob defended, "and call it what you want, but at the end of the day the purpose remains the same. I help those who can't help themselves. It's admirable, if I do say so myself."

"Locksley's most notorious delinquent is actually a good guy in disguise," I mused. "Who would've thought? By the way, your reputation is ruined now that I know. Never again will you be intimidating. Congratulations."

"Yeah, yeah. Keep it a secret and I get to keep my bad-boy status intact. What do you say?"

"Me? Keep your alter ego a secret? Why would I do that?"

"Because I'm Rob Hood, babe," he said, putting his arm around my shoulder. "The man, the myth, the mystery."

Sleeping Beauty Syndrome

ali novak

CHAPTER ONE

Asleep

I **WAKE TO A DARKNESS** *so thick I feel it pressing against my chest.*

I don't know where I am except that it's underground somewhere. The air is damp and heavy with the smell of earth and decay. Beneath me is a bed of dirt, and twisting roots dig into my back like the knobby hands of an old woman.

Dread traces an icy claw down my spine. Even without my sight, I know I am not alone. There is someone else, something else, lurking in the shadows that surround me.

I hold my breath and pray the feeling will pass, but then I hear it—a low, throaty growl. The sound jolts through me like a strike of lightning, and I scramble to my feet. Arms extended in front of me, I stretch and reach until I find what must be a rock wall. It's jagged and slick with moisture, and yet it's my only grounding element. I race forward along it, moving as fast as the dark and my feet will allow, until the suffocating blackness recedes.

When I emerge from the mouth of a cave and spill into a forest, I gulp down the first fresh air I've had since waking. My lungs burn, and I don't know if it's from the frigid air or running. Maybe it's from the fear. All around me, the trees are dipped in the silver of the moon.

They're breathtakingly beautiful.

But I still don't feel safe.

I never feel safe anymore.

CHAPTER TWO

Awake

F RIDAY MORNING.

Right now I should be cursing my alarm clock. Dragging myself out of bed so I don't miss the nine a.m. lecture that I thought was a good idea those many weeks ago. I should be nursing a hangover from last night and tugging on a sweatshirt and yoga pants, the uniform of college girls everywhere.

But I'm not. Instead, I'm sitting on the couch in my mom's Upper West Side apartment, trying to find something entertaining on Netflix. Which is a major challenge. I've already seen everything good. For a moment, I consider *Gilmore Girls*, but I've already watched all seven seasons . . . *twice*.

Millie glides into the kitchen wearing what she calls her work armor: stilettos and Giorgio Armani blazer. I haven't called her Mom since Dad left. Probably because she's been more of a businesswoman than a mother.

"Morning, darling. You're up early," she greets.

"And you're late," I respond. I don't tell her that I never went to bed. She wants me to stick to a normal routine since sleep deprivation can trigger an episode, but "normal" and I don't coexist anymore.

"Didn't I tell you?" she says, pulling a carton of orange juice from the fridge. "I'll be in London for the weekend. My flight's at eleven."

Millie's the best event planner in New York City, but she travels all over the world for her clients. Last week she did a wedding in Tokyo, and the week before that it was LA for a charity ball. Her schedule has been so hectic lately, she hasn't bothered telling me the whens and wheres of her job.

Not sure how to respond, I pick at a snag in my sweater. I'm not upset that she's leaving, but I'm not throwing confetti either. Because if she's gone, that means—

"Don't worry. Hannah will stay here until I get back."

My shoulders slump. *"Fantastic."*

"Her last class ends at three," Millie says, oblivious to my sarcasm. "Think you'll be okay until then?"

I press my lips together and look away. When I'm not in an episode, I don't need to be watched like a child. I'm a perfectly healthy adult who can take care of herself—something Millie has yet to grasp. It's been two years since my diagnosis and she still doesn't have a thorough understanding of my condition. I don't think she ever intends to really try to, either.

"Rory?"

"She doesn't need to come home. It's only three days. I'll be fine."

Hannah is a freshman at NYU, and I hate that my problems are affecting her life almost as much as they do my own. She should be hanging out with her friends on the track team or partying with her roommate. I'm afraid if she spends one more weekend here playing Monopoly and having Harry Potter movie marathons, she'll resent me. And more than the guilt and fear, I have this overwhelming sense of shame.

No twenty-one-year-old wants to be babysat by their little sister.

"Don't be ridiculous, Rory," Millie scoffs at me over her glass of vitamin C. "I'm not leaving you unsupervised."

A sigh escapes my lips and I turn toward the window. There's a breathtaking view of Central Park from my spot in the living room. Sometimes I like to pretend I've been whisked away to another land, and that the stretch of greenery below is an enchanted forest.

I suppose that makes this apartment my tower prison.

CHAPTER THREE

Asleep

*T*HE SOUND OF A BLARING HORN *wakes me, and I open my eyes in a field of roses.*

It's nighttime. The stars hang low in the sky, like fireflies frozen in time, and the air is sweet and humid. A gentle breeze sweeps across the meadow, making the flowers ripple and sway.

Everything seems peaceful, but my skin is prickling. I know in my gut something isn't right.

The horn blasts again. Only, it's not a horn. It's a blood-curdling roar that rips through the dark.

I throw my head back and blink. Soaring above me is a creature with scaled wings and a tail dripping in spikes. A dinosaur brought back to life. A dragon. I watch for a horrified moment as it glides over the moon.

How is this real?

. . . Is it real?

Another thundering roar answers my question.

A painful feeling rises in my chest, and I realize a moment too late that what I'm hearing is my own scream. The dragon twists toward me before tucking its wings and falling out of the sky with the precision of a dive-bomber. I jump to my feet. Thorns as thick as branches reach out to grab me, tearing at my skin as I flee. They slice my arms and legs, and I leave behind drops of blood like a trail of rose petals.

Faster, I urge my legs. Faster, faster!

But it's too late—I can already feel the dragon's hot breath on the back of my neck.

CHAPTER FOUR

Awake

THERE ARE ONLY TWO THINGS in this world that truly terrify me.

The first is sleep and the hallucinations that accompany it. The second, and more prominent, of my fears is waking up—because what if I do and another month of my life has slipped away, just like the last time and the time before that?

I wasn't always like this, afraid of something as trivial and ordinary as sleeping. But a few weeks after I turned nineteen, I came down with the flu. Instead of recovering, I became increasingly exhausted. I remember skipping a Shakespeare lecture one afternoon to catch up on some sleep, hoping that when I woke I'd feel better. But the next time I opened my eyes, fifteen days of my life had disappeared.

It was my first KLS episode.

KLS, Kleine-Levin syndrome, is a rare sleep disorder. It's characterized by episodic bouts of hypersomnia along with cognitive and behavioral problems. The media, when they run one of those "Hey—a Rare Disorder!" stories, call it Sleeping Beauty syndrome. But nothing about my condition resembles a fairy tale. It's more like being trapped in a repetitive nightmare.

During an episode, I can sleep anywhere from twelve to twenty hours a day and only "wake up" to eat and use the bathroom. But even when my eyes are open, my brain is never fully awake.

When I'm in an episode, I can't do anything: leave the apartment, shower, cook my own food. I can't hold a conversation, or even think, for that matter. I don't act or feel like myself. I say things I don't mean. I'm always famished, but too exhausted to eat. I'm a prisoner inside my own body, as if someone else has taken control. And that's only in the fleeting moments when I'm awake—for the rest of the time, it's as if I don't exist.

My old college roommate, Beth, was the one who found me during my original episode. Unable to wake me for class, she panicked and called an ambulance, thinking I'd slipped into a coma. Nobody at the hospital could figure out what was wrong with me, why I wouldn't wake up. My mom was even less inclined to believe that something was actually the matter. She thought I was faking to get out of my exams.

Of course, I don't remember any of that. I hardly ever remember what happens during my episodes. It's as if my brain is wiped clean. After that, it took two more occurrences, an MRI, and a revolving door of doctors before I received my diagnosis.

For me, the worst part about KLS is the division it creates between myself and the real world. While having an episode, it's impossible for me to tell whether I'm dreaming or hallucinating—or if I'm even alive. Everything about my surroundings seems wrong, distorted somehow.

Nothing seems real.

But nothing is a dream. It's a constant nightmare.

CHAPTER FIVE

Asleep

W HEN I WAKE, I'm lying at the edge of a thorn thicket.

But these aren't normal thorns. They're as wide and as long as hunting knives, swords even, and when I climb to my feet, I realize that the tangled bushes are taller than me.

The panic of not knowing where I am lodges in the back of my throat, and for a moment, I can't get any air into my lungs. It's as if I've swallowed a rock. A few feet to my left is a boulder, and I clamber up to get my bearings. The thicket stretches farther than I imagined, like an ocean of broken glass. At its center sits a stone castle with three crumbling towers, still trying to stretch toward the moon.

A sudden shadow passes over the fortress, and when I crane my neck back, my heart drops like a stone. The dragon has returned. As if to welcome me back to her domain, she does a lazy loop in the air and lets out a tremendous roar. I nearly fall off my rock when a blast of fire streams past her jaw. Then, with a flick of her tail and another loop, she's diving toward me, dropping out of the sky at an alarming pace.

I need somewhere to hide. Somewhere the dragon's flaming kiss can't reach me. Looking around, I know there's only one place that can offer any sort of protection. The castle.

I take a deep breath and plunge into the razor-sharp labyrinth.

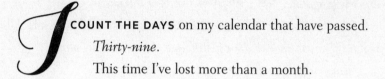

CHAPTER SIX

Awake

I COUNT THE DAYS on my calendar that have passed.

Thirty-nine.

This time I've lost more than a month.

CHAPTER SEVEN

Asleep

I SHIVER AWAKE.

The bed below me is as hard and freezing as a slab of ice cut from a winter lake. A second later I understand why. I'm not in bed, but lying on the cold, hard ground of the castle entrance hall.

Like the rest of my nightmare world, this place is not inviting, to say the least.

The air tastes stale, and I feel as if I've been sealed inside a crypt, forced to breathe in the powdered bones of the dead. Cobwebs drip from pillars like drapery, and the vaulted ceiling is clouded in shadow.

This place must have been magnificent, I think. At one point . . .

As if the castle can hear my thoughts, the curtain between me and the afterlife is lifted, and I can see them—the gentry who once lived here, dancing and laughing, adorned in the finest silk and jewels. They swept across the room like phantoms, fading in and out of existence. Another involuntary shiver rips down my spine. I don't belong here. Not with these spirits of the past.

I back out of the room as stealthily as possible, but before I reach the towering oak door behind me, I hear it—my name.

"Rory," a voice calls.

Every muscle in my body tenses. Besides the ghosts, I thought I was alone.

"Rory," the voice sounds again. "Rory Briar."

It's deep and silvery. A man's voice.

I glance around, wild with fear, and on my second pass of the room, I spot him. How I ever overlooked such a presence is mystifying. He stands across the entrance hall, smiling down at me from atop a flight of stairs. Golden warmth radiates from every inch of his body, as if he's bottled up the sun and slipped it into his pocket. Just the sight of him makes my breath catch, and a feeling I've nearly forgotten blooms in my chest like a rosebud in spring—safety.

In this place of darkness, he is a prince of light.

CHAPTER EIGHT

Awake

I MUST STILL BE DREAMING, because when I open my eyes, the most beautiful guy I've ever seen is gazing down at me. His dark hair is wavy and thick in a way that makes me want to run my fingers through it. And his eyes. A light brown, almost golden color that reminds me of liquid amber. Something about him is familiar, although I'm positive we've never met. It's almost as if I know him from a dream.

A smile jumps onto his lips when he notices I'm awake.

"Hey, Rory!" he says, and his level of enthusiasm is daunting. "Welcome back to the world of the living."

I want to say something witty to this beautiful creature, something that will keep the smile on his face, but when I open my mouth, "Who the hell are you?" is what comes out.

It's Kleine-Levin speaking, not me. That's how it normally is with KLS patients, the filter in our heads is switched off. I may have woken up, but my episode isn't over yet. It takes a few days to come down from, time when the wall between myself and the real world has yet to be lifted.

Despite my rude greeting, his smile doesn't falter. "I'm Phil."

"What are you doing in my bedroom, *Phil*?"

Good looks don't make up for the fact that it's insanely creepy waking up to a stranger hovering over me.

He must realize this, because he takes a few steps back and plops into my computer chair. "I was about to try and get you to eat something. It's been twenty-two hours since you last had anything," he answers. "But you're up on your own. That's great news!"

He knows about my condition, I realize, and warning bells instantly go off in my head. *Is he . . . taking care of me?*

"Where's my sister?" I demand, pushing myself up into a sitting position.

Phil hesitates, but then says, "She left for Germany last week."

His answer makes my heart twist. I know Hannah planned to spend her summer semester abroad, but she wasn't supposed to leave until May first. I quickly count the days in my head. Last time I was awake it was March . . . which means I've lost two months of time. My longest episode yet.

"What about Mil—my mother?" I ask. "Where is my mom?" She promised to cut back at work, only accepting jobs in New York in order to look after me while Hannah was away.

"Chicago, I think. She's so busy, it's hard to keep track."

"You mean—she's *working* while I've been out?"

"Well, yeah. Isn't that normal?"

My lips purse. "I suppose it is."

God. I should've known better than to trust her, I think to myself. Because if there is one thing about my mom I can count on, it's that she will always be more dedicated to her job than to me. It wasn't always like this, but Millie threw herself into her work once Dad was gone. I forgave so many things because of her broken heart, but I don't know that I can let this go—that *she left me.*

"So . . . I take it she hired you as my caregiver?" I ask, uncomfortable with the situation. Just thinking about Phil helping me do something as simple as eating—or anything, for that matter—makes the tips of my ears burn. Plus, I'm not wearing a bra and haven't showered in God knows how long.

I really hope he hasn't sponge-bathed me . . .

Raising my arm as stealthily as possible, I take a whiff and—*yuck!* Okay, that answers that question.

"Yup," Phil says, drumming both hands against his legs.

"Right now I'm studying to become a nurse. I need real-world experience outside of a hospital to graduate, so this was the perfect opportunity for me."

He's only trying to be friendly, but a bitter tang fills my mouth. "Glad my *real-world* problem is helping you earn a degree," I tell him. I know I sound bitter, which is probably because I am. Ever since I was little, I've dreamed of becoming a doctor. KLS robbed me of that future. I tried to go to college, but after my first episode I realized it would've been impossible for me to get the grades I needed for med school with all the time I'd miss.

Phil's hands instantly go still. "Rory, I didn't mean it like that."

"I can't believe she pawned me off on a total stranger," I mutter, shaking my head in disbelief.

"Oh, don't worry. I know your mom," he says, as if that makes it okay. "I work part-time for Beyond Bread. The catering company she always hires for her New York events? I don't have any aspirations to go into the catering business, but the gig pays well and I'm putting myself through school, so a little extra cash never hurts. Anyway, I was part of a crew who catered the silent auction your mom planned at the Plaza two nights ago. We ran into each other, got talking, and when she heard I was in nursing school, she offered me this job."

"That's a wonderful story," I say, trying as best as possible to control my tone. Which is almost impossible since I'm seething on the inside. "But it doesn't make up for the fact that I don't know you. Did you ever stop to think how traumatizing it might be for me to be left alone with a stranger when I'm not in my right mind?"

Cringing, Phil rakes a hand through his thick waves. "It's not like I'm totally incompetent. I have my EMT certification," he says. "And I told your mom it wasn't a good idea for me to start before we met properly, but she insisted you'd be fine. I think she was worried about a gala something-or-other, so she wouldn't take no for an answer."

"No offense, but how's that supposed to make me feel any better?" I ask. He opens his mouth to respond, but I hold up my hand. "I know you're only doing the job you were hired for, but can you please get out of my room? I just want to be alone right now."

Shoulders slumping, he nods. "Yeah, sure."

I watch in silence as Phil stands and exits into the hall, closing the door behind him. Once he's gone, I collapse backward onto my pillow. My brain is sluggish, still waking up from its sixty-day nap, and it takes me a while to process everything that's happened. When it finally hits me that my mother has abandoned me, tears gather in my eyes like fluid crystal.

I've lost so much to my condition: huge chunks of my life that I can never get back, a future career in medicine. And now it's clear I'll lose people too. First it was my boyfriend, Nick, who wasn't interested in waiting around for Sleeping Beauty. Then Hannah, who left so she didn't have to babysit me anymore. Now even Millie is gone.

I know I'm bitter, but I hate KLS so much. It takes and it takes and it takes. I don't know if I have anything left to give.

CHAPTER NINE

Awake

THERE'S AN AUDIBLE GASP from the other end of the phone. "She did not."

"Yup. Millie's in Chicago right now."

Hannah is quiet for a moment, but then whispers, "God, what a bitch."

This makes me feel a little bit better. After meeting Phil and learning that I'd been deserted, I needed to hear a familiar voice, one that would cheer me up. It's nearly midnight in Germany, but thankfully she answered my call.

"If I'd known she was going to dump you with the first random cater-waiter she ran into at a charity event," she continues, "I never would have—"

"Never would have what?" I interrupt. "Studied abroad? I'd have been pissed if you gave up this opportunity for me. You shouldn't have to keep making sacrifices for me. It was supposed to be Millie's turn." As sad as I am that Hannah left, she deserves this trip. I don't want to be responsible for holding her back.

"Thanks, Rory. That means a lot," she says. "But I'm still worried about you. I mean, you don't even know who this Phil guy is. What if he's a psychopath or something?"

I snort. "Don't worry. I still have a mean swing from my tennis days, and there's a racket buried somewhere at the back of my closet. I think I can handle one psychopath."

"Well, is he cute at least?"

"No," I tell her. "A more accurate description would be 'beyond gorgeous.'"

"Good." Hannah giggles. "Then I don't feel so bad for you anymore."

⁓⟡⁓

AFTER SAYING GOOD-BYE to Hannah and taking a much-needed shower, I wander into the kitchen looking for something to eat. The TV is blaring in the living room, and I look over to find Phil sprawled out on the couch. His T-shirt and socks are strewn across the floor as if he tossed them any which way, and six Chinese takeout containers clutter the coffee table, along with multiple soda cans.

Sure, just make yourself at home . . .

He's watching a baseball game, the Yankees versus some team I don't recognize. When one of the players gets a hit, he sits up slightly, leaning toward the screen as if a closer view will help the outcome. Two seconds later, he throws his hands up in the air.

"Are you freaking kidding me?" he shouts. "He was clearly safe!" Then, after a rude gesture to the TV, he slumps back into the cushions.

"Comfortable?" I ask, stepping into the room and crossing my arms. I want to tell him he can go home now, that I don't need him anymore, but given our last conversation, I don't want to be too rude.

"Oh! Hey, Rory." Phil sits up and flashes me a full-face smile. Clearly our earlier encounter didn't deter his amiability. "How you feeling? Hungry, I hope. Your mom mentioned that

Jade Kitchen is your favorite takeout, but I don't know what you like, so I just ordered a little bit of everything."

"Oh." I'm completely taken aback by his thoughtfulness. "Um, thanks."

I peek at Phil's bare chest as I cross the room. *Maybe this won't be so bad*, I think. But when I move around the couch and see what's lying at his feet, I freeze.

"What the hell is that?" I asked, pointing at the big white mop of hair that's drooling on the floor.

"This is Samson," he says, reaching down and scratching the creature behind the ears. "Haven't you ever seen a dog before?"

I shoot Phil a pointed look. "Don't be a smart-ass. What I meant was, why is it here?" Millie would have a field day if she knew.

"Where else would he be?"

"I don't know. Maybe your apartment?"

"About that . . ." Phil says. He rubs the back of his neck, and I can tell he doesn't know how to say what's coming next. "Well, um. I kinda live here now."

"WHAT?"

"Your mom didn't know how long you'd be out for, so she asked me to move into Hannah's room for the summer," he explains, words pouring from his mouth as fast as possible. "Told her that Samson and I are a package deal, and she agreed to let him stay so long as he doesn't chew on the furniture."

I momentarily consider the possibility that I've woken up in an alternative dimension. Because under no circumstance would she ever allow an animal in the house. I wasn't even allowed to have a goldfish growing up. *Unless*, my mind whispers cruelly, *she was that desperate to be rid of you . . .*

Phil mistakes the shock on my face for fear. "You're not afraid of dogs, are you?"

"No," I say, although I take a spot in the armchair as far away from the huge animal as possible.

"Allergic?"

"Not that I know of."

"Then don't worry," he says with a dismissive wave of the hand. "Samson likes everyone. You guys will be best friends in no time."

In response, Samson lets out a loud snore, and I surprise myself by laughing.

Later that night, I pull my sketchbook out from the drawer in my nightstand and climb into bed. Since the start of my episodes, I've taken to illustrating the tiny fragments I can remember from my hallucinations: a castle on a hill, foot-long thorns, the wings of a great beast. The collection of drawings looks like some kind of demented fairy tale.

I'm not very good, but putting the nightmares down on a page helps me cope, and I find the sound of scratching pencil soothing.

My sketches are normally rough and out of focus, half-realized images that will never come to full fruition. But tonight I have a clear memory. Tonight I can see every detail of my subject from the gleam in his eyes to the freckle on his temple.

I flip to a new page and draw my prince of light.

CHAPTER TEN

Awake

THE NEXT MORNING, I'm in the process of making coffee when Phil pads into the kitchen wearing nothing but a pair of low-hanging athletic shorts. He yawns and does one of those over-the-head arm stretches, and I try not to drop the can of Folgers clutched in my hand. Before he can catch me staring, I turn back around and focus all my attention on getting myself some much-needed caffeine.

"Morning," I mumble.

"Morning!" he greets, full of his usual cheer despite the fact that it's not yet eight. I hear the refrigerator door open. Then, "How do you like your eggs?"

I grin. "Doesn't matter as long as I don't have to make them."

Five minutes later, we're cooking breakfast together. While Phil mans the omelets, I slice up some fresh fruit. We work quietly, and although I feel a bit uncomfortable, he seems completely at ease.

"Tomatoes, peppers, and onion okay?"

Glancing up to answer, I'm momentarily distracted by the line of definition between Phil's shoulder blades. I wonder if he doesn't own many shirts, if he hates doing laundry, or if he's just trying to drive me crazy.

"Rory?"

"Huh?" I shake my head to clear the fog. "Oh, right. Yeah, that's fine." When the food is done, we sit at the counter bar stools to eat.

"So," I say, no longer able to stand the silence. "You mentioned yesterday you're studying to be a nurse. How come?" I'm still not sure what to think of Phil, but if I have to live with him for the next few months, I might as well make an effort to be nice.

"Promise not to tell?" he asks, pointing his fork at me.

Casting my gaze around the empty room, I say, "Who could I possibly tell?"

"Okay, point taken. I've always had a strange obsession with blood. Needles too. I don't know what it is, they just get me going."

I rear back and Phil laughs. Despite my sudden horror, it's a beautiful sound. "Relax, Rory. I'm just messing with you."

This makes me scowl. "I'm still coming out of my episode right now. You shouldn't mess with someone who struggles separating hallucinations from the real world." Earlier this morning while I was brushing my teeth, I saw a shadow monster lurking on the edge of my vision. It took me an entire ten minutes to calm down. Sometimes the things I see are so real looking that it's impossible not to be paranoid.

The pink color in Phil's cheeks drains away. "Oh, shit. You're totally right."

"Some nurse you are," I grumble.

"Aspiring nurse," he corrects. "And I'm really sorry. I wasn't thinking."

"No," I say simply, flatly. "You weren't."

Phil goes quiet, poking at his food without actually eating anything, and it occurs to me that I may have been too harsh.

"So what is it, then?" I ask, trying to get him talking again.

"What's what?" He stabs at a stray grape, sending it shooting across his plate.

"The real reason you wanted to be a nurse."

Finally, the smile that I'm already growing accustomed to returns. "My Mamey."

My eyebrows pinch together. "What's a Mamey?"

A deep laugh barrels from his mouth, more musical and beautiful than the first. "My grandmother," he clarifies. "When I was growing up, both my parents were in the navy and stationed at sea, so she raised me. My grandmother is the kindest, most badass lady I know. Most kids idolize their parents, but she's always been my hero."

"How come?"

"Because she spent her life saving people. First she was a nurse in the Vietnam War, and then she worked in an ER for years. I want to do the same thing. Make a difference in people's lives."

Any doubt I have about Phil melts away, and something warm unfolds inside my chest because I *get it*.

"I wanted to help people too," I confess. "My plan was to be a doctor, although I don't think I would've cut it in an ER."

"Mamey always says it takes quick thinking and a strong stomach." His lips quirk for a second before his face turns serious. "You know you don't have to be a doctor to help people, right? There's lots of things you can do. You just have to find what that something else is."

I'm slow to respond. "I know," I say at last, "but I'm not in the right place to do that yet. This will probably sound stupid, but when I gave up on going to med school, I feel like I lost a part of myself, and I think I need to grieve for that loss before I can move on."

CHAPTER ELEVEN

Asleep

THIS TIME, *I wake on the edge of a jagged canyon, and a moment of stupidity compels me to peer over the side. Whatever lies at the bottom is too far down for me to see, shrouded in a river of darkness.*

Out of nowhere, a battle cry echoes through the ravine.

Jerking my head, I glance to the other side. It takes me three long seconds to process what I'm seeing, and when I do, my chest seizes. Crouched against a backdrop of rugged rock face is the dragon, her deadly tail poised in the air like a cobra ready to strike. And below her, sword clutched in hand and teetering dangerously close to the end of the cliff, is the prince made of light.

Nothing happens.

And then, suddenly, everything is happening.

The dragon moves so fast it's as if I'm watching a clip on fast forward. Her head darts down, powerful jaws snapping together, but the prince jerks his weapon up to meet her teeth. The polished metal catches a moonbeam, flashing like a bolt of lightning before clashing with my nightmare.

"Run, Rory!" he shouts. "Run!"

But I can't. His voice is so familiar that I'm rooted to the spot.

He risks a glance over his shoulder to see if I've obeyed, and in the moment before it happens, I know I've killed him. Because while he's distracted, the dragon attacks. The prince stumbles backward until there's no ground left to stumble on, and then he's falling.

As I scream, recognition finally dawns on me—it's Phil I see disappearing into the abyss below.

CHAPTER TWELVE

Awake

"TELL ME ABOUT YOURSELF."

"What is this? An interview?" I ask. Phil and I are sitting in my favorite spot: the rooftop patio of the apartment building. From here you can see all the best parts of Manhattan. The sun is blazing, but I don't mind. Light weaves through Phil's hair, bringing out shades of color I didn't know were there: caramel, copper, and chestnut.

"No," he says, lifting his shoulder in a half shrug. "I just feel like I don't know anything about you."

"Sure you do," I say, my face screwing up in confusion. "I have KLS. I've always wanted to be a doctor. I was at Columbia before I was diagnosed—"

"No, no. Not that stuff," he interrupts. "I want to know about who you are *now*."

His question throws me off. "Like what?"

Another half shrug. "I don't know. Any hidden talents? Can you sing?"

Tilting my head back, I close my eyes and let the heat of the day warm my skin. "I would probably break your eardrums if I tried to sing."

"So seems like a no on the hidden-talent front."

"Does being a Netflix marathon athlete count? Because I can square away entire seasons in a day," I tell him. We both laugh, and after it turns quiet again, I say, "In all honesty, the only thing I was ever gifted at was getting good grades in school. I enjoy drawing, but I'm crap at it."

"What do you draw?"

My face burns as I think about the sketch of him inside my notebook. "Oh, you know. Just stuff."

Phil cocks an eyebrow. "Do I get to see any drawings of this mysterious stuff?"

I bite back my smile. "Not a chance in the world."

⁂

PHIL LUNGES ACROSS THE COUCH, trying to snatch the remote from my hand, but I hold it just out of reach.

"Come on," he grumbles when I turn on my all-time favorite movie, *The Princess Bride*. "You got to pick last time."

Samson jumps up on the couch and settles next to me instead of Phil. I smirk and pat his head. Over the past few weeks, I've grown more and more attached to the old English sheepdog. The last time I had an episode, he could tell something was wrong and cuddled in bed with me for the five days I slipped out of reality. It was a greater comfort than I ever imagined possible.

"That's because it's my house," I tell him.

"But I live here too!"

"So does Samson, but you don't see him mauling me for the remote, now, do you?"

⚜

MILLIE COMES HOME every once in a while, but mainly she stays in hotels wherever she's working. And I'm okay with that now. As I slowly get to know Phil, I realize it's better this way. He treats me like the adult I am, not a child who needs watching, and the apartment is starting to feel like a home again instead of a cage.

On the few occasions Millie does grace us with her presence, we always end up arguing. It's always about the same thing: her inability to treat me like an adult. Today our fight is particularly bad, so Phil kidnaps me before I can retreat to my bedroom and hide for the rest of her visit.

"Where are we going?" I ask as he hails a cab.

He grins over his shoulder at me. "To get the three Feel Better Foods. Pizza, ice cream, and chocolate. You get points if the last two are combined."

My mouth waters at the thought. "That sounds amazing right now."

"I know," he says, flashing me a cocky smirk. "And when we're done, we're going out to Brooklyn."

"What's out there?" I ask as a yellow taxi finally pulls up to the curb.

"My Mamey." He opens the door for me. "She wants to meet you."

❧

WE'VE FOUND A SECLUDED BENCH in Central Park and are finishing our lunch of PB&Js.

"So there's no cure for KLS?" Phil asks before shoving the rest of his sandwich into his mouth.

"Nope," I say. Jelly oozes out of my remaining bite, and I quickly lick it away before the purple goo falls on my lap. "There are different meds that help with certain things—the mood changes, for example. But there's no way to prevent or end episodes." If I feel one coming on, the only thing I can do is warn my family. And when I enter an episode, the only way to come back around is naturally.

Phil presses his lips together like this is the most frustrating thing in the world. "Do you think they'll find one?"

"Don't know," I answer, twisting my hands in my lap. "But I really hope so. I wouldn't wish this on anyone."

He casts a sidelong glance at me. "Not even your mom?"

I know he's only joking, but I answer seriously. "Not even she deserves this kind of torture."

Phil drapes his arm around the back of the bench and hugs me against his side. "I'm so sorry, Rory. I wish I could make it better for you."

"It's okay," I say as I stare out at the trees surrounding us. What I don't tell him is that he already has.

CHAPTER THIRTEEN

Asleep

I **WAKE IN HIS ARMS**—*my prince of sun and light.*

The haze of sleep quickly melts away, and just the feel of his arms around me is enough to make my blood sing. At first, all I can do is stare up at him and his beautiful golden eyes. I hardly notice the world around us, that for the first time it's day during my dream and wisps of clouds drift across a brilliant blue sky. We're lying in a soft patch of grass outside the castle, and the thorn thicket has bloomed into an endless wave of roses.

"How?" I finally ask. "How is this possible?"

"What do you mean?" He runs his fingers through my hair, gently massaging my scalp, and a shiver racks my entire body.

"I saw you die."

He laughs. "Nothing here is real, Rory. You know that."

I open my mouth to argue, but the sky suddenly goes dark, almost as if the sun has been plucked from above and replaced with the moon. And just as quickly, the dragon appears, swooping through the clouds, bringing with her darkness and doom and death.

"Don't worry," Phil says as we clutch each other. "Everything is going to be all right."

CHAPTER FOURTEEN

Awake

*J*UNE. JULY. AUGUST.

The months go by quickly, easily, like tearing a page from a book.

Hannah will be home from Germany soon, and while I'm excited to see her again, I'm also terrified of the change her return will bring. Because if my sister is home, why would Phil need to stay? For the past two years of my life, I've let KLS rule me. I've lived in fear of my condition and its terrible effects. But Phil has changed that. He makes it bearable.

Now the only thing I fear is losing him, because . . . I think I love him. What if I fall asleep and never see him again?

CHAPTER FIFTEEN

Ever After

*W*HEN I WAKE *I know I'm about to die.*

I'm lying in the dirt in what must be a courtyard of the castle. Perched on the roof twenty feet above is a woman draped in a scaley purple cloak. She's watching me as if she's been waiting for me to wake up.

"Morning, darling," she says, baring her teeth in a knifelike smile.

Something about her is familiar, but before I can figure out what, she leaps into the sky, transforming into a dragon.

I look around for an escape, somewhere to hide, but it's hopeless. All the exits are blocked by overgrown rosebushes. The flowers are long past dead, and all that remain are the painful thorns.

My monster swoops through the dark sky. I know I should run, should try to escape, but I'm so tired. She must know I've given up, because she circles overhead, mocking me.

Just get it over with! I want to shout. Then I hear his voice.

"Rory!" Phil calls. "Rory!"

I glance around my small stone prison. On the other side of the square, right where a wall of thorns has grown in front of the door, I see a bright shining light. It's as if the sun has risen behind the dead bush, illuminating the brown vines and shriveled leaves. I know that it's him, here to save me.

"Rory!" he shouts again. "Get up! Please, I need you to get up!"

So I do.

The dragon roars in outrage as I push myself up out of the dirt, but I can't let her win. Hearing Phil's voice has reminded me of this.

I'm across the courtyard in a second, but there's nowhere for me to go. I'm trapped behind the lifeless roses. I try to rip through the branches but only succeed in slicing open my palms. Drops of warm blood stain the ground. A glance over my shoulder tells me that I only have seconds left.

"Phil, help me!" I call in desperation.

He doesn't respond, but I hear his sword as it's unsheathed. Foliage starts to fly as he hacks through the barrier, but he's not going to reach me in time. The sound of the dragon's wings beating in the air matches the pounding of my heart, and I fear her claws will sink into my back at any moment. I can already feel the heat of her breath.

But instead, the last twisted branch falls away and—

A pair of soft lips press against my mouth, kissing me awake.

I open my eyes in my room and see Phil smiling above me. A lock of his dark bangs falls into his eyes, and I can't help but reach up and push it back.

He catches my hand against his cheek and holds it there. "Welcome back to the world of the living," he says, just like the first time we met. "I've missed you."

"You're still here," I whisper in amazement.

A goofy grin spreads across his face. "Where else would I be?"

"I thought you were going to leave me."

"Rory," Phil says. "I'm never going anywhere."

About the Authors

Danielle Banas grew up in Pittsburgh, Pennsylvania, and received a Bachelor of Arts in communication and advertising from Robert Morris University. She began posting her work online in 2014, and it has since been viewed 2 million times. When she is not writing, she can be found fangirling over superheroes, spouting off Walt Disney World trivia, and snuggling with her puppy. Follow her on Wattpad as @tasting_stars and on Twitter as @daniellebanas.

Mikaela Bender has always had a love for modern stories with an impossible twist. Her first novel won the Royal Palm Literary Award as well as the Candice Coghill Award in 2015. On Wattpad, her story "Expiration Date" has held the number-one spot on the Science Fiction Hot List multiple times and has reached over 8 million reads. Every day she's thankful to God, her parents, and readers for all they've done. Find her on Wattpad as @MikaelaBender.

J. M. Butler is an adventurer and attorney who never outgrew her love of Disney or fairy tales. Her passion for writing began when she was five and couldn't find the story she wanted to read. She is a Wattpad Featured and award-winning writer. While she enjoys cooking and dancing with her husband, she also dabbles in knife-throwing, warrior-dashing, and mud-running. She once proposed marriage to a stranger with a Ring Pop and knows from experience which hurts more: a camel bite or a giraffe bite. If you'd like to know more, you can visit her on Wattpad and Twitter as @JessicaBFry or at www.jessicabfry.com.

Debra Goelz is a refugee from Hollywood. She served for ten years as a financial executive for such companies as Universal Pictures and Jim Henson Productions. Her performing career began and ended with her puppeteering a chicken during the closing scene of *Muppet Treasure Island*. Her short story "Redirection" was published in an anthology titled *Imagines: Celebrity Encounters Starring You*, published by Gallery Books in April 2016. Her YA humorous fantasy, *Mermaids and the Vampires Who Love Them*, won a Watty in 2014. She lives in a redwood forest in rural Marin County. You can reach her on Twitter as @DebbieGoelz and on Wattpad as @BrittanieCharmintine.

Shannon Klare is an aspiring YA/NA writer with a love of quirky characters and witticisms. Four years ago, she shared her first story with the world. Since then, her stories have earned over 10 million reads, and two have been featured on Wattpad. When she isn't writing or working, Shannon can be found spending time with her family or daydreaming about new storylines. Occasionally, she tries to craft. The results always vary. You can find her on Wattpad as @liveandlove10.

R. S. Kovach is an art historian by training and a senior financial administrator by trade who has worked at universities across three continents. A Wattpad Featured Author with over 3 million reads, she has also written commissioned shorts for *The Gallows* and *Crimson Peak* movie campaigns. After winning the inaugural XOXOAfterDark.com flash-fiction contest, Pocket Star Books will publish her debut contemporary romance, *The Last Resort*, in March 2017. She lives with her husband and three boys in the greater Washington, D.C., area, but you can find her on Wattpad and Twitter as @rskovach or Facebook as @rskovach.author.

Ali Novak is a twenty-five-year-old Wisconsin native and a graduate of the University of Wisconsin–Madison's creative-writing program. She started writing her debut novel, *My Life with the Walter Boys*, when she was only fifteen. Since then, her work has received more than 150 million hits online. When she isn't writing, Ali enjoys Netflix marathons, traveling with her husband, Jared, and reading any type of fantasy novel she can get her hands on. You can follow her on Wattpad, Snapchat, and Twitter @fallzswimer and on Instagram as @alinovak.

Tammy Oja lives in the Metro Detroit area with her husband, Alan, teen children, and dog, Buster Brown. She has always been a voracious reader, and though she is new to writing, she feels like she has been chasing stories her whole life. Her writing journey started on Wattpad, where she began with the joy of finding a place to read to her heart's content and ended up taking the brave step to trying to write herself. She cannot express how much Wattpad and the people there mean to her. You can find her on Wattpad as @tamoja.

Christine Owen, penname of Joy Moll, writes exclusively via an outdated iPhone. (Consequently her right thumb is gargantuan and her texting skills are outstanding.) She grew up TV-less and started writing in high school when she ran out of things to read. In her free time (who are we kidding, she has kids) she re-arranges her tiny Illinois apartment and spray-paints things she finds on the side of the road. But mostly you can find her tossing peanut butter crackers and cheese sticks at children (usually her own) and begging them to nap. You can also find her on Wattpad as @Christine_Owen.

Jesse Sprague is a speculative-fiction writer whose accomplishments include publishing her short story "Little Cracks" with Acidic Fiction and being a finalist in the PNWA's literary contest for sci-fi (2015) and short story (2016). In the fall of 2016, her story "Outwitting Alexa" will be in a sci-fi anthology of Wattpad authors titled *Nemesis*. Along with Wattpad (@jessesprague), she can be found on Facebook, her website jessesprague.com, and on Radish Fiction.

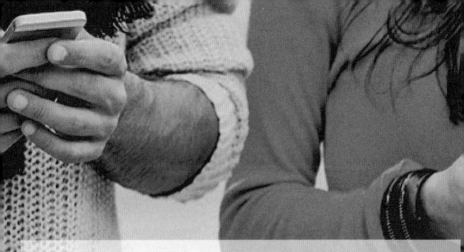